I0618340

The Moonstorm Series

Special Thanks:

Peter Gawtry
Stephanie Gawtry
Ren Johnson
Chris Mayer
Pat Sullivan
Jack Svenningsen
Ricki Terry
Tracy van der Leeuw
Christopher West

DEATH

IS

THE

DOOR

A. P. Malloy

The Moonstorm Series

Ardilla Blanca

Copyright © 2020 A.P. Malloy

U.S. Copyright Office Registration Number
TXu 1-944-883

All rights reserved,
Ardilla Blanca Publishers, LLC.
Reproduction or storage of this work
in part or whole for commercial use
prohibited without written permission.

ISBN-13: 978-0-578-32006-9

Cover design and artwork: Mari Fridley Larsen
marilarsen.com

Learn more about the series
and order promotional copies:
moonstormseries.com

The author welcomes correspondence:
apmalloy1@gmail.com

CONTENTS

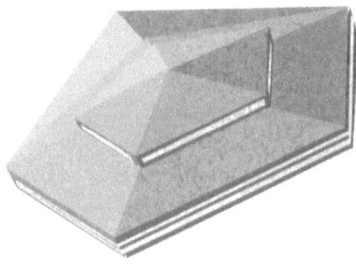

CHAPTER ONE
Trip

WHEN HE LEARNED the news of Maya's pregnancy, Watt, who had been brushing his teeth, stopped what he was doing and stared at her where she sat on a small stool, his mouth foamy and his eyes wide like a rabid weasel. She had told him they needed to talk, and she knew he expected she was going to break up with him, tell him she would not accompany him on the *Destiny* expedition. This turn shocked him. His mind was less a mystery to her with every passing day, and she sensed him floundering to grasp what the news meant.

He rinsed his mouth and dried his hands.

It's OK, she thought. *I was surprised, too.*

Who's surprised? he replied. *Heck.*

He sat on the toilet. Then stood up. Then sat.

Heck.

She tried to take his hand, but he pulled away and looked at her out of the corner of his eye.

Are you sure?

Yeah, of course.

Did you...do you want this? We weren't trying...

We weren't exactly not *trying.*

This is my fault.

Maya scowled.

I'm not looking for someone to blame, Watt.

No, Moses, no, of course not. I'm sorry. But...

Watt rose to his feet again and began inexplicably

rapping his knuckles against the wall as if sounding for a hollow spot or keeping time to an unheard tune.

Watt, please sit down.

But instead, he left the room, came back with her specs in their case and handed them to her.

If you're breaking up with me, he thought. *Write me a letter. I can't take it any other way.* And he turned as if to leave again. But Maya reached out quickly, and she grabbed the hem of his pajamas.

Watt, you dummy! I'm not breaking up with you. But I will if you don't sit down.

He stayed in the room, but he didn't sit. He looked down at her and chewed on his mustache.

Then what? he thought. *The world's longest long-distance relationship? Or have you changed your mind about coming with us?*

I can't change something I haven't made yet.

Argh. I'm not really cut out to be a father.

Maya smiled wanly.

When I first met you, I would have gladly agreed.

And now?

And now... She held his gaze for a time, then looked away, considering carefully. What did she feel now? What was her heart telling her?

For God's sake, she snapped. *Please sit down.*

He did, his beard twitching, and they sat like this in silence, their thoughts their own. Maya felt a decision rushing at her; she could see it charging like a hungry tiger. There was no point trying to run or fight. It was meant to consume her one way or another. And so, she took a deep breath and let it come, watched it pounce, waited for the teeth. But she felt calm, serene even, and when she reached for Watt's hand, he did not pull away. When the tiger pounced, she felt neither claws nor teeth, but, a rough, muscular tongue, wet and warm, running up the side of her face like a sandpaper kiss, and she imagined purring, wholesome as a kept promise. When she opened her eyes, the feeling was gone, but the certainty remained.

She looked at Watt; he looked down at her hand.

I will come with you, she thought to him, and she pressed his hand to her belly. *We both will.*

+ + +

Janet leapt to her feet and clapped her hands like a schoolgirl at a sporting event.

"I'm going to be an auntie," she exclaimed and set aside her case studies to spend the afternoon with Maya. They sat in the chaplain's office, adjacent to the modest, non-denominational chapel, Maya bemused and drinking tea, Janet asking her many questions ("When did you find out?" "How does it feel?" "What did my brother say?"). When these had been exhausted, she briefed Maya on *Destiny's* mission protocol and any details of the upcoming expedition she deemed helpful.

"I'm glad one of us is…buoyant," Maya said, trying to temper her friend's enthusiasm. But Janet was having none of it. She squeezed Maya's hand and smiled.

"It's OK," she said. "The universe is opening a door for you—for all of us! It's natural to be scared, all the literature suggests it. But I'm here for you, and Watt, and—oh! Have you told the major?"

"About going? He invited me ages ago."

"No, about…" Janet pointed to her mid-section.

"No. Not yet."

"Then here we go!"

Maya had never known anyone who actually danced a jig, but when Javon learned the news, he did just that, his smile wider than ever. He had shaved his beard—a pre-mission ritual—and his skin was smooth and smelled like mint. He hugged her like a rag doll, lifting her from the floor before checking himself and gently releasing her, as if afraid she might break.

"Sorry," he said, running his hand over his head and looking at her like a foreign specimen.

"I take it," said Janet, "this means you approve?"

"Approve? Chaplain MacLean! That's not the word

for it. I wouldn't have it any other way!" He hugged Maya again, more discreetly. "You'll be our zoologist."

"You already have one of those," Maya reminded.

"A minor detail," said Javon, and he called for Charlotte. "We'll find something for you to do."

"La benediction," Charlotte murmured, smelling of lavender and motor oil, and she placed her hand on Maya's belly, kissing her on both cheeks, precisely the boon she needed, though she hadn't known it until then.

+ + +

When the time finally came for departure, Maya had the feeling she should be more appreciative of the honor she was being shown, about to partake in the maiden voyage of her father's grand vision. She worried that she hadn't written to Sindi, felt sad that Carl had not been allowed to be uploaded. But all of this was driven from her mind, for she was perpetually ill to her stomach and confined to her quarters, ministered by Watt when he wasn't occupied (rarely) and the tireless Sister Janet, without whose help she would have been lost.

"Nausea gravidarum," the chaplain diagnosed, clinical like an experienced obstetrician but enthusiastic like a first-year med student. "So fascinating!" She worked as a liaison between Maya and Doc Foster, the ship's chief physician, delivering advice and medication and disposing without comment whatever undigested food found its way back out. As Maya convalesced, Janet told her stories of the ship, the progress they were making, and the imminent engagement of the astral drive, key to their mission and as much Rathi Sharma's child as Maya herself. She listened absently, glad for the company but more tuned in to the nascent life inside her than the workings of the ship or its crew.

"Tell her about Willie," Watt suggested.

"Oh, she doesn't care about that," Janet frowned.

"I might," Maya said, and she rose from bed, critiquing her disheveled appearance in the mirror.

"Janet's got a suitor," Watt said, and he offered her a cup of soup, which, at the moment, was the perfect choice. Five minutes from now, that might change.

"Acetone Willie?" she guessed.

"The one and only."

"We share a fondness for the workings of the astral drive," said Janet. "Nothing more. As an engineer, he is extremely knowledgeable about the practical demands of the drive, far beyond what the specs can tell."

"Of course," said Watt, "that's how *you* feel. But I know Willie. He's got other interests, so watch out."

"I have nothing to watch out for," Janet said with great certainty. "Come," she motioned to Maya. "Join me on the observation deck while we still can. Non-essential personnel will be sequestered to quarters once the drive's engaged. Not that I consider you non-essential."

About as essential as the baggage, Maya thought to herself. But she did want to stretch her legs.

They were five days out from Triton when Javon gave the order to engage the drive and the cold reality of Maya's decision set in. They were going to a place so far away no one could be certain of their return. And yet, what did she care? All that mattered to her either walked *Destiny's* corridors, hung on a silver chain around her neck, haunted her memories, or grew like the future inside her. She had no reason to stay.

Will I feel anything? she asked Watt.

When the drive engages? Only if you really pay attention. Little vibration in the walls, maybe. A humming sound if you put your ears to the ventilation. But it won't last long. The drop into distorted space-time lasts less than a minute if everything is going according to plan.

If?

Watt's mustache twitched.

Ninety-seven point nine percent success in all the tests, he soothed, and he sat next to her at the desk they shared. *For the record,* he said quietly, *I always had a... I never told anyone, but I was always... I don't want to use the word 'scared,' but...*

Death is the Door

She poked him.

You? Scared?

Heck! It's only natural. Anything that requires a twenty-four hour recovery time—for the ship and the people, that's the rule; a full twenty-four hours has to pass before it's considered safe to re-enter distorted space-time. Anything that powerful is bound to cause the jitters. But I'm over that! As soon as you agreed to come, it was like all my doubt vanished.

Ninety-seven point nine percent of it?

One hundred.

But no one accounted for Acetone Willie.

+ + +

The first indication of trouble came in the form of wailing sirens that woke Maya from a dream she immediately forgot. She rose too quickly, got dizzy, sat back on the bed—in which she was the only occupant—and she listened to the sound of running feet in the corridor and shouting voices.

"Watt," she said, using her voice because she assumed he had fallen asleep at the desk. "What is it?"

But he was already awake.

"I don't know," he said, entering their sleeping quarters and fumbling into his lab coat, buttoning and zipping like a race. "Where's Janet?"

"I... She said she was going to see Willie. What is it? What's happening?"

But Watt merely grabbed his tool kit, not bothering to tie his boots.

Stay here, he thought, kissing her so quickly he barely made contact before dashing from the room.

Maya listened carefully, her heart racing. She felt a faint vibration in the floor that should have been gone by now, heard a humming sound that continued long after it was supposed to. A mad desire to comm the major nearly overwhelmed her, but she forced herself to sit and think, coaxing her sleepy brain to do its job. Perhaps she should put on her space suit? What good would it do?

The alarms fell silent, but the vibration and humming continued. She sat huddled in her blanket, useless and terrified, and she waited.

And waited.

The opening door startled her from a light, unintentional sleep, and she sat up, her eyes bleary. Watt escorted Janet into the room, his face pinched and pale. Janet's frock was torn, her cheeks smudged, and she wore a blank expression, the look of deactivation, as if someone had simply flipped a switch.

"Watch her," is all Watt said, then he hurried away again before Maya could speak.

"Janet," she said. "What happened?"

But Janet did not respond. She moved to a chair and sat down. Her eyes closed, and her simulated breathing ceased. She was motionless as stone and remained that way until long after the vibration and humming had finally stopped and Watt, looking sick to his soul, had returned to crash into immediate sleep.

We'll be OK, he thought when he woke, which made Maya believe the opposite. Janet remained frozen.

What happened? What's wrong with her?

Watt shook his head, sweeping the hair away from his eyes and pouring himself a liquid breakfast.

I'm going to need some time, he thought. *I'll tell you everything I know as soon as I know it.* He sat down in front of Janet and opened his tool kit.

God, Watt, you've got to give me something, Maya exclaimed. *I'm freaking out here!*

Watt's head bowed and he released a heavy sigh.

Willie's dead, he thought. *Fell down a service shaft into the drive electronics. I don't know how, but he managed to hit every major node on the way down. Argh. He fused the drive, Maya. It wouldn't disengage.*

What does that mean?

It means the major had to eject it to keep us from going even farther off course—or burning up. I wish I could tell you more, I do, but that's all I know. His face scrunched as if he was trying to smile, but it was a lost cause. *Janet was there*, he thought. *If I can wake her up, she'll tell us what happened. But I need time, please. And no one can come in here, OK? That door needs to stay locked.*

Maya nodded her understanding and backed from the room, unable to force her gaze from Janet's blank expression. Locking the door, she began wandering the corridor, not sure of her destination. Crewmembers hurried by, ignoring her, or slouched past wearing haggard looks and hastily donned uniforms. No one said a word to her. After a time, she realized she was moving toward the major's quarters, but once there, she found Javon out and Charlotte just about to leave.

"Ma chere," she said, and she hugged Maya. "Are you OK? Where is Watt? Have you heard?"

"I heard...some. Not enough."

"Is Janet OK?"

"I don't know. Watt is with her."

"La pauvre chérie," Charlotte pursed her lips. "Elle a failli perdre la tête." She hoisted a pack to her shoulders, filled with tools and meters. "The poor dear was nearly out of her mind when I saw her." She closed the door to their quarters and joined Maya in the corridor. "I'm going to the engine room if you want to walk with me. But I have to hurry, and you won't be allowed in. Too much radiation—and too many anxious bodies."

Maya walked with her for a time.

"Are we adrift?"

"We are."

"Can you fix it?"

"Perhaps."

"What can I do?"

Charlotte's smile was forced, her eyes tired.

"Take care of yourself. Make sure Watt gets some sleep. And watch over Janet. I worry..."

But she didn't specify about what.

They reached one of the lifts.

"I have to go," Charlotte said, kissing both cheeks lightly. "We will be OK." Then she stepped into the lift and was whisked away, leaving Maya to wander the corridors until hunger and fatigue called her back to her quarters. And yet she feared to return, dreading what she would find when she unlocked that door. Would Janet be disassembled, would her machine parts be exposed like nakedness? Would Watt need her support, or would he snap at her and drive her from the room?

In the end, she decided against fear, made her slow way back to their quarters, and placed her palm against the lock, opening the door.

"It's just me," she said.

She entered timidly, with the feeling of someone interrupting lovers or an interloper at a confession. Watt knelt before Janet, his head on her lap, his hair a mess. Janet's face was streaked with tears, and her frock was open at the back, but life had returned to her expression. She ran her fingers through Watt's hair in a perfectly sororal fashion. She looked up when Maya entered.

"It's OK," she said. "Come in."

Maya did, and Watt, rising slowly to his feet, escorted her to a chair.

"Sit with her," he said. "I need to talk to the major." And he left them, locking the door on his way.

"Willie," Janet said to Maya. "He's dead, isn't he? That's been confirmed? I calculated less than two percent likelihood of his survival."

"As far as I know."

"And the drive is ruined?"

"I think so. I mean, Javon ejected it, so..."

"Then I've stranded us in the middle of open space," Janet said grimly. "I must look a mess."

"Would you like me to button you up?"

"I think Watt still has work to do. But thank you."

"I'm so sorry, Janet. But you don't have to talk about it if you don't want to."

Janet's synthesized breathing resumed.

"What is there to say? Willie liked me. I knew that. I just wanted to see the drive in action. The field is a spectacular study, you know, unlike anything else. Your father was a special man, and Willie understood that. He had a favorite place, shielded, but with an observation platform. I suspect we weren't supposed to be there, but he said it would be OK, and I wanted to believe him. We were just sitting there, watching. And he held my hand."

She wiped the tears from her face.

"Do you understand how I was designed, Maya?"

"To...emulate humanity?"

"To be indistinguishable to the naked eye. And more! To pass basic security tests—x-rays, retinal scans, palm readers. Even the generation of simulated brain waves." Janet's brow furrowed. "I can eat and drink, excrete waste, and generate various odors. And it wasn't just an elaborate game Watt was playing, to see if he could get away with something, like I was some kind of proof. He never does anything without a purpose."

Maya didn't know where this line of thought was headed, but she didn't interrupt with questions, merely sat and listened, her hands on her lap.

"A good job he did," said Janet. "But no one, not even the most discerning machine mind, can predict everything. And I wanted Willie to like me. So, I went with him to the observation platform, and I let him hold my hand. Eighty-two percent likelihood that was a mistake. We were bathed in exotic light, he leaned in to kiss me, and he saw something. I could tell. Something about the light coming from that drive reacted strangely with my eyes, and when he looked into them, he knew, I could tell. He knew right away what I was."

She looked squarely at Maya.

"Why do you not hate me?"

"Why would I? Did you kill my parents?"

"Someone like me did."

"No," Maya shook her head. "No. Not like you. Watt made sure. I know."

"Nobody knows anything, dear Maya. All we have are various levels of uncertainty."

Maya felt a lump in her throat.

"What happened to Willie?" she asked.

"He screamed," Janet said. "Like an animal. He was stationed on Mars, you know. When it happened. I've never experienced someone in pure terror. And I was the cause of it! He...scrambled to get away, and when I stood up to calm him, he slipped on the stair and fell. He tried to grab my tunic, but it tore. Five point two seconds he fell, with seven different impacts on the way down. He stopped screaming after the third one."

"God, Janet."

Her friend methodically pulled her mousy brown hair back into place and returned the coif to her head.

"I calculate a forty-nine percent likelihood that God does not exist," she said. "I am close to failure. I need to assimilate. Will you stay with me?"

"Of course."

"I'm scared."

"It will be OK," said Maya, hoping she sounded more convincing than Watt or Charlotte. "I won't leave you," and she moved her chair closer.

The android's eyes closed, she sat motionless, and she did not respond. They sat like that until Watt returned—and for a long time after.

+ + +

"I want that report," demanded Magister Healey, who accosted Javon the moment he set foot on the bridge. He stood close enough to the major that Javon could guess what the stout little man ate at his last meal.

"And you'll get it," Javon replied coolly. "In due time. But at the moment, I'm sort of occupied trying to save our lives." With a respectful but firm hand on Healey's shoulder, Javon moved the man from his path and continued toward his station.

"Have you interviewed our chaplain?" Healey asked, following close behind.

"Informally."

"What was she doing in one of the service shafts? With our assistant engineer? Or do I have to ask?"

"You don't have to."

"She's relieved of duty, I assume."

"Yes, but only because she's under medical supervision. When she's given a clean bill of health, she'll be put to work. We need all hands on deck."

"For all you know, she's a saboteur!" The magister's face grew red, and his cheeks puffed out.

"Oh, stop it, Chuck." The major paused to review a tablet shown to him by a dutiful ensign who saluted smartly and moved off. "She's not been charged with any crimes, and I'm not interested in a witch hunt."

"I could have her arrested."

"Not while we're in a state of emergency, and you know it. Listen." Javon looked up from his readouts and fixed the magister with an unblinking gaze. "I know you're just trying to do your job, so yes, I will double and triple check to make sure our chaplain isn't trying to sabotage the mission. But for now, she's sequestered and being cared for. That's the best I can do."

Magister Healey took a deep breath, loading up a string of objections, but Javon cut him off with a chopping gesture before toggling the comm's microphone.

"All hands, this is Major Monroe. As you may have heard, we're working on an unexpected issue that might put us a little behind schedule. The details are irrelevant, so I won't waste your time. What I will do is ask that everyone stay on task and go about your duties like professionals. When this issue is resolved—and it will be, you can count on it—we'll be back underway. But that will only be possible if everyone stays focused on their job. As always, I'll keep you informed with regular updates. Until then, business as usual, people. Monroe out."

He toggled the switch.

Magister Healey sneered.

"'A little behind schedule?'"

Javon manufactured a weary smile.

"I'm putting you in charge of Willie's funeral service," he said. "Sister Janet would normally get the job, but..." He waved absently. "I want a guest list and an itinerary by the end of the day. Understood?"

"I'm not a mortician."

"Don't worry, Chuck. There's nothing left to embalm. His remains are in the infirmary. They'll handle the casket, etcetera. You just make sure the event is laid out smooth and proper. Give people a chance to say goodbye. Willie was well-liked."

"How long will that last," the magister wondered, "once people learn the truth?"

"Which is?"

"That's your job to find out! I want that report!"

"In due time." Javon placed a hand on the magister's back, amply cushioned, and he ushered him from the bridge. "In due time."

+ + +

They remained adrift for days, then weeks.

Javon reassured the passengers and crew, but when the rumor began to circulate that the astral drive was not simply damaged but jettisoned, panic set in, and he was forced to arrest some and confine others to their quarters. Food and water they could synthesize and harvest as long as their fuel lasted, but that wouldn't be forever, and they were, in the words of the major, "in the middle of a whole lot of nothing."

Maya felt life burgeoning inside her, or imagined she did, and wondered what Janet would calculate as the likelihood of its ever seeing the outside world.

Hum ko man ki shakti dena, she sang in her mind, thinking to soothe the cluster of dividing cells in her womb—though it was she who needed comfort.

The chaplain rarely left their quarters at first. When time allowed, Javon questioned her in detail, getting the same story Maya had. He reckoned her guilty of entering a restricted area, but acquitted her with minimal scolding. She had, after all, been escorted by a high-ranking member of the engineering team, and that absolved her in his eyes. But he was decisive in deeming her unfit for duty—"Temporarily," he assured, "until you feel better"—sensing she was more in need of a counselor than able to be one. He suggested a guard outside their quarters, but Watt's objections were vehement.

"That's just Healey talking," he snapped.

And so, Javon dropped the matter, insisting only that if Janet left her quarters she would promise to do so escorted by either Watt or Maya. This she did, though initially, no escort was needed, as she spent most of her time seated in her darkened room, her eyes closed.

Finally, as weeks of drifting through the fathomless black turned into the first month, Janet arrived at some resolution to her personal crisis.

"Will you walk with me?" she asked Maya. The latter's nausea had largely passed, and she gladly accepted the invitation, feeling anxious and pent up, eager to move and perhaps serve some purpose. They spoke rarely as they walked but often held hands. Janet asked about Willie's funeral, which she had not attended, and Maya assured her it had been appropriately honorable, the chapel overflowing.

"You were missed," she added, which was true.

Janet sighed, a perfectly human but entirely unnecessary thing to do. And yet, the gesture conveyed a world of meaning, and Maya squeezed the warm hand she held. Her heart swelled, but her words, as often happened, stuck in her throat.

Healing, she thought to herself. *She's healing.*

This first walk led to many others, meandering, contemplative affairs that wound throughout the ship but often led them to the bridge—comforted for different reasons by the blinking lights and dutiful crew. Watt rarely joined them, occupied most waking hours with helping to fabricate another drive, but the major occasionally did, as the bridge was, after all, his office. This is where the three of them were at the end of the second month, trying to buoy each other's spirits.

"Refitting at sea," Javon said, seated at the helm. "It's not my first choice, but there you have it."

"Is that even possible?" Maya asked.

"We're about to find out."

"Do you... how badly lost are we?"

Javon glanced at Sister Janet, as if weighing his answer against the effect it would have on her.

"Not so badly that a Monroe can't find a way out," he said. "Just you watch. We've got a brilliant crew—and we launched all our distress buoys first thing. One way or another, we're going to get through this."

Janet turned to him.

"You may believe the time is past for such feelings, Major, but I am wracked with guilt and shame. I know the rules. You should be punishing me."

"There are some who agree," Javon ran the back of his hand over the stubble on his face as if he missed his beard. "But what good would that do?"

"It would make me feel I was paying for my sins."

"I don't want to bruise your pride, Chaplain, but you aren't the first lady Willie invited to one of his private love nests. He had...a reputation."

"That strikes me as irrelevant."

"Perhaps. But at the moment, locking you in the brig for being lured into seeing a pretty light show also seems pretty irrelevant. You want to pay? Take care of Maya. And get your head back in the game." He lowered his voice to a whisper. "I have a feeling we're going to need a chaplain very badly if we don't..." He let that idea go unfinished. "Just get better."

"What about me?" Maya lamented. "I'm useless."

"That makes two of us," said Javon.

But Janet did not appear to be listening. She looked past Maya, across the bridge to the comm station, and she tilted her head and removed her glasses as if concentrating to see a distant object.

"There's a ghost on the bridge," she said.

"Excuse me?" Javon's brows arched.

"There," Janet said, and she pointed. But they saw nothing more than the young comm officer on duty, his bald head making him look twice his age, his hands-free display casting a glow across his smooth features.

"Listen," said Javon. "Are you sure you're OK?"

Janet looked away from the comm.

"I'm sorry," she said, and she returned her glasses to their home. "I'm not sure what that was. You're right, Major. It's clear I continue to suffer residual trauma. If you don't mind, I think I'll go back and rest."

+ + +

Javon and Maya exchanged worried glances as Janet left the bridge. But neither said anything, for a moment later, they were both overwhelmed by two very different, utterly compelling sensations, short-lived but awesome, and so beyond description they made no remark, but simply stood, rapt and helpless.

Javon had an impression he would later describe to Charlotte as, "power, pure and simple, like a blind man in the middle of an elephant herd. I didn't dare move, scared as I've ever been and glad to be blind—because they weren't elephants, Char, and I didn't want to see what they were. Power. Fearful power."

And that's all he could say about it.

But for Maya, the feeling was not one of power but of grace, and it settled over her womb, found its way *inside,* and spread outward from there, like chocolate melting over ice cream. She laced her fingers and rested her hands on her belly, still not evidently pregnant, and she stood there, staring at nothing. Her heart stirred, and she knew, somehow and certainly, that they were OK.

"Grace," she murmured, and so named the child.

Then the sensation passed for both of them, gone as quickly as it had appeared, and it was replaced by a chiming at the navigation console.

"Major," said a voice. "We've got something."

Javon blinked and shook his head as if waking from an unexpected nap. He turned to the navigator.

"Something good?"

"Too early to say, sir. But it might be. Whatever it

is, it's within range of sub-light engines."

Javon stood up from his chair.

"Johnson, if you're playing a game..."

"Negative, sir. You need to see this."

"Well, then," Javon waved impatiently. Taking this cue, the navigator selected a few commands and a holographic image sprang to life in front of the helm station, a tiny ball of white light.

"It's a star, sir. Confirmed: G-class."

"And?" Javon pressed.

"Still scanning, sir."

Javon gripped his armrests, knuckles whitening as he waited, and when Maya placed her hand on his forearm, she felt the tension of a trap about to spring. Then: one, two, and finally three elliptical rings appeared around the holographic image of the star, each marking the path taken by a single spherical object. A hush fell across the bridge. All eyes were on the images, all minds bent toward a single hope.

"Please," someone said.

"Working," the navigator assured, selecting commands and interpreting data. The images resolved and clarified, and a collective gasp could be heard from one end of the bridge to the other.

"How in the name of justice did we not see this earlier"? the major demanded.

"I'm sorry, sir," said Johnson, throwing up his hands. "I can't explain it. But there it is. Plain as day."

"It," riding the second of the three ellipses, was an earth-like planet, tidally locked to its star.

+ + +

"If this is real," said Javon, and he moved to the navigator's station, "and not just a phantom, I accept your apology and promote you."

But all indications, from every scan *Destiny* could perform, was that the planet was very much real, the outermost of two rocky worlds, its neighbor much smaller and devoid of life. One gas giant patrolled the far reaches of the star system, the whole of which was banded by a dense ring of asteroids many kilometers wide. Two days of sub-light travel brought the ship close enough to see their target with the naked eye, and all doubt vanished. Those who viewed the spectacle from the observation deck, and those whose view was mediated by a holo-screen on the bridge deep in *Destiny's* heart, all responded with a similar mix of cheers and weeping.

"That's the second prettiest thing I have ever seen," Watt said, his mustache twitching, and he kissed Maya and hugged his sister.

Another day passed before they were close enough to distinguish details of the planet, a day that required careful navigation, for they were within the orbital paths of its satellites, all five of them. Few were as large as Luna, but all were much closer to the planet, and one was a contrarian—mottled brick red and traveling in a highly elliptical, retrograde orbit.

Maya, like many aboard *Destiny* who had spent their share of time on Earth, could scarcely tear themselves away from the observation deck, though there was plenty for everyone to do.

"Storms," said Janet, and she pointed at the wildly swirling cloud formations sweeping across the planet's surface. "It's to be expected."

"Sure," Watt agreed. "With all that energy transfer from the sunny side to the dark." He bit his lip, growing pensive. "My physics teacher used to say, 'a tidally locked planet is...' Well," he looked at Maya and shrugged. "He liked to swear a lot, so use your imagination. But he wasn't keen on settling one. 'Radical climatic oscillation,' he would say. 'No guarantee of liquid water,' et cetera."

"You're being a downer," said Maya.

"Ready an atmospheric probe," the major ordered, and they all waited throughout the day as the probe circled the planet, gathering and transmitting data. Shonda Abara, *Destiny's* chief scientist, was called to the bridge to analyze data and offer advice. For their part, Maya and

Janet stayed out of the way, happy to be distracted from recent trauma by the sight of the cloud-wracked jewel hovering just outside.

"Keep your hope in check," Janet advised, and Maya tried, but it felt wrong, somehow, as if it were an insult to her earlier feeling of certainty and well-being. The residue of that feeling had never left her; it had, in fact, grown like multiplying cells in a Petri dish, and she felt it was impervious to any 'checking' on her part. A calm bliss had settled in her heart and had no plans of leaving.

Home, she thought.

The results of the probe were not long in coming, but Javon shared nothing with the ship's crew and passengers at first, huddling with his science team and swearing them to secrecy. Even Magister Healey was kept from the bridge, though he huffed and puffed resentfully. First was the analysis of the electro-magnetic field that enveloped the planet. Viewed two-dimensionally, its arms arced outward and around, looking on all the digital readouts like the embracing legs of an arachnid.

"Aranea," said Chief Abara. "It's Latin for spider."

"Could we swap the vowels?" asked her assistant. "I think Aranae sounds better."

"Aranae," Javon said, brushing the hologram with the tip of his finger. The name fit like a comfortable shoe. "Clever and pretty," he conceded. "But no naming until we know if it's habitable. I don't want people getting attached to a puppy we can't bring home." He squinted at the image. "How strong is that field?"

"As strong in relative terms as Earth's," Chief Abara replied, and her assistant agreed, nodding.

"It's been a long time since this planet rotated," the assistant said. "But at its core, it's clearly liquid, spinning enough to be one giant field generator. It's shielding the atmosphere from roughly the same percent of radiation as Earth's field."

"Gravity is point nine four that of Earth," Chief Abara added. "Most people won't notice the difference. Atmospheric composition and pressure are safely within tolerances. But the stratospheric turbulence is unlike any-thing we encounter on any of the System colonies."

"Windy," the major murmured.

"To say the least," said Chief Abara. "But not con-stantly so, I wouldn't think. There are lulls between storms—you can see one here, and here—and it looks like there are high pressure systems that clear the skies every once in a while. And this, too: it seems the orbits of the moons have created a sort of meteorological resonance. Their gravitational forces and the temperature difference caused by their passing shadows seem to be stirring the weather pot. We would need to examine for several lunar cycles to identify the exact rhythm, but there is one."

"Next step? Can we probe the surface?"

Chief Abara's smile was wide and eager.

"Yes sir, Major. We sure can."

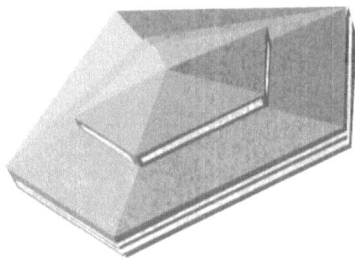

CHAPTER TWO
Double

IN THE PAST, when Lightning got over her surprise at their unexpected relocation, fear quickly followed—and fury. She looked at the plain, windowless walls of their prison with fire in her eyes, cursing when Joy's attempt to open the lone door failed.

What happened this *time?* she demanded, *We did everything we were supposed to do! We saw the picture of the moon cave, we concentrated on it...it should have sent us there. Why didn't it work?*

Because it's Moondweller trash, Thunder scowled. *We should have known better than to trust anything they put their hands on. We would have been better fighting back through the kish. At least they make sense.*

When, instead of where? Joy thought to the artifact riding in her sling. *What does that mean?*

It means, said the Book, *that our transporter trip didn't just take us across space. It took us across time as well. Into the past, to be precise.*

When Joy shared this idea with Lightning and Thunder, their confusion was written in wrinkled snouts and pinned ears.

Like...before the Red? thought Lightning.

Farther back, I guess, Joy tried to explain, though what she was being told made little sense, and her head had begun to ache long ago from being the conduit for so many different modes of communication.

Death is the Door

Can't you tell them? she implored the Book.

I'm afraid not. They aren't designed for it.

Can you simplify then?

You be the judge. Our matter stream from the Hold transporter was obviously redirected and intercepted, and my own energy was co-mingled with the active field of a functioning astral drive. I presume that of the human ship Valiant, *purportedly held by the android, Sister MacLean. If my suspicions are correct, we are in orbit around Aranae—but several hundred red moon cycles ago.*

Aw, put a lid on that stink! thought Lightning upon sensing Joy's painstaking translation. *Who cares who did what with the mingling, and the fields, and all that? Not me! The question is, how do we get back?*

When asked this, the Book had a simple answer.

We can't, it said. *Not without her help.*

And at this, a bipedal figure dressed in a simple brown tunic and headdress appeared before them with no warning, though how she got there they couldn't say, as the door to their cell remained tightly sealed. Joy quickly took refuge behind Lightning, whose spikes flared. But Thunder didn't hesitate; he lunged at the newcomer, his jaws snapping shut around one of her legs. All they caught was air. The figure remained standing, unperplexed by the attack even as Thunder wheeled and lashed viciously with his tail. The blow passed through the figure as if it was smoke, no more affected by the tail than by the kick Thunder next aimed at its chest. He landed awkwardly, snarling and cursing.

You're wasting your time, Lightning thought. *Use your nose! It's obviously not real. Like the pictures in that transporter. They look like something, but they're not.*

"Imanee nona ramham," the robed figure said, extending her hands, palms forward.

What is she saying? Joy asked of the Book.

She claims she means us no harm, it replied. *She is Sister Janet MacLean, if you hadn't guessed.*

Upon sensing Joy's message, Lightning bared her teeth and took a step toward the figure.

How can it claim anything? she demanded. *It's not real!* And she swiped her claws through the image.

It is the representation of a real being, the Book replied when Joy repeated this question. *A hologram. We see it as it appears—somewhere on this ship. And of course, we can hear it. But as you have noted, the image itself is just that—an image.*

It can hear us? Joy asked. *And sense our minds?*

Hear, yes, via microphones located throughout this room—but not sense. Sister Janet was designed to communicate in vocalizations much as the sapiens named Captain Monroe. But even if she were not, thoughts are not transmissible via hologram.

The robed figure began speaking again, her voice quite different than that of the captain's. But the sounds she made were just as indecipherable and crude.

"Niggi innahac woffingcur," is what they sounded like. "Huv ruv niggi. Gwonoweh piktikkit jerta hunga jink." And more like it. But with help from the Book, the verbal nonsense took the form of words in Joy's mind, and through her, the kezel were also able to understand—although not appreciate.

"You are angry and confused," the image said. "And I am sorry for that, I sincerely am. I promise that all your questions will be answered, and that, if it lies within my power, I will return you to your home."

If? Lightning curled her lip. *What is that supposed to mean? You brought us here! You can't bring us back?*

But this was a one-way conversation. No one spoke the language being used except their translator, and it had no voice.

"If everything goes according to my plan," the robed figure continued, "you will be free of this confinement and among friends very soon. I expect food and water and a thorough explanation will go a long way toward soothing your nerves. Nothing would make me happier. Kezel are among my favorite of all Aranae's creatures. Again, I mean you no harm. But I must ask your patience a while longer."

Death is the Door

Then she turned to address Joy.

"And you—I believe you are called Joy—I now speak directly to the device you carry. I know it can understand me through you. This is my message, Petros, and you can believe it or not as you choose. I know you are already guessing at my motivation and judging my decision to come here. Yes! We have traveled back in time, just like you told me not to do so often when I begged for your help. You refused me then, but I no longer need your permission. Before you judge harshly, understand: this decision doesn't stem from my own desires, unless you count among those desires wanting to save Aranae from the destruction that approaches. You know what I refer to. And you know time is short. But if my plan succeeds, Aranae will be saved—and so much more!"

The robed figure looked behind her as if responding to a signal only she could hear.

"I have to go," she said. "But I'll be back, I promise." The image flickered and faded, but just as it seemed about to vanish, it re-stabilized, and the figure looked at each of them in turn.

"You will be heroes," she said. "You'll see."

And the image disappeared.

+ + + + + +

While the entire ship waited, it seemed, with breath held, Javon ordered *Destiny* maneuvered into position and a surface probe made ready. But the probe had scarcely been gone a day when a young ensign, working the third shift at the helm, delivered an urgent message to the major via the comm, waking him from the best sleep he'd had in weeks.

"Sir," the young man said, after double, then triple-checking his readings. "I'm sorry to disturb you, sir, but there's another ship out there."

Javon sat up and leaned forward, as if by getting closer to the speaker he could understand the message. Charlotte woke and rolled over, looking at him.

"Another ship?" she repeated, incredulous, but Javon only rubbed his eyes, trying to shake the last of the sleep from his foggy mind.

"Is this DJ?" he asked.

"Yes sir."

"Level of certainty?"

"One hundred percent, sir. It's hailing us!"

Javon rose to his feet, slipping into the uniform Charlotte handed him and fastening his belt.

"Patch it to my quarters," he ordered.

"Sorry, sir, but there's no audio. It's text only."

"Text..."

"Yes sir, and it's coded. 'Major Monroe. Eyes only,' is all I can read. Whoever it is knows System coding—and knows you're on board."

This inspired Javon to pause, looking at but not seeing his wife as he considered the news. She got into her own uniform, watching him closely.

"Any hostility?" he asked.

"None evident, sir. It's holding at a distance of ten thousand kilometers. No shields at the moment, but it appears to be armed."

"Identity?"

"Unknown, sir. Unfamiliar configuration."

"Where the hell did it come from?" Javon growled as Charlotte tossed him his boots, lacing her own.

"Sorry, sir, I can't say. It's a small ship, smaller than a frigate, but the scans are clear: it's definitely super-luminal. It could have dropped into our space-time on the dark side of the planet."

"Shhh... Alright, ensign, thank you; that will do. Send the message to my quarters and sound yellow alert." He paused. "And ensign..."

"Yes sir?"

"Keep this to yourself, understood?"

"Yes sir."

The message, when it arrived and was decoded, was simple enough:

"System Starship *Destiny,* do not attempt to land

on Aranae. Great peril. Galactic Starship *Valiant* requesting audience with Major Javon Monroe. Utmost urgency. Absolute secrecy required."

Javon read and re-read the message as he made his way to the bridge. The senior staff was assembling or was on their way; Shonda, Watt, and Deputy Kim had each taken their stations, marveling at the arrival of this new ship. Magister Healey hadn't bothered to put on his uniform, but he was the first to arrive.

"Do you want to tell me why I've been knocked out of bed by a bunch of flashing lights and alarms?"

"Yes," Javon frowned. "But not yet." And he ordered a secure channel opened to the conference room, the scans of the mysterious arrival sent there as well. Leaving his staff to guess amongst themselves the cause for it, he closed himself in the conference room. There, he laid eyes for the first time on the ship calling itself *Valiant.* The holographic image was of a wide, triangular nose and broad wings, angled forward, an unfamiliar design, and worrisome. What kind of guns were those? He took a deep breath and opened the comm.

"Galactic Starship *Valiant,*" he said. "This is Major Javon Monroe of the System Starship *Destiny.* Please identify yourself and your purpose."

There was a pause that seemed to last ages, but which was likely no more than a few seconds. Then, a voice, disguised and unfamiliar came from the speakers.

"Are you alone, Major?"

"I am. Who is this?"

"And this line is secure?"

"It is. Who am I speaking to?"

"May we switch to video?"

"Yes, please. The mystery is wearing on me."

Moments later, an image appeared before him, life-size and three-dimensional, and so unexpected was the form it took that at first the major stared at it with his mouth open and his brain gone slack.

"I apologize for the secrecy and the surprise," the image said earnestly, looking for all the world like a white-haired Sister Janet MacLean after weeks without a good cleaning. "I assure you, Major, it is justified."

"Whoa," he replied, holding up one hand. "Whoa."

"Yes," she said. "I understand. But I can explain, if you will let me." And then, adding to his bewilderment, she began to weep, tears streaming down her face. "I have missed you," she said.

+ + +

But Major Javon was unmoved.

"Who are you?" he demanded. "What is this?"

"I'm sorry for my emotions," the image replied, and it wiped its tears on the sleeve of its tunic. "I know you have many questions. But first and foremost: I am not here to cause trouble for you or *Destiny*. The opposite, in fact. I'm here to save you."

"Maybe you didn't hear me," Javon said, and his voice was hard. "Who are you? And don't say Janet Mac-Lean, because we already have one of those."

"Yes, Major, I know. As I know every person on your manifest, from their talents to their failings, all the things a good chaplain should know. You can test me if you want. I don't mean to be defiant, but I am Janet Mac-Lean. I'm just not the Janet you know."

Javon glanced over his shoulder, aware of the people waiting impatiently outside the door.

"You have one solid minute to start making sense," he said, "or this conversation is over."

"Oh Major! If only I could. Nothing I'm going to tell you will seem plausible. And yet here I am. One 'solid' minute? I'll do my best. Let's get the worst part out of the way first. I came here from the future."

Javon thumped the conference table with his fist.

"Cock-a-doodle! Who are you? Why the ruse?"

"It's true, Major. Ask me anything."

"I just did!"

"This is no ruse, Major. I've lived through everything you are currently experiencing, and I've come here

Death is the Door

to save you from making the catastrophic mistakes that are going to doom this expedition."

"I've had enough." Javon pressed a button on the table. "Chief Abara, get in here."

"Please, Major," the image begged him. "If you're going to reveal this to anyone, have it be Maya Sharma. No one else is more qualified to judge the truth of what I say. If my mission becomes common knowledge, it is likely to fail—and *Destiny* with it."

"What does Maya have to do with this?"

"She's pregnant, isn't she?"

Javon answered with silence.

"The child is a girl, has she told you that?"

"What does that have to do with anything?"

"Has she?"

Javon's brow furrowed, and he opened his mouth as if about to speak. But he checked himself and pressed the switch again.

"Belay that order, Chief. Send for Maya Sharma. Have her join me here ASAP."

"Aye, Major," came the reply, obedient but laden with question marks.

Javon pointed a finger at the hologram.

"Just so we're clear: I don't believe a word you're saying. But I'm going to let you talk until Maya gets here. Change my mind—if you can. Start with that joke about coming from the future. Prove it."

"There may be no way to do that, Major. But you've scanned my ship. You know it has the markings of a human vessel, but you've never seen anything like it. You know—or your crew is beginning to piece together— that it's a fifth the size of *Destiny* but has an astral drive that's twice as powerful. How can you explain that?"

"It's not my job to explain! It's yours!"

Javon never raised his voice, but the words were like a shout, and the holographic figure hugged itself against their force, closing its eyes.

"Please, Major," it said. "I am trying. Should I re-cite the names and ranks of the entire crew? Would that be convincing? Should I tell you about Commander Terry Rickles? First Mate. You like him because he makes you laugh, and you trust him because he saved your life. Lieutenant Commander Shonda Abara, Chief Science Officer. You think she's the smartest human on board, with the possible exception of the civilian Watt MacLean, your chief programmer and my creator. Magister Charles Healey, in charge of overseeing the Company's assets and organizing the colony. You don't hate him, sometimes you even enjoy his company. But he is the one person on this expedition most likely to rub you the wrong way."

"Until you showed up!" Javon collapsed into one of the padded chairs arranged around the table. "Enough with the personnel list. You look like Sister Janet and you know some things. That doesn't prove..." But he couldn't make himself express the preposterous idea. "That doesn't prove your story. What is it you want from us? What are these 'catastrophic mistakes' you're going on about, and how do you propose we avoid them?"

"By coming with me to my time."

"Your time..."

"Yes. I know, Major, how spectacular this all sounds. But it's true. In my time, *Destiny's* already been re-fitted with a new astral drive. We've established a mining compound, a refinery, a research facility. We've even built a hydroelectric dam."

"It sounds like heaven. If everything's so great, why bother with us? It seems like we did OK."

"No Major, respectfully not. The tension between you and Magister Healey recently came to the surface when he tried to have me arrested for hobbling the ship. Am I wrong? It will only get worse. Early in the colony's existence, there will be an argument about energy acquisition. You will lose—capitulate, perhaps is a better word. You will grieve that decision the rest of your life, as it is the first in a chain of events that leads ultimately to civil war and the imminent destruction of the planet."

Javon threw up his hands.

"If you know me so well, you have to know I'm not

buying any of this without proof—and I don't like being called a capitulator!"

"Yes, Major. I do know. But if you will allow me to board *Destiny,* I can provide that proof."

"Absolutely not."

"I understand your reluctance. But aboard my ship there are beings who may convince you of my story."

"Beings...from the future, I suppose?"

"Over two centuries in the future, in fact. And when Maya gets here, she will know, I believe, in her heart, the truth of what I am saying."

"Yes, well, we'll see." Javon was about to toggle the comm once again, but the door chimed, and on his order, it opened to admit a hastily dressed Maya. Her eyes were only half open, but that changed when she saw the hologram standing in the center of the room.

"Oh!" the figure said upon seeing her, its tone one of someone in great pain. And indeed, it clutched for a moment at its heart, rocking back and forth, never taking its eyes off Maya. Then it reached forward, though of course, it could not touch her, and its hands seemed to stroke her head and run lovingly across her cheek. "Maya...dear Maya," it said, then faltered, its eyes losing focus and its limbs stiffening.

A moment later, the figure collapsed.

+ + +

Maya stood silently. She examined the fallen figure, the holographic image of someone—something?—that looked beyond all explanation like a badly-worn replica of her friend—a friend who was in their quarters with Watt, recharging and de-bugging.

"What is this?" she coaxed the words out at last. "What am I seeing here?" Javon remained seated in his chair, his arms crossed and his eyes closed.

"That," he said with no irony, "is future Janet."

"She came in that ship?"

"So she says."

A.P. Malloy

"What happened to her?"

"You mean why did she buckle? I have no idea."

"Javon," Maya puckered her lips. "What is this?"

"A trip down the rabbit hole, if you ask me."

"But it's not real, is it? I mean...time travel?"

Javon's customary smile was nowhere to be seen. "Did your high-paid professors tell you that?"

"I thought it was common knowledge."

"Practically impossible, yes. But theoretically?" Javon looked from the motionless figure to Maya. "If we had the energy and understood the process... You know, the Doctor—sorry, your dad—talked about it all the time."

"Not with me."

"Yes, well, it was just fireside chat. How would it work, what would be the results, all that. He didn't take it seriously. He had a lot of other things on his mind. But this...this he would take seriously."

He patted the seat next to his.

Maya sat.

"How long do we wait?" she asked.

Javon shrugged.

"I hope not long. But who knows? She claims to be over two hundred years old. Maybe she wore out. Either way, we need to remain in a holding pattern until I know more. She was pretty adamant about us not setting down on that planet. Tales of doom and gloom."

"She came here for that?"

"So she claims."

Maya absorbed this information. The clinging strands of sleep tangled her thoughts, and she wondered if she looked as dull as she felt. The crumpled form lying before them begged to be interpreted as a dream, or perhaps a hallucination brought on by stress. Maybe she was having this experience all on her own, still lying in bed with her eyes closed. Pinching herself proved nothing, but she did it anyway, hard enough to bruise.

"How is the baby?" Javon asked suddenly.

"It's...fine."

He peered at her from the corner of his eye.

"Do you mean *she's* fine?"

An offended tone colored Maya's voice.

"Foster told you? I haven't even told Watt."

"No Maya, our visitor told me."

"No."

"Yes. And she knows a great many other things too, with all the precision you'd expect from an android chaplain. Whoa!" He stopped and uncrossed his arms.

The image had moved.

"What do we do?" Maya asked.

Javon gripped her forearm and pressed a finger to his lips, urging her to silence.

The figure's hands trembled. Its fingers flexed and extended, and with mechanical deliberation, it raised itself to a sitting position.

"Let me do the talking," Javon whispered.

"Works for me."

The figure did not rise to its feet, seeming content to remain seated. Looking at both of them, it made small, precise adjustments to its tunic, straightening the coif covering its white-streaked hair.

"I must look a mess," it said.

"You asked for Maya," said Javon.

"Yes. Thank you. I'm sorry... I took the precautions I thought necessary to shield myself from the emotional strain of seeing you again—seeing you both—but I calculate a ninety-six percent likelihood that nothing less than complete disconnection from my affective sub-routines would have sufficed. That's a thing I've never been able to do." She clenched her hands as if praying. "I've missed you, Maya, much more than I had anticipated. The pain..."

"It's OK," Maya said, in spite of herself. Javon made a hissing sound of disapproval, but what could she do? She had to offer some consolation to the pathetic figure, didn't she? "What can we do to help?"

"Allow my passengers and I to come aboard. Speak with them. Then you will know the truth."

"Who are these passengers?" Javon demanded.

"Denizens of Aranae—my Aranae. Three of them. Two kezel and a sui generis."

Javon arched his brows.

"That mean anything to you, xenobiologist?"

Maya shook her head.

"Kezel? No. Sui generis means one of a kind. But," she asked the image, "a kind of what?"

"A hybrid," the image spoke. "Part human."

"And part what?"

"A species called scion. You will see."

"And meeting them will prove what?" Javon asked, leaning forward, doubt in his voice.

"Everything I've been saying, Major." And with what appeared to be great effort, the figure rose to its feet, in a slow, methodical straightening of its limbs. "And there is another, a fourth, you will most want to meet."

"Oh?"

"Yes, Major. Please. Time is so very short."

"Who is this special fourth?"

The image that was—and wasn't—Janet, cocked its head the slightest, and its eyes adopted a tighter focus, its voice a tone of carefully suppressed intensity.

"You won't believe it until you see it, Major, but for what it's worth, its past self, the thing it was over two hundred years ago, has already made itself acquainted with you—with you both."

"Now you're playing games!"

"No, Major. Never. Not with you. His—its—name is Petros. And he's here, with us, in this room."

+ + +

As was his habit when in charge of the bridge, Commander Rickles eschewed the seat reserved for him, pacing slowly from station to station, rarely making eye contact. He hardly ever spoke, but was often watching, or if not watching, running his hand back and forth over his pale, bald head, mumbling to himself and staring at the floor until he had completed one full circuit of the bridge.

Death is the Door

That done, he turned and began the process again, this time in reverse. He was ambling past Deputy Kim's station when Maya appeared from the conference room, followed shortly by the major.

"No changes, sir," Rickles was quick to report. His voice was as gravelly as his appearance suggested. "But Kim here thinks he's gotten a good scan. Looks like there's life forms on board. Three of them."

"But is no idea what they are," the deputy was quick to add , self-deprecating as always.

"It's OK, Mr. Kim," Javon said. "We're going to meet our visitors in person, if you don't mind."

"Yes sir! Is not minded."

Javon moved closer to his second-in-command, speaking in a low voice. He stood a foot taller than the man and outweighed him by twenty-five pounds of muscle. But he also had just as many years less experience, and when he spoke, his tone was one of authority, but also great respect.

"What's Foster's status?"

"Doc is wrapping up surgery," said the commander. "Emergency appie. She'll be done soon."

"Good. The second she is, I want you to work with her to quarantine cargo bay four."

"We're letting them on board?"

"We are."

Commander Rickles rubbed his head like a genie's lamp and stared at the floor for a moment.

"Kim says we're perfectly compatible for docking."

"We are. But don't ask me how that's possible."

"He also thinks they're armed beyond just the guns we can see."

"I don't think it's their plan to harm us, Terry. If they had wanted to poke us full of holes, I suspect they could have done that from the first. We need to speak to these characters face-to-face, and I would rather have them on our turf than vice versa."

"OK, you're the boss, Major," Rickles said, which meant, 'I don't like this one bit.' He ground his teeth, and his voice grew rougher. "Deputy Kim! Prepare a security detail and meet me in bay four."

"Aye, Commander. Is what kind of situation?"

Rickles deferred this to the major.

"Four in number," Javon said. "An android, a small, humanoid alien, and two..." He looked to Maya, who had gone to stand by Watt at his station. She only shrugged. Left on his own, the major did his best to describe the images the future chaplain had shown them. "Think a mini tyrannosaurus rex crossed with a wolf and a porcupine," he said. "About the size of a large bear."

Deputy Kim's mouth opened, closed, then opened again. He looked at Commander Rickles as if hoping he would say something. He did not.

"Are two of these, sir? Are dangerous?"

"I imagine so. But we're told they're sentient—the humanoid alien as well. And they're coming aboard under terms of peace, so be prepared, but keep your cool."

"Aye, Major."

And with that, Commander and Deputy left the bridge, filled now with wide eyes and open ears.

"Can I be there too, Major?" Shonda asked, so much like an eager child that Javon's smile returned to its proper place and turned a second later to laughter.

"Would I be able to stop you?"

"I'm hoping you won't try, sir."

"I won't. In fact, I have a very special role for you. Go to the galley, get those steaks, and thaw them out. Don't cook them—they need to be raw."

"All of them, sir?"

"I know."

"But the landing celebration..."

"They have a more noble purpose now. Our guests are hungry, and that's the best we can do."

The moment Shonda had left, Major Monroe's gaze swept the bridge, taking in each of the remaining members in turn. Magister Healey, growing puffier and redder with each passing second, finally spoke.

"This sounds like a disaster in the making."

Death is the Door

To which the major offered no disagreement.

+ + +

In the modest confines of *Valiant's* belly, Lightning leaned against the door and strained to smell or hear any sign of their captor.

When this door opens, she thought, *we can't hesitate. Everybody through quick, and whoever kills the Moondweller gets a prize.*

Prize or not, thought Thunder, *I guarantee I'll be the first one to her worthless throat.*

Joy buzzed an uncertain tune.

Does that sound good? she asked the Book.

Terrible, actually, was its reply. *If my surmise is correct, we are floating in the essential vacuum of space with no one but Sister Janet to get us home. Killing her would likely be killing ourselves.*

Neither kezel was pleased to learn this news.

You mean we're supposed to let her get away with this? Thunder bared his teeth.

To stay alive, yes, Joy replied.

But Lightning wasn't convinced. She turned away from the door, her ears pinned back.

What does that stupid thing care about 'home?' Aranae isn't its home. I bet it could float around out here for a thousand cycles and be just fine. I'm getting tired of its advice, and I'm getting tired of the only thing I sense from your mind being whatever it tells you.

Joy rubbed her fingertips to her thumbs, soft and raspy, and her antennae drooped.

Just trying to help, she thought.

You are, I know, but I wonder about that thing.

Joy kept her thoughts sheltered.

Get over here! Lightning ordered her oti-mu. *Pay attention and let me know if you hear anything.*

Thunder moved to take her place at the door, and she, tense with growing fear, returned to pacing the limits of their cell. Confinement was a new experience for her; it had a surprising, corrosive effect. Though the space was hardly warm, her tongue lolled as if she was panting, and the more she paced, the more wild her gaze became. Joy felt her rising panic as if it was her own, and she struggled against the feeling at the back of her throat, a shrieking whistle seeking to escape.

You're just wasting energy, Thunder advised. *I have some experience being locked up, and what you're doing isn't going to help.*

He held out a clawed hand to stop Lightning when she paced by, but she snapped her jaws and swiped at him, coming a spike-length from drawing blood.

Don't touch me!

Thunder backed away, returning to attend the door, but his worried gaze remained on Lightning. When Joy attempted to approach and console her, she rounded on her so fiercely, snarling and squint-eyed, that Joy cowered, sure she was about to be bitten.

I said stay away from me!

And so, Joy did—as much as it was possible in that confined space—and Lightning continued her pacing, round and round, growling to herself.

What can I do? Joy asked the Book, miserable at the suffering she saw and felt before her.

Few things are worse to the kezel mind than captivity, it replied soberly. *She must be given the certainty of eventual freedom, or I fear she may damage herself.*

What certainty is there?

None. But there is likelihood. And it may be enough. It will give her something to think about, something to plan.

So, what is it?

Think. Consider what you know about Sister Janet's motivations, what it is she needs.

How would I know?

Because she has shown you.

Just answer the question! Joy clicked angrily. *She hasn't shown anything!* But as she should have known, the Book offered no reply to her statement. Spiraling hair around her fingers, she worked to relax and concentrate.

Death is the Door

What had the one called Sister Janet shown them? What did she need? Well, she hadn't killed them, there was that. Just the opposite. She seemed to have worked especially hard to bring them to this place intact, had in fact, alluded to an indirect need for...

Epiphany.

She needs you, *yes?*

She does, the Book replied in an approving tone. *But something more. Something every Book needs.*

Joy considered.

She needs me, too. Her eyes flashed. *She's not a Reader.* This revelation seemed helpful, but incomplete. *But what about freedom?*

As I said, not a certainty, but you haven't solved the entire puzzle. Yes, she needs you, because she can't communicate with me otherwise. But you could refuse to co-operate. Consider her response if you did.

That's hard to say, Joy replied. *Would she hurt me?* Then a worse idea. *Would she hurt Lightning?*

Your kezel companions have a saying: assume the worst. Sister Janet is, in my experience, not a sadist. She does not relish the pain of others. But her mind has been damaged by grief and loss of faith. If she believes it is the statistically expeditious means to a desired end, she may resort to violence of the worst sort—torture even.

Joy absorbed this information, watching as Lightning paced the cell, wrestling with her internal demons, chafing at the stale air and windowless room.

Has torture already begun? she asked.

I suspect not. We have given her no reason.

You're saying we shouldn't?

I'm saying that, based on what I know of her, there is good likelihood that, if she gets what she wants, she will eventually release all of us.

What does she want?

She's trying to buy time, the Book replied. *Seeking to be reunited with people she dearly misses. But of course, she is going about it all wrong—and somewhere in her mind, she knows that. Still, she is obviously convinced this is the best she can do. She will pursue the plan to the end.*

And in the meantime?

Trust nothing she says. But do not indicate that lack of trust. Go along with what she proposes and bide your time. You will see your opportunity.

Joy thought about all she had learned, yearning to offer its consolation to Lightning, to ease her distress. But her head, already achy, felt like it was being stretched and reconfigured, like a body outgrowing a vest. The thought of relaying all this information one quartet after another seemed daunting to the point of failure.

Can't you do it? she pleaded to the Book.

You know I can't.

It's getting too hard, she insisted, eyes dimming.

The Book did not reply.

Why won't you help? she chastised bitterly.

I already have, in ways you haven't discovered yet.

How is that useful?

Relax and search your mind. Something new has been happening; you have simply overlooked it because of long habit. Look closely and consider: the more you Read, the better you get. The better your Reading, the better your thinking. Remember how you communicated when you were very young.

I just repeated everything.

And so, you learned what things were. Now recall how it was after your transformation.

I...made new thoughts, Joy replied. *But always in fours.* She whistled a wry tune. *Slow and really hard.*

Yes, but excellent practice. And finally, consider how you communicate now.

Now? Nothing has changed!

No Reader is unchanged by contact with a Book. Perhaps you are scared to try.

Joy's antennae straightened, and her eyes ignited.

I'm not scared of anything! I am kezel!

And just like that, something in her mind snapped, a pleasant sensation, like a crick in the neck popping free, and ideas bottled up to be doled out in fragments now flowed twice as easily. She couldn't contain her elated buzzing.

Ami-kan! Amoti Thunder! I have learned good news! Both kezel turned their attention to her, and Lightning's lolling tongue retreated into her mouth.

Don't keep us in suspense, thought Thunder.

Joy didn't. In half the time it would normally have taken, she shared what she had learned, and the sense of hope it inspired in her companions was immediately evident. Lightning stopped her pacing and moved to the door, taking Thunder's place. She didn't apologize for her outburst, but her ears relaxed and her snarl softened.

Just a matter of time, then? she asked.

Joy's tone was certain.

Yes. I don't know how long, but yes.

As if in reward for their patience, the image of Sister Janet again appeared in their midst not long after. This time, they were composed and calm, waiting for the news they felt certain their captor bore, eager to find in it the path to their freedom. The message was simple.

"We are about to move again," the image spoke. "But have no fear. Through the door that will open behind you, there will be food and friends."

And a door did open behind them, in fact, a pair of them, first one, then the other, pressurized air hissing.

Mere seconds passed, but painfully breathless.

Then a voice:

"Simona. Cofers ka loo mobalilly," it said, which, when translated by the Book meant: "Hello. Welcome aboard *Destiny*."

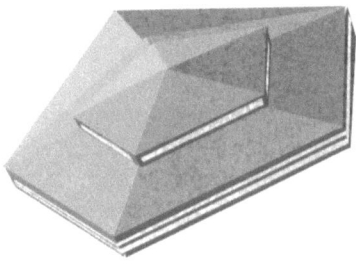

CHAPTER THREE
Escape

IN THE PRESENT, Delta One, Ensign Carmela Morales—
on whose back the battered android rides—and Captain
Julius Monroe stand on the modest runway overlooking
Ozag's Hold. Together, they appraise the shuttle that is
parked there, a craft meant to take them to a rendezvous
with the starship *Destiny* on the planet's dark side.

"It's nothing fancy," Delta One says in its tinny
voice. "And perhaps it will be too old-fashioned for you to
pilot—very little A.I. and few creature comforts."

"Don't worry about us, Shiny," the captain replies.
"Comfort means different things to different creatures.
How about that security you mentioned?"

"Of course," says Delta One, and the ensign leans
forward to allow the android to reach the touchpad situ-
ated left of the personnel hatch. With the push of a few
buttons, the hatch opens slowly, the gangway lowering
like a tongue from a gaping mouth. The captain's face
lights up, and he runs his hand over the gangway's rail-
ing, looking up into the shuttle's darkened interior.

"What are you thinking, Ensign?" he asks.

What she is thinking she keeps to herself at first.
Instead, she peers under the shuttle's belly, which easily
clears her head, examines its wheels, three double sets,
each standing taller than her waist, and scans the vehicle
from cockpit to tail, taking extra time with the broad
wings and triple port engines.

Death is the Door

"Morales," the captain prods. "Report, please."

"Sorry sir," she snaps to attention. "It's like a museum piece, you know."

"Which would be great if we were nine-year-olds on a field trip, but..."

"Yes sir. Well, I won't be able to say for sure until we're inside, but everything I see here is immaculately maintained. If the rest of the craft is in similar shape, there's every reason to believe it'll fly."

"Into orbit?"

"Yes sir."

"Then what are we waiting for?" The captain fixes his gaze on the android whose head peers over the ensign's shoulder. "No objection to us boarding?"

"None at all, Captain. Beta Three is waiting."

"And what do we do with you?"

"Why, take me along, of course. I, among all the Deltas, was most highly versed in the details of our mission. Beta Three can monitor our flight and provide support from the ground. It is his specialty."

"Fine. Then call to your buddy and have him come out. I don't like a crowd."

"Do you mean to say you don't trust him?"

"I've never met him. I'm sure he's a great guy, a bunch of laughs. But if he's done prepping the ship, there's no reason to have him on board."

"As you wish." And with that, Delta One sends a transmission that is beyond the captain, but which the ensign senses perfectly well. Moments later, a chrome-plated work-bot, scuffed and squeaky, exits the shuttle and climbs down the gangway, its joints stiff and its steps cautious. Captain Monroe watches carefully, his fingers idling at his side as if itching for a weapon. But his concerns are unfounded. The android pays them no heed, attending only to its partner.

"To the control center," Delta One orders. "Inform me when you've reached your station and prepare to run pre-flight tests on my command."

"Understood," says Beta Three, and off it shuffles,

like an old man wishing for a cane.

"How much," the captain asks, "do you think some fat cat on Luna would pay to add Grandfather Time there to his collection? A real, working antique!"

"Beta Three is my friend, Captain," chides the mangled android. "He's not a thing to be collected or sold—at any price. Nor, for that matter am I, though I am also what you term an antique."

"Sure, no, of course not," the captain holds up a hand to show good will. "I'm just impressed is all. That he's still ambulatory? Amazing!"

"So would I be! We have all been given the best care possible under the circumstances. Shall we board?"

"After you," the captain waves, and he follows Ensign Morales as she climbs the gangway.

The ship would have been a playground for the student of aerospace technology, but Captain Monroe wastes no time. Once inside, he orders the android temporarily placed on one of the seats in the passenger compartment so he and the ensign can conduct a thorough examination of the vehicle.

"Don't leave me!" Delta One frets.

"Wouldn't dream of it, Shiny," the captain replies, and he pats the android on its dented shoulder. He and the ensign move from compartment to compartment, until every inch has been surveyed and found free of danger. Before they re-join Delta One, however, they pause to converse near the aft firewall separating the passenger compartment from the engines.

Captain Monroe closes the hatch.

"Away from prying ears, if you know what I mean," he whispers. "So, what have you learned?"

"Not enough," the ensign replies, "until we have electrical systems powered up and I can get a look at the readouts. But on the surface, everything seems as advertised. It's old but remarkably well-maintained. In fact—" But she doesn't finish this thought. Her eyes drift out of focus and she tilts her head as if listening.

"What is it, Carmela?"

"Sir," the ensign's eyes snap into focus. "It's *Valiant*. Someone activated the astral drive. She's gone!"

"What? Gone where?"

"There's no way to tell. But…"

"But what?"

"Sir. The locator badge we left with the one named Joy. It's stopped transmitting."

Captain Monroe thumps his forehead with his fist.

"Tell me that's a co-incidence!"

"It's possible sir, but…"

The captain clamps his jaws shut. His temples bulge, and he closes his eyes as if the bad news was something visible. BAM! He kicks the bulkhead.

"Morales!"

"I know, sir. This isn't good."

From the front of the ship they hear Delta One's tinny voice, tremulous with concern.

"Is everything OK back there?"

Captain Monroe shoves the hatch open.

"Just fabulous, buddy! We'll be up in a minute."

He turns to the ensign.

"Hypothesize; what's our chaplain doing?"

"I'm sorry, sir, there's not enough data for anything but wild conjecture. Maybe she felt there was no hope with this plan to avoid the lunar collision and took *Valiant* to some other planet. For all we know, she's on her way back to Earth. Or maybe she's just testing the drive and will re-appear in the next five minutes."

"Dammit! How sure is this this collision?"

"Assuming the information we were given hasn't been fabricated or altered in some way, very sure."

Before the captain can respond, a panel of lights springs to twinkling life, and they hear two sounds. One is the outer hatch closing; the second is low and sustained, like a motorboat crossing a distant lake.

"The engines are being ventilated!" the ensign says, but the captain has already guessed as much, for he has studied these craft for years. Ventilation is the first stage of the cycle, leading eventually to combustion—and then launch. He hurries from the engine room, followed closely by the ensign and a trail of creative profanity.

They pass Delta One on their way to the cockpit.

"Dear me!" he says, his arms flailing. "Beta Three has misunderstood—or he is acting on orders other than mine. He initiated the auto launch sequence!"

"Or you gave him the order, and you're just putting on a show," the captain glares. But when Delta One pleads his innocence, the captain hisses like a snake and waves him to silence. He motions for Ensign Morales to move on to the cockpit without him.

"How do we stop it?" he demands of the android. An automatic launch function was not part of the shuttle's original design as he understands it, and he is suddenly out of his reckoning.

"We can't," Delta One replies. "The controls will remain inoperable until the craft is safely in orbit."

"There has to be a manual override."

Delta One shakes its head, neck creaking.

"Disabled except in the case of emergency."

"A power cut-off, then."

"I'm sorry, Captain. Once the cycle has begun it can't be stopped without damaging the engines. It will continue to its conclusion."

The distant motor boat becomes an approaching flotilla, and the floor begins to vibrate.

"Ensign?"

"Primary ignition, sir," the ensign replies from the cockpit. "Controls are non-responsive."

"I blame you for this," the captain points to Delta One. "Don't go anywhere." And he turns away, fists clenched, hastening to join the ensign.

"Oh dear," says the android. "Please, won't you at least strap me in before take-off?"

"We're not taking off!" the captain shouts.

"Actually," the ensign says when he arrives in the cockpit. "We are. And there's nothing I can do about it."

"Then blow that hatch and let's jump for it."

"No good, sir...there isn't time. We're wheels up in

sixty seconds." Concern clouds her brow, but she moves calmly as she rises from the pilot's seat, leaving it for the captain and taking the navigator's position. But Captain Monroe returns to the crew compartment before sitting. Delta One flails and creaks, his proclamations of innocence waved away with curses and scowls.

"Just sit still and be quiet," the captain says, and he adjusts the safety straps to secure the android as well as his damaged frame allows. "I'm only doing this to prevent you from bouncing around back here and busting up our ride. We're not friends, got it, Shiny?"

"But Captain, I swear, this isn't my—"

The Captain turns his back.

"Not friends!"

And he returns to the cockpit.

"You'd better strap in sir," advises the ensign, and she stows the pack under her seat. It's an old runway and not long. Acceleration will be rapid and bumpy."

"Sure, sure," the captain grumbles. He takes his seat and straps his safety harness as the flotilla becomes an armada and both seats jiggle merrily.

"Well," says the ensign as the craft begins to roll. "I guess this is what we wanted, yes?"

"Not under these terms." The captain grits his teeth and squeezes the helmet over his head, lifting the faceplate. "I'm a great pilot. I'm a terrible passenger."

A moment later, the armada fires all its cannon, and an implacable force presses them both back into their seats; the conversation must wait. The runway rushes away beneath them, faster and faster, soon becoming a blur. Then the captain's stomach drops and they lift, nose first, from the ground, rising into the air, trailing white smoke and roaring off into the blue.

+ + + + + +

In the lofty heights of Cyclonia's lone tower, Queen Allura grants audience to the farmer drones responsible for bringing her a most unexpected offering.

A.P. Malloy

Flying machine, then falling vumierre, explains the highest numbered farmer, Four Thousand Seven. *That is all they know, Queen.*

Yes, Queen, thinks a second farmer, and it bows low. *They know nothing else.*

Nothing, assures a third. *Flying, then falling.*

Yes, thinks another. *That is the way it happened.*

Queen Allura has heard enough. She clicks impatiently, and the drones still their chittering.

Before them on the ground lies the motionless form of an alabaster vumierre clad in gray, its head injured, but—according to the drones—not as badly as it had been upon first being discovered. In fact, even now, where the gaping wound is its worst, scorched and open for the world to see, its edges seem to smooth, almost imperceptibly, and the hole begins to reform and fill. Unlike any vumierre she has ever heard of, the creature before them seems to be repairing itself.

And the flying machine? Allura wonders.

Off to the northwest, Four Thousand Seven thinks, gesturing with his antennae.

Yes, his partner agrees. *Fast and loud.*

Yes, thinks the third. *The fastest and loudest.*

And they are certain nothing else was dropped?

Nothing else, Queen.

No. Nothing.

No—not that they saw.

Then they have done well and will be rewarded. Allura whistles twice, shrill but short notes that summon her magister at once to the chamber. Strikingly blue and bristled, he is graceful and confident when he bows, standing before his queen respectful but uncowed, eyes dim and antennae leaning forward. At his arrival, the farmer drones sink even lower to the ground.

How may he serve? the magister asks.

These are to be re-numbered. They have done work worthy of a promotion, and will now gain twelve steps.

As she commands, the magister bows, and the farmers chitter and buzz.

They are grateful, thinks Four Thousand Seven, for he will now be in the three thousands, and who would have expected that after a simple day of tending lova?

Yes, agrees the second. *So much gratitude.*

And honor, thinks the third. *Very honored.*

No queen is more generous!

No. None in any of the hives so regal and kind.

And they bow and bend their antennae with such enthusiasm that Allura must whistle them to silence and order them from the chamber, accompanied by her magister for the detailed work of re-numbering.

She turns to the silver scion, a princess, sitting all the while at a distance, observing in silence.

Summon her pluripotents, she thinks. *And inform her soldiers: none are to disturb them.*

The princess bends her antennae slightly in reply and rises from the ground, the sound of her wings fading as she exits the chamber. In moments, she returns, joined by six bronze flyers. Together, they settle in a ring around their queen, who rests on an elaborately woven mat, silky and plush. Her eyes settle on each of them.

Royal chronicle, she orders simply. *They will attend carefully and check each other's recollection so that not a word is forgotten or misunderstood.*

It will be their pleasure, as always, thinks the princess, and the pluripotents assure her it is so.

Allura pauses to gather her thoughts. Chronicling is one of her least favorite duties. Very little happens in Cyclonia, and documenting the commonplace hardly seems worth her precious time. Events of the past moons, however, have made the chronicle much more interesting—and necessary.

The most recent tey Ramota, she begins, *was typical. The tower held fast, and no damage was recorded. Predictions were that the arrival of the vumierre flying device—and its crash into the bay—would lead to disruptions of the climate and worsening of the quakes. But that has not been the case.*

However, there have been other happenings. While

the device sat dormant in the bay, Albion was beset by devastation from the sky, and the Circle was destroyed. No explanation exists. Shortly after, two vumierre rose from the depths of the bay, naked, but bearing parcels. They left Cyclonia on foot, traveling toward Albion. They were not followed, but she regrets this decision now.

The watch on the device was doubled. The vumierre did return, this time with a third, but stayed to the north of Cyclonia's border and escaped to the upper land. Albion's Old Magister arrived then, with news of all that had happened in that doomed hive. Towers filled with hungry larvae waited untended, but remarkably, a princess survived. For unknown reasons, she did not remain in Albion, but was last seen moving north toward the Mouth of Ozag, already transforming to a queen. Allura believed her to have lost her senses, perhaps engaged in a mad quest to seek the Undying.

Old Magister went in pursuit of the vumierre, with Allura's blessing, and with his leave, she sent what tenders she could to Albion, for she is resolved to claim the towers as her own, to raise the larvae there as her loyal subjects. So planning, she was disappointed to learn that her soldiers failed in their guarding of the sunken device. An entire company allowed it to be drawn from the bay without a single bite. And most recently, it has once again taken to the air, leaving behind a remarkable but baffling specimen, a vumierre of a type unknown in legend.

Allura whistles softly, and her antennae dip.

She is weary, she thinks. *This chronicle is complete.* Princess and pluripotents buzz an obedient tune, rising to leave the chamber. The bronze flyers lead the way, the silver princess close behind. But before she has disappeared, Allura's clicking stops her.

She will inform her soldiers, she thinks. *They will remove this vumierre from her presence. Have them store it safely in the Royal Garden—let no harm come to it! Bring it vumierre food and water—assuming it ever revives—and command that they watch over it more closely than they did the flying device!*

Death is the Door

She will make it so, thinks the princess, and she turns in a twinkling to deliver the message.

+ + +

What, thinks the royal gardener, *is he supposed to do with this?* He examines the biped, its legs and arms bound, its eyes frozen and apparently sightless. It makes no response when the team of soldiers places it on the sparse, rusty turf, and it seems to all of them lifeless.

Queen desires it be cared for, the lead soldier replies. *Fed and watered and not harmed.*

A vumierre? In the Garden? It is unheard of! Should it not be sent at once to Albion? He understands they have a vumierre there that has been well-trained.

Had a vumierre. Does he not know the news?

He does not and is quite beside himself upon hearing of the Circle's destruction and the tale of other vumierre roaming free. He chitters nervously and paces small circles, his gaze wary and always on the bound figure laying before him.

Are they certain? Is there no other way?

Queen insists!

Does she say what it should eat? Drink?

Vumierre food. This is obvious. And water.

The royal gardener continues his agitated pacing, considering all he has heard of vumierre legend. They were said to eat almost anything, were even reputed to have enjoyed scion during the time of enslavement, boiled in great pots by the dozens. He whistles forlornly.

It is hideous...must it be kept?

It must, thinks the lead soldier. *No more delay!*

And so, clicking orders to a team of subordinates, the royal gardener has the biped unbound and carried to an empty enclosure—he refuses to touch it himself—and placed inside. The globe is larger than the one Joy had found herself in moons before, but the design is the same. Perfectly spherical and scored with tiny ventilation holes, it has a door that locks from the outside, and this is made secure the moment a pair of skinned virbles and a lova leaf have been placed inside.

They will leave it now, the royal gardener orders to his followers, and this they do, although they steal many fascinated glances at the wonder as they depart, chittering to one another in great excitement. But the royal gardener himself is not so sanguine. Once his team has left the space and sealed the gate, he climbs to the safety of his observation post and waits to see what, if anything, the vumierre will do.

+ + +

What Lieutenant K does, initially, is invisible to the outside observer. He seems to be lying unconscious or dead in his spherical prison. But inside, in flowing electrons and binary data, tremendous work is being done. The most complex of the labor took place after his violent run-in with Sister Janet and his own plasma pistol. Damage had to be assessed, ruined components rebuilt— essentially grown from within, using the universal template in each of his thirty trillion synthetic cells. Some mass was inevitably lost to the pistol's trauma; anyone making a precise measurement would have found him a full two kilograms lighter now than he had been only one Earth day earlier.

Power test, he thinks, though he is unaware of the thought on a conscious level. It is stored, of course, in his long-term memory, but at the moment, he is incapable of accessing that. Everything that is happening at this point is autonomous, like a post-surgical patient sleeping while they recover.

Primary systems power confirmed.
Secondary systems power confirmed.
Emergency power confirmed.
Input/output systems test.

The lieutenant's eyes open and close. Yes, he can see. His hands clench into fists and release, and his toes wiggle inside his work boots. Yes, he can feel. He inhales through his nose, licks his lips, makes several low sounds, barely audible.

Yes, he can smell, taste, and hear.

More complex sensory tests follow, including sub- and supersonic, x-ray, infrared, ultra-violet, and radio. His long-range communication has been restored.

Operating system test.

Open eyes no longer simply take in data. They deliver it to the lieutenant's synthetic brain where it is interpreted and evaluated. The core of his memory is accessed and opens to him slowly like the time-lapse of a blooming dahlia. He remembers his name.

I am Nikoli Ilyich Khristorovdestvensky.

I am a lieutenant, formerly in the Galactic Guild, Enforcement Division, assigned to Captain Julius Monroe.

Precise location: unknown.

Current mission: Destiny *salvage.*

Mission status: jeopardized.

Immediate threat assessment: low but persistent.

Health assessment: ninety nine percent.

Higher-order personality comes online.

Son of a gun, he thinks. *That nun shot me!* But then he settles. *Easy, Nikki. You're being watched.*

And so, he lies motionless, until, bored or called to other duty, the scion watching him from atop the northern wall leaves its post and disappears. But Lieutenant K is cautious; he waits patiently to see if the watcher will return, and while he does, he evaluates what data he can, limited as he is by his awkward position. Coastal Mediterranean climate, dancing waves close at hand, exotic flora, scion construction—a single tower, rising from the sheltering arms of the cove—a spherical prison, synthetic and tough, but no concern to an enforcement unit like himself. Sharply rising walls, rocky and weathered by the sea. The sun at thirty degrees, due south. And there, at the far end of the cove, kept separately in two large enclosures, a pair of spike-covered animals, a species he knows.

Kezel adults, identically enormous and orange.

A.P. Malloy

+ + +

Crag! thinks Rock. *Wake up!*

He pokes his snout through one of the many holes that allow him to see and smell the world outside his six-sided prison, its rough walls not thick, but strong like stone. The hole isn't large enough to accommodate his entire head, but through it, he sees his oti-mu, similarly confined, lying on the dirty floor of his own cell, mere strides away, his eyes closed.

Crag! Rock concentrates fiercely, the thought like a shout in his mind. *Wake up! You need to see this.*

His oti-mu stirs, groaning as he rolls over and opens his eyes.

Lunch time already? he thinks wearily.

You'll see if you sit up. C'mon!

C'mon yourself. I'm done.

Not until I say you are! Now up, kezel! Look!

Yeah, yeah. Looking. And Crag takes a deep breath, raising himself to his haunches. He peers through tired eyes across the cove, in the direction his twin points, and he blinks to clear his vision.

Ever see one of those before? Rock asks.

'One of those,' to Crag's astonishment, is a bipedal figure lying curled at the bottom of a clear, hollow ball, perforated but—he assumes from having seen other scion prisoners kept in similar contraptions—impregnable. The figure is at first difficult to make out clearly, but then it stands, slowly, and when it does, the twins share matching exclamations, looking quickly at one another, then back to the newcomer.

Looks like... Crag thinks.

...just like... Rock agrees. *Two legs...*

...two arms... Crag adds.

...one head, they think at the same time.

But it can't be, Crag objects. *A Moondweller...*

...wouldn't get caught so easy, Rock agrees. *Not if they're as amazing as we've been told. But look at that head. Just like Ancian...*

Death is the Door

...always described, sure, Crag thinks. *Small teeth, small eyes, small ears, small nose, but...*

...but big brains, Rock finishes. *And fur on top.*

Can't count the fingers from here, thinks Crag.

Can't smell it, either, Rock adds, nose twitching.

Just a matter of time... Crag rises to four legs.

...cuz here it comes, Rock finishes. He pulls his snout from the hole as the mysterious biped walks his spherical prison across the cove toward them. Its stride starts out uncertain and slow, as if it is remembering how to walk, but it soon gains confidence—perhaps it was bitten like they had been and is recovering from the poison. Whatever the case, it observes but does not pause before any of the other creatures held captive throughout the cove. Instead, it moves directly toward them until it has drawn close enough for them to count its fingers.

Five on each! Can't count the toes, Rock notes, looking at the biped's sturdy boots. *But Ancian...*

...always said they liked to cover their feet, Crag finishes. *And most of the rest of their body.*

The biped stops his mobile prison, standing between the two cells and appraising them both.

Don't suppose it... Rock begins.

...knows how to think? Crag asks. *Try it.*

You try it.

You saw it first.

You're the oldest.

Crag sniffs.

By a few breaths, sure! Got a funny smell, doesn't it? Smells like it's...

...like it's not alive, yeah. But obviously...

...obviously it is. OK. Fine. I'll try.

Crag focuses on the biped, wondering what an appropriate greeting might be, when, to their great, mutual surprise, the creature bends in the middle, bowing.

Whoa, thinks Rock. *That looks like it's...*

...looks like it's saying hello, Crag finishes.

The figure steps its prison a few paces closer, now one pounce away were pouncing an option. It opens its mouth—tiny teeth, indeed—and beyond all expectation and understanding, it begins to generate sounds, familiar and inexplicable.

Pull my tail! thinks Crag. *Are those...*

...kezel voices? Rock asks. *They sure are. But where are they coming from? Are they coming from...*

They are. The sounds are coming from *inside* the Moondweller, but who can say how that might be?

I don't understand, thinks Crag. *Is that...*

...yes, it's Bliss, thinks Rock, and his ears angle forward. *It's her voice for sure. And there's Yellow!*

The twins lean forward, hungrily taking in the sound of kezel. What an outsider might sense as nothing but growls and grumbles, yips and murmurs, is to Rock and Crag a clear set of ideas being expressed by no fewer than eight distinct voices in conversation. Though divorced from context—the real heart of the message would have been expressed in thought—the cumulative effect is the creation of a tone that shifts but ultimately settles on something hopeful.

> Surprise.
> Wonder.
> Fear.
> Awe.
> Relief.
> Solicitude.
> Comfort.
> Food.
> Honor.
> Gratitude.

The recording—for that is what it is, an audible documentation of every second spent by the lieutenant in kezel company—comes suddenly to an end.

The biped turns and looks toward the lone scion tower as if expecting someone to appear. Moments later, both Crag and Rock hear the pincing steps and chittering voices of their captors. Quickly, the biped jogs his globe away from the kezel and parks in the sun fifty strides away, taking a seat with his legs crossed and his gaze neutral. The scion enter the cove, twelve of them, two carrying long, sharp sticks, two carrying parcels of lova and virble. They spend some time gathered around the biped, clicking and buzzing to one another at the unprecedented sight, but eventually, seeming to recall their duties, they leave the wonder and approach the kezel, stopping at Rock's enclosure first.

What do you suppose? he thinks. *Howling, or...*

*...maybe standing on two legs...*Crag thinks. *Or...*

...or maybe today's a roll over and play dead day...

...or a tumbling day...

The two scion with the food hold their prize in clear sight before Rock's enclosure, while the two with the sticks put them to work, jabbing and poking from opposite sides. The intent isn't to injure as much as inspire, and Rock knows the implied message is a simple, "Do! Do! Perform! Perform!"

Because he is hungry, but also because he wants to give his captors no reason to stay any longer than necessary, he scrolls through his entire repertoire, demeaning though it is. He puts his head back and howls, then stands on two legs and does a fine pirouette. This is followed by the best somersault his cramped quarters allow and some rhythmic clapping.

The scion chitter appreciatively and pass some of the food into the enclosure, suspended from one of the sticks. Rock doesn't bother grabbing the weapon. Crag had done that the first time, moons ago, and had gotten nothing but trouble for his initiative, a long, painful period without food or water.

When Crag, too, has put on his little show and been given just enough food to keep him alive, the scion gather one last time around the biped. But they eventually grow tired of the novelty—so boring! All it does is sit there!—and they take their sticks and their incessant chittering and leave the cove.

The twins waste little time downing their food.

I've had better, thinks Crag.

And more, Rock adds.

But for the moment, hunger is not the primary concern. All their attention is fixed on their new acquaintance. With the scion safely moved on and the cove left unattended, the biped rises to its feet and rolls slowly back toward the kezel, getting so close its spherical prison bumps against Crag's enclosure.

It reaches its fingers through the vent holes. It touches the surface of the enclosure.

As if gauging its composition, it brushes the stone-like substance lightly with its fingertips, then taps at it with its nails, as useless and non-threatening in appearance as its teeth. The twins watch, fascinated, but neither expect what happens next. The biped, expressionless, leaves off with its survey of the kezel enclosure and focuses instead on its own. It runs its palms over the inside of the globe, then puts a finger through one ventilation hole and the thumb of the same hand through another. It looks up at the kezel, and—miracle!—it pinches the clear substance with such force that a small fracture appears with the sharp cracking of a chewed bone.

Stronger than it looks, thinks Rock.

Well done, thinks Crag.

And they both make a low bow to the biped.

It returns the gesture.

+ + +

There is no time for more. Word of a vumierre being held in the Royal Garden soon spreads, and before long, a line of blue files into the cove from the ground level of Cyclonia's lone tower, ushered by scion soldiers careful to keep the line moving and ensure that no one disturbs or does damage to the queen's prize. One by one, they pass by the kezel enclosures, rarely pausing—kezel aren't new and exciting any more—on their way to the amazing spectacle in its spherical prison.

Except the vumierre, up close, is not so spectacular. It sits looking at them without a motion or sound, its eyes unblinking, and it seems quite content to do so indefinitely. A pair of soldiers jostle the globe to inspire some kind of response, but the creature merely braces itself to keep from being tumbled over and never once gets to its feet. Had it, they would have noticed hidden beneath it a very interesting thing indeed, and unprecedented: a small but distinct crack marring the globe's otherwise unblemished form.

What is the use? thinks one of the spectators.

Yes. What is the purpose? another agrees.

Yes, thinks a third. *Long wait in a long line.*

Yes. Too long. For what? Vumierre are supposed to walk upright and make speech. Poke it!

No, thinks a soldier. *Queen will not allow.*

No. Not allow, agrees its bristly companion. *To be looked at only, not touched.*

Maybe not a vumierre, one spectator dares to suggest. *Maybe an imposter.*

Yes, thinks another. *Fake vumierre, or defective.*

Yes, others agree, growing disenchanted. *Five fingers and two feet—what is the use?*

No use, others think, and so they move on, clicking disappointedly and returning to the tower, allowing others to take their place. These are similarly amazed at first, but like their peers before them, high expectations are soon dashed by the sheer dullness of a subject they had expected to embody all the dreams and fears of a legendary past.

No walking, thinks one.

No talking, thinks another.

No Power, no Command, thinks a third.

It is not a real vumierre, someone echoes the growing sentiment. *Not a real slaver.*

Yes, others come to agree. *Slavers had Power.*

Yes. They had Command.

And so it goes, the kezel generally ignored and looking on until it seems every scion in the hive has had a chance to pass by and judge as lacking the newest addition to the Garden. In time, clouds darken the horizon, and a brewing storm announces itself with crackling thunder. The line grows short, then simply comes to an end, until the last underwhelmed scion shuffles off, buzzing to itself. The soldiers, their oversight no longer needed, induce the kezel to some tumbling and howling for scraps of virble, then become bored themselves—or anxious of the storm—and leave the cove, clicking, and whistling, and never looking back.

Lieutenant K sits quietly.

He has been busy during the visitation, acquiring and analyzing data. Once the cove has been vacated, he rises to his feet and rolls his prison to where the sand meets the lapping waves. He scans the steep, jagged walls that run into the sea, looks out to where they become toothy shoals, exposed and battered by the tide. To a lesser observer, it might have appeared hopeless. But Lieutenant K scans and analyzes every meter of the rock faces with the cold, calculating gaze unique to the machine mind. Soon enough, he identifies three different zigzag paths up the curved wall, measures their relative difficulty, and chooses the best of the three.

Looks like we're swimming, he thinks to himself, an unnecessary habit of his programming. Where are the captain and ensign? Where should he go once free? *One thing at a time,* he thinks. *We've got a storm on the way and a lot of ground to cover.*

He rolls his prison close to the kezel enclosure and bows once again. They watch him closely.

He waits.

When the sky is dark and the wind whipping, he strikes the globe with a fist like a hatching chick, puncturing the shell where it had earlier been cracked. In moments, the door is broken to shards, and he crawls out in an easy motion. The kezel bare and clash their teeth. But the best is yet to come. Stepping close to the first enclosure, Lieutenant K runs his hands across the rough surface and leans in, as if listening. Then, in one explosive motion, he pivots at the waist and strikes the enclosure with the back of his elbow directly between two of the holes. Crack! Two well-placed kicks follow—crunch!—and

Death is the Door

that portion of the wall breaks away.

Now both kezel are on their feet and turning frenzied circles, hope and anxiety pent up with no outlet. But not for long. Several precise blows widen the hole until the first of the caged beasts is free. Its partner soon follows. Once out onto the rain-peppered sand of the open cove, they look about wildly, unsure of which way to go. But Lieutenant K has no doubts. Turning decisively, he waves for them to follow and treads into the shallows.

Freedom tastes like salt water.

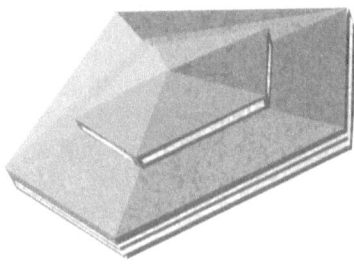

CHAPTER FOUR
Contact

IN THE PAST, Doc Foster, a hard, unsmiling woman with emotionless, dark hair, took meticulous care to sterilize and seal cargo bay four. She and her team, overseen by Commander Rickles, left only one service door accessible, via a series of zippered containment barriers and a mobile purification unit through which everyone entering and exiting the bay had to pass. In the galley, Chief Science Officer Shonda Abara was equally diligent as she supervised the ship's steward and his crew in making sure the water, steaks, and containers—as well as the people transporting them to the bay—were contaminant free. The process was painstaking and nerve-wracking for everyone involved (most had been roused from other duties or a deep sleep) but no one complained, and eventually, the job was complete.

Their reward was a once-in-a-lifetime sight.

Maya stood in the control room next to Watt, clutching his hand, while they and Commander Rickles, each dressed in a decon suit, looked through the barred window at the creatures who had entered the cargo bay through the docking hatch on the other side. She gasped at what she saw. Standing in the final containment barrier, just outside the service door, Shonda, wearing her own decon suit and attended by an armed escort—also sterilized and suited—peered through the door's small window and clapped her gloved hands slowly.

Death is the Door

"Yes!" she exclaimed. "Gorgeous!"

But Maya could give no voice to words. She no longer felt she was dreaming or hallucinating. But simply accepting events without some objection seemed impossible, dangerous, even, like a freefall of trust. The quadrupeds were amazing enough for a lifetime of study—they were wearing vests, for God's sake—but it was the other one, the blue one, who really tilted her world. This creature, bug-eyed and naked, had the look of a child in costume. But the antennae atop its head were vitally expressive, not at all prosthetic, and those eyes...

She has your hair, Watt observed, judging from pictures he had seen of her in her youth. Maya instinctively moved her hand toward her head but was blocked by her hood. She recalled the curly locks she had long ago shorn and incinerated.

"We're a go, Major," the commander spoke into his comm. His gravelly voice didn't match the spectacular thing that was happening before them, too business-like by far. "All three aboard."

"OK, Shonda." Javon's voice came over the speakers, and Maya imagined him on the bridge, watching every detail. "Dinner time."

The science chief took one last look through the window to where the newcomers stood in the middle of the bay, and slowly, so as not to startle them, she opened the door and wheeled into the room a giant salver of bloody steaks and a stainless-steel kettle filled with water. She had her orders, and dared not remain, but she couldn't resist one look at the aliens—aliens!—standing less than fifty feet away. The spiky ones turned to face her, the smaller of the two baring a mouth of teeth unlike any in her years of experience. The blue creature stood between the others, and it held up a hand, for all the world a human hand, palm out and fingers up.

"Get out of there, Shonda," Javon ordered.

And she did, but not before returning the gesture.

When the door was again locked, Shonda and her escort both passed through the sanitizer and zipped themselves out of the last containment barrier. The look on the chief's face when she removed her hood was nothing short of beatific.

"OK," the commander waved to the others. "Clear out of the control room."

+ + +

"Your passengers are aboard," said Javon to the hologram of Sister Janet. "It's your turn."

"Are they OK?"

"As far as I can tell."

"The cargo bay control room, then?"

"Yes, and if you appear anywhere else, you'll be shot on sight. Understood?"

"Of course, Major. There's no need for threats."

"Then call it fair warning."

The image flickered and disappeared. A moment later, the commander's voice abraded the air.

"She's here, Major. Smokes! A transporter beam! Just like in the movies."

"Keep her there, Terry." Javon got to his feet and straightened his collar. "No one talks to her but me."

But of course, he said nothing about gathering around the door and staring through the window, which is what Watt, Shonda, Doc Foster, and the commander were all doing when Javon arrived at the cargo bay wearing his own decon suit. Maya sat nearby, her hand on her belly and her gaze distant.

"Are you OK?" Javon asked; she didn't reply.

Watt turned from the door.

"You're not going to hurt her."

"Not unless she gives me a reason."

"Promise me!"

"The major already gave you the best answer you're going to get," Commander Rickles grumbled. "Step aside, MacLean."

Watt did, chewing on his beard, watching every move the major made as Javon stepped closer to Shonda and Doc Foster, joining them in peering through the window. A dirty and disheveled Janet MacLean, her glasses lensless and bent, sat inside, hands on her knees.

"What can you tell me, people?" the major asked.

Shonda spoke first.

"She's clean as far as I can tell, sir. If she's hiding any threats, I can't find them."

Doc Foster turned her stern gaze from the control room to the major, her accent British and her tone professional to the point of humorless.

"Assuming my sensors are properly calibrated, I'm detecting no pathogens, either on the biologics or the android. I still recommend suits if you're going in."

"I'm going in," Watt said, "suit or not."

Commander Rickles looked poised to remark, but Javon held up his hand.

"I can't imagine how this is making you feel, Watt, and I know you mean well, but I need to know your emotions aren't going to get in the way of making good decisions. Whatever she is, whoever she is, she isn't *your* Janet. And until I trust her one hundred percent, you'll interact how I say and when I say. Understood?"

Watt's face scrunched up tight and sour, and his fingers twitched at his sides. Maya could read him brewing a hot reply, and she reached out, pulling him close to her and looking up at him.

Please, she thought. *Just do what he says.*

And like that, Watt's fuse was doused.

She's in our room, he thought, and he slouched in a chair next to her. *She wants to know what's going on.*

And we'll tell her as soon as we can.

What is *going on?*

I don't for sure know.

You know more than you're telling.

Not for long, I promise. Please...

Meanwhile, two armed and suited guards had entered the control room and, according to the pre-arranged agreement, clapped a pair of restraints around the chaplain's wrists and ankles. She bore this placidly, making no comment except to thank each of the guards by name. They glanced awkwardly at one another, but their orders had been clear, and they gave her no reply. They moved from the room and stood watchfully as Javon addressed his second-in-command.

"Take the bridge, Terry. Not a word to anyone. And post guards; no one enters this area without my permission. Loose lips, you know..."

"Yeah," the commander replied. "I do." And he left them, his scowl looking apt to become a fixture.

"You know," Javon said to Doc Foster, "you're done here if you want to get some sleep." But her face told him she had no plans of leaving. "Forget I mentioned it," he waved. "Work with Shonda and monitor the situation from here." He paused. "If something should happen, I want you both out of here immediately. Let Terry handle it. Clear the area and comm for back-up."

"Nothing is going to happen," Watt mumbled.

But something already had happened, Maya knew, and would continue happening, whether they understood it or not. She expected they might look back some day and view Janet's inexplicable appearance as the least remarkable part of that something. She could feel Watt's fear, but she had none herself.

Javon gestured to them both.

"Here's your chance," he said, and he led the way through the sterilization compartment and into the control room, Maya and Watt following close behind. The door was sealed, and the room was silent, the wide window giving them a clear view of the alien creatures in the bay, tentatively exploring their new surroundings and sniffing their way close to the salver of steaks.

"I don't suppose there's any point in introductions," Javon said. But Watt surprised him.

"Yes," he said to the Janet seated before them. "Heck yes there is. Who am I?"

Janet looked as though he had spat on her.

"The person who is trying to make me cry."

"Not if you are who you say you are."

"Watt! How do I convince you of that? Do you wish to open me up and run tests?"

Inside his decon hood, Watt's jaw jutted forward.

"Who am I?"

"You're my brother! You've been dead for over a hundred years, and I miss you every day. But you're my maker, too, and I need your help."

"Maya says you know about the baby."

"And your fear of heights, and her grandfather Sujan's creation of the first Halo, which freed billions of people from their devices and made the family fortune that would help build this ship, and how your mom thought you had cute toes, and your dad called you a weakling. I also know that, only moments before you sighted Aranae, Maya and the major felt an awesome power they couldn't explain. 'A ghost,' I joked at the time, but it was weak humor, because I was devastated by my role in Willie's death, and I thought my senses were failing. I know now it was no ghost."

Her chin dipped to her modest bosom.

"I know too many things."

"What was it?" Maya asked, desire for an answer overshadowing her reluctance to speak. "The power?"

But when she spoke again, Janet addressed the major, and her tone was cold.

"You don't like telepaths."

Javon leaned back.

"What does that have to do with anything?"

"Then you admit it?"

"I've never met one! How would I know?"

"Simply, major. The me you know—the one who is, at this moment, waiting in her room and calculating the odds that you are all discussing having her shut down, that me agreed to never divulge the secret. That me agreed the risk was too great. But all the while, that same me wondered: 'Major Monroe has always respected me, never said a bad word about androids. Why would he tolerate me and naturally dislike a telepath? Why not tell him?' But I respected the wishes of others and never did."

Now it was Javon's voice that hardened.

"Tell me what? What 'others'?"

"I'm sorry, Major. That remains someone else's prerogative. I merely raise the point because I can't answer Maya's question without...revelation."

"Revelation of what? I'm getting tired of games."

"Oh, Moses!" Watt spouted. "I get it! You didn't break the promise in the past and you're not going to break it now." He tried to tug at his beard but bumped into his facemask. Maya felt his tension rising and wondered if he might do something stupid like remove his headgear. Instead, he once again surprised them by sitting down next to the new Janet. "Major Monroe," he said. "I'm sorry, Major. I wanted to tell you. There were times I thought you guessed, thought you knew. I was...I was scared and stupid. I should have trusted you."

"Bullspit," said the major.

"It's true," said Maya.

Javon wheeled on her.

"How would you know?"

"How would you not?" Maya snapped. She took a deep breath, knowing she would get only one chance to say this. "From our first date, you knew I was different. You said I 'tickled your brainy parts.'"

"I know what I said! Were you reading my mind the whole time? Were you spying on my thoughts?"

"You know I wasn't."

"Are you reading them now?"

"It doesn't work like that." Maya closed her eyes. So many words, so much energy. "Help me here, Watt."

Watt clenched his fists.

"I can't speak for anyone but myself. I can read thoughts if someone is able to send them. Otherwise, all I get are moods, emotions."

"Then this should be easy," said Javon. "How am I feeling about your so-called 'revelation?'"

"Betrayed," said Watt, and he sounded like a sad little boy. "I feel a distance that wasn't there before."

"Well?" Javon pressed. "Can you blame me?"

Death is the Door

No one could.

"Let's say for the moment," said Javon, "that I buy this and am OK with it. What does it have to do with what happened on the bridge?"

"Everything," Janet replied. "Whatever power found you—found us—adrift out here, responded first to the distress buoys you were wise to deploy. But when they saw we were an acquisitive, colonizing species, they at first intended to leave us there to fend for ourselves."

"Too bad for them," said Javon. "Whoever they were. We found a planet without their help."

"No, Major. Just the opposite, in fact, though it was their intention to make us believe we had done it on our own. In truth, they moved this ship as easily as a human helping a turtle cross a road."

"Why? What changed their minds?"

"They sensed me," said Maya, guessing, but a moment later she corrected herself. "No. The baby."

"Yes," Janet sighed. "She's what they call a Reader. Or she will be. You will name her Grace, but everyone will call her Abuelita, 'Little Grandmother,' because of how wrinkled she'll be when she's born. And the name will stick, because she'll be wise beyond her years. She'll grow up to be my best friend. Ahh!"

And Janet clutched at her chest, her bound hands wringing at her tunic as she began to sob like a dam rupturing. Javon watched suspiciously, but Maya felt her heart breaking, and something shifted uneasily inside her—was it too early for a baby to be kicking? It was Watt, in the end, who cast away his doubts and flung his arm around the distraught creature, holding her until she once again grew calm.

"I'm sorry," he said, his hood making it sound like a whisper, and then, despite not having permission, he tore the thing from his head and threw it to the side. "Heck!" he cried, and he removed Janet's glasses, using his sleeve to wipe at her tears. "What do you need from us?" he asked. "What should we do?"

"Meet my passengers," she said, and she gestured

through the window, where several of the steaks had vanished and the alien creatures, their spikes no longer flared, seemed huddled in conversation.

"And what will meeting them do for us?" Javon wanted to know. "And for that matter, how will we be able to understand each other?"

Janet sat up and accepted her glasses.

"Meeting them will help establish trust in the face of a common enemy. The blue one—her name is Joy—will translate. She is the hub." And here, Janet looked at Maya. "She's also your...I guess we would say granddaughter. Child of an experiment wrought by the baby you carry, and the best Reader I've met."

"Reader of what, exactly?" Javon demanded.

"The artifact she carries." Janet pointed at Joy. "It calls itself a Book. And...well, we shall see."

"Oh, I don't think so," Javon growled. "If you've got something on your mind, let's have it."

"It's not for me to give, Major. Please. Lower the partition. You needn't worry about their health; they have been exposed to humans, directly and indirectly, many times. That way, we can all get some answers."

+ + +

Lightning and her companions adjusted slowly to their new surroundings. The place was as sterile as the one they just left, but it was several times larger and had a world of scents circulating through it; warm-blooded creatures inhabited the spaces outside.

Moondwellers, Lightning thought as she walked the periphery of the room, sniffing at its corners.

Lots of them, Thunder agreed, and he rose to two legs to get a closer smell of the air moving in from a ventilation register. *I know Ancian wouldn't want to hear this, but they smell so delicious!*

Joy sat with her hand inside her sling.

Please don't try to eat them, amoti Thunder.

Moments later, a door opened at the far end of the

room, and an odd figure peeked inside, shaped like a Moondweller but covered head to toe in a baggy orange suit. The kezel backed away, their spikes flaring, but the figure didn't stay long, didn't even come all the way into the room. Instead, it pushed a wheeled cart inside, on top of which rode a large, metal tray, filled with cuts of red meat. This was followed by a metallic basin of water. The figure waited only a moment to hold up its hand in response to Joy's greeting. Then it quickly turned and left, closing the door behind it.

You see? thought Thunder. *I didn't eat anybody.*

Yes, heroic restraint, Lightning replied, and she stepped carefully toward the containers. The water smelled safe, but it had no character. Water in the accrete took on the flavors and scents unique to its varied sources. It could be salty or sweet, loamy or herby, seasoned by the rocks through which it was filtered or the scales often found steeping on its surface. Aerated and frothy or stagnant and stale, water had a personality, and any self-respecting kezel could identify its source simply by its taste or its smell.

Reckon it'll quench thirst, she thought, curling her lip. *But it's the most boring water I've ever smelled.*

Who cares? thought Thunder, and he stepped boldly up to the salver of meat, red, marbled slabs with one small bone in their middle. Each was roughly the size of one of his hands, and about as thick.

Go easy, Lightning cautioned. They could neither of them smell any reason to be suspicious of the food—in fact, it smelled fantastic—but it came from some foreign animal. Who could say what unpleasantness might result from overconsumption? Thunder snatched one of the slabs from the pile and slunk away to a corner of the room. He showed great self-control, tearing away a hunk and actually chewing it a couple times before swallowing.

Say, he thought. *That's pretty good.*

Before taking one for herself, Lightning offered Joy a strip of awl from her pack. Joy nibbled on the rubbery flesh, walking idly about the space, her mind deep in thought as Lightning became briefly engrossed in the pleasure of a novel food. Thunder wasn't mistaken: this was quite a treat, richer than talihew, softer than babelrack, not nearly as bitter as a sneer. The bone was its own type of delight, like an egg filled with marrow. Thunder helped himself to a second, and Lightning, despite her caution, followed soon after.

Let's hope we don't have to be here long, she thought. *I don't care how tasty, this is still cage food.*

Hey, thought Thunder, and he gulped the last of his steak. *Look! I think we're being watched.* He pointed to the opposite side of the room where vague reflections could be seen moving on the other side of a large rectangular panel, smooth and featureless.

Lightning's snout wrinkled. The figures were difficult to make out, but she could see three, perhaps four of them, Moondwellers, if she were forced to guess. She did not care to be observed like some kind of display, and her appetite vanished.

Come in here, she thought angrily. *We're done waiting around for you!*

I don't think they're able to understand you, Joy offered, leaning over the cauldron and taking a drink.

Well, thought Lightning, her patience evaporating. *Maybe they'll understand this.* And she stepped toward the panel, intending to give it a good rapping with her fist. But before she could, the reflective partition slid open from bottom to top, revealing behind a linked barrier four bipeds, one the troublemaker named Sister Janet and three others dressed in orange.

+ + +

"Moses," Watt whispered. "Will this grate hold?"

"They're not here to hurt you," Janet said quietly.

Maya leaned close to the barricade. She sensed at once that each of the miraculous creatures she faced through the heavy chain link was loaded with thoughts of its own about her, her companions, and the situation they found themselves in. At first, emotions and moods were what she read, general and inexact, as if she was trying to make words out of the clouds. The smaller of the two—kezel? Was that the name?—was angry and scared, the larger, distrustful and defensive, but also hungry and thinking of the remaining steaks. The third creature, the blue one, was also scared, but she—it was clearly female—was either better at hiding her fear, or was too busy with other thoughts. For Maya could sense her mind working at a furious pace, as if she were carrying on a conversation with several people at once.

"OK," said Javon to Sister Janet. "What do we do?"

"Introduce yourself."

"How?"

"As you normally would. As I said, the blue one is called Joy. She can't understand System English, but the device she carries will interpret for her. Through her, the two kezel will also be able to understand you."

"And how will she be able respond?"

"Through Maya—or Watt. Using her mind."

"If she doesn't know English?"

"It's true, Major. She'll be sending clear ideas in a universal language of thought. And what's more, not only can she understand telepaths from other species, she engenders comprehension between them as well."

Maya gasped.

"You mean we'll understand the...those..." She pointed vaguely, hoping to not insult their guests.

"Kezel, yes, if they choose to share."

Which is getting less likely the longer you keep us here against our will, came a thought.

Stunned, Maya and Watt reached for one another at the same time. They felt something in their brains shift, like reluctant puzzle pieces falling at last into place, lining up neatly and locking together. The thought couldn't be mistaken; it clearly came from the smaller of the two kezel. It stepped forward, its prodigious snout only inches from the grate. They could see the simple stiches of its primitive vest, could count the claws on its hands when it paused to remove the mask from around its eyes. Then, to everyone's surprise, it rose to two legs and bowed. And when it did, they could see a belt strapped around its waist, from which hung a sheathed blade.

That's one of mine, thought Javon to himself, but he had no chance to ask how that could be.

The bow is for my gami-kan, the creature thought, and a picture appeared in Maya's mind of a very old kezel in a faded vest. *It's the last one you're getting unless you start sharing some answers.*

Oh, thought Maya, delighted but also aware of the stress in the creature's tone. *Yes, we will try,* she promised. *We are confused too. But we'll do our best. We mean you no harm.*

Then you'll have no problem bringing us home. The creature's lip drew back to reveal jagged, white teeth.

I...I hope we can do that, Maya glanced at Javon.

"What's happening?" he demanded.

"They want to go home," said Watt simply, looking at Janet. "And they're very upset with you."

"Yes, they have every right to be. But I needed them—specifically, the blue one and the device it carries. The others could not be conveniently separated. And I couldn't risk explaining my plan. They may not have co-operated and I would have had to attempt...I hate to use the word abduction, but..." She shrugged. "You haven't properly introduced yourself yet, Major. Kezel are a surprisingly formal species. They will respect you more if you identify yourself as the leader."

"You'd better hope so," said Javon. He took a deep breath and addressed the kezel. "Hello," he said, and he held up his hand as Shonda had. "My name is Major Javon Monroe. I'm in charge of this ship."

At the mention of this name, Maya was struck by the way light danced in the blue creature's eyes, the one named Joy. And then:

We know another Moondweller who has that name, the creature thought, clear as polished glass.

"Well?" thought Javon, who of course could sense

nothing. "Did it work? Did they understand me?"

Maya nodded.

"And?" Javon pressed. But Maya deferred to Watt, having no energy for voice. When he translated, Javon scrunched his lips and glared at Janet.

"What does that mean? 'Has that name?'"

"It seems," she said, "that one of your more enterprising descendants has—in our time—finally located where the original *Destiny* mission ended up. We met him and his two-person crew before coming here."

"One of my descendants..." Javon squirmed as if something itchy had crawled inside his suit.

"So he claims."

"And what in the world is a Moondweller?"

"It's what kezel refer to as humans. Their explanation for your arrival on their planet is that you came from one of their moons. Some kezel hold humans in contempt, some in high regard, as these do."

Not so fast, thought the smaller of the two kezel. *We were taught all sorts of things about Moondwellers, wherever they come from, but let me say: I've never run into anything good they ever did. Dead things, poisonous things, unnatural things... Oh, sure, throwers can be useful—until the wrong kezel gets their hands on one, or they stop working. No insult intended, but we'll hold you in 'high regard' when you return us home.*

Watt scrambled to translate this, repeating words as fast as his mind could formulate the ideas. Even still, what Maya heard from his voice was a rough, flat version of what she sensed in her mind. There, the thoughts were rich with tone and complex imagery, a treat to her brain.

Do you have a name? she asked at last.

The creature resumed a four-legged posture.

I'm Fire of the Storm, she thought. *That's my otimu, Sound of the Storm. And this is Joy. Who are you?*

But Joy answered the question first.

She is my gami-kan. Her name is Maya.

Yes, thought Maya, subdued but incredulous. *But I can't explain how or why...or anything!*

A.P. Malloy

I bet that one can, thought the one calling itself Sound of the Storm, and it pointed at Sister Janet. Its ears pinned back and its eyes grew squinty. *It's got all sorts of big plans—and secrets.*

But when Watt translated this and Javon turned like an accusation to face Janet, she merely returned his gaze and nodded slightly.

"I have done what I had to do. But I have no secrets, I promise. You can ask me anything. I welcome it! The sooner you see the truth in what I am telling you, the better for all of us."

Javon closed his eyes for several moments.

"I was having such a nice sleep," he said after a time. "And then, in the span of an hour, a time-traveling android, three telepathic extra-terrestrials, and stories of God-like aliens who consider us no better than turtles."

"Not stories, Major," Janet objected. "Truth."

"Then show me the proof."

"It's not mine to show. Ask the girl."

The one named Joy seemed to understand immediately she had become the center of attention. The larger of the two kezel, who had helped itself to another steak, paused in its chewing to join the other in looking at her. She lowered her gaze and dipped her hand inside the crude sling strapped over her shoulder. She made no reply, but Maya was certain she was thinking all the while, locked in a conversation that was tightly sheltered. She made no attempt to pry—wasn't sure she could have had she wanted to—and merely waved Javon to silence when he began to grow impatient. The blue creature had a light in its enormous eyes that sank deep into its head while it thought, and its hand moved in slow circles, caressing whatever rode in its sling.

How? Maya thought to herself. *How in all the world?* She looked at the creature's cascading raven hair and could imagine nothing but pictures of her ninth birthday, taken by her mother when Shantikar had spent an hour first playing in, then napping amid her glorious tangles. But...antennae! No common ground there. And it

Death is the Door

was blue—many different shades. What was that about?

The creature looked up at her.

Krishna, Shiva, and Rama are all blue, yes?

Maya's mouth opened soundlessly.

Say something, Watt urged her.

But she struggled for the words, images of Daada and spicy clouds of incense filling her mind.

Yes, she thought at last. *How do you know that?*

My friend told me. He knows many things. And the creature's hand moved lovingly, tracing an irregular shape as its antennae bent forward.

What is that? Maya asked. *What is in there?*

The reason that one brought us all here, the creature thought, and it tilted its antennae toward Sister Janet. *She wasn't even nice enough to ask us.*

She claims she was afraid you'd say no.

The creature fixed Maya with a sharp, glittering gaze and made a low clicking sound.

She can't understand us if you stop translating.

Maya's heart wiggled in her chest, and she glanced unintentionally at Watt. He returned the look, but only for a fraction, before taking the hint and allowing the thought to remain untranslated. When the creature offered another thought, he didn't translate this either, and Javon and Janet were left to assume that nothing was being shared. But something was.

Our planet is in trouble. You can help, the creature thought. *But you should be careful. Don't trust her.*

How? In what way? Please, I don't understand.

She means well, but she's been badly damaged.

So, what do we do?

Let her explain. See how honest she is.

How will I know?

I'll tell you—as much as I'm able. The creature buzzed like a weary kazoo. *I'm afraid my brain is getting very tired.* Even as it thought, it moved to sit next to the smaller of the kezel, leaning against its spiky coat.

Maya turned to Watt.

I think it's time for someone to do some explaining.

A.P. Malloy

Watt agreed; he shared this with the major.

"OK," Javon said to Janet. "This is your big chance. I'm going to give you ten minutes."

She smiled, a sad, tired expression.

"Ten hours wouldn't be enough," she said. "But I'll do my best." She took a deep breath.

+ + +

"In my time, long ago, I wandered off with the Assistant Chief Engineer and scared him into damaging the drive—and killing himself."

"We know all this!"

"Yes, Major and you know that a sentient power beyond description interceded on our behalf."

"So you claim."

"So I hope to prove. For now, assume it is so."

She paused, gathering herself, and she began her tale slowly, often hesitating between ideas, grasping for the most important points. This is what she said:

"The planet was a difficult place to colonize, the habitable zone was small and crowded, and resources were scarce—this led to the First Great Mistake. Magister Healey pressed you into mining on the smallest of the five moons. There was an explosion that, over time, resulted in a slight alteration to that moon's orbit. But that went unnoticed for a long time. What was more contentious was the relationship between the people who were aware of the great sentient power you encountered, and those who were not—or, more precisely, the talisman those beings left with us before going on their way. Suffice to say the talisman is a tool of power, but only some can access it. The ones who couldn't grew suspicious and jealous, and many years after colonization, when *Destiny's* astral drive had been repaired but before there was sufficient fuel refined to return to the System, there was armed conflict known as the Rift. Maya's daughter and I were exiled from the planet and forced to live aboard *Destiny*. During the exile, the humans on the surface learned that the alteration of the smallest moon was likely, over time, to result in a catastrophic perturbation of the intricate orbits of the other moons."

Javon wagged a finger.

"Halfway there. You'd better hurry up."

But Maya placed her hand on his forearm, and he released a slow breath.

"You have five more," he said.

Janet looked as if she might cry again, but instead, she clenched her hands and continued.

"In their fear, the humans on the surface made the Second Great Mistake, inciting an uprising among the native species called scion. There were no survivors—or so we thought. And so, we returned to the surface. There we learned of the survival of three young colonists. With their help, we re-fueled *Destiny* and made a plan to use her to deliver a payload that would drive the rogue moon from harm's way. But the moon is ejecting mass at an unpredictable rate, and when it next returns, I don't know exactly where it will be or the ideal location to deliver the payload. The device this creature carries allows travel through time, and I intend to go to the future to learn what I need so I can return to my time and execute my plan. I came here because that artifact has been depleted over the years and can't make another jump without the help of...I guess you would say kin, but in fact, it is the new, young version of itself that was left with you."

She fixed Javon with a hard stare.

"Ten minutes exactly," she said.

Major Javon looked at Maya. Maya looked at Joy.

The creature shrugged its diminutive shoulders.

I didn't understand all of what she said. It patted its sling gently, as if comforting a friend. *But we didn't catch anything that was dishonest.*

Javon revealed no emotion at this news.

"Everything hinges on these mysterious artifacts you keep alluding to," he said to Janet. "A talisman? And yet, when I ask to see it, I get 'it's not mine to share,' and the like. You had no problem hauling these...people...

away from their home because you were afraid they'd say 'no.' Why the sudden courtesy?"

"Oh, Major, I wish it was courtesy, I surely do! I wish I could act like I used to, to trust in courtesy, and kindness, and the good nature of a loving deity. But I have seen horrors, been lied to, and lied. If I could simply take you and *Destiny* with me back to my time, I would, without reservation. But I cannot. The artifact that creature carries is a greatly reduced version of its earlier self, and I did not need its permission to use the little energy it has to travel through time this once."

She pointed at Maya's belly.

"That, however, the talisman that resides like a protective shell around your unborn child, is a power beyond me. I can do nothing without its permission."

Maya drew away from Watt's touch, and lines creased her forehead. An urgent need to deny this claim rose inside her, so strong it had to be cast into words.

"That's wrong," she said. "Nothing's in there."

But no sooner were the words out of her mouth than she felt a feathery touch inside her, as if a pressure on her bladder had been released. The next moment, incredible as a dream but real as a blow to the head, a ball of golden light leapt from her midsection, landed on the floor between them, and quickly solidified, taking human form. A young man stood before them, his dress boyish, his hair unruly and blonde, his smile mischievous. But his eyes were old, so old, and Maya was unable to determine their color.

Major Javon stepped forward, standing between the newcomer and his crewmembers.

"Who are you?" he demanded.

"My name is Petros," the young man smiled, and he bowed theatrically, winking. "I am a Book."

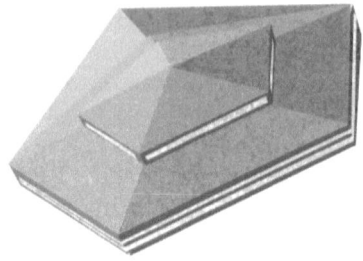

Chapter Five
News

CLIFF AND FLUVIAL step out of the transporter and make their way out to the island accrete just as Lightning had explained they should. There they find Piedmont waiting for them and tending his injuries. His mood is still somber, but the experience of traveling by Moondweller transporter is too much to keep bottled up. The kish poison slows his speech but doesn't stop it.

Whadda thing! he thinks. *Real whirly-giggin' tummy droppin' noise maker, sur-ee, but whaddayaknow? Worked just like we's told it would. WHOOSH! off ya's go, like the bottom just dropped out an you's a fallin' and spinnin'—or that's how it feels anahoo—and then KABUMP! you pop out in another one o' them cavey sorta rooms ceptin' it aint the same one, no siree, different one altogether, and Weaver's Web! One breath we's at the foot o' that ol' Colosser, (durned ol' place! Never gonna have no good feelins 'bout it no matter how fancy all their Moondweller business. Poor ol' Pounce! Poor big fella!) and next ya's walkin' outta from under a fine purply fan and how did that happen? Bunch o' thousands o' strides we took and never took a one, if yunnerstand.*

Yes sir, thinks Cliff. *That's how it was. So, I guess we should wait here for the others?*

Oh, sur-ee, that Lightnin', now that's one saucy Sugarfoot, that. She's a remindin' me a Big Fork when he was just a Little Fork, see? Always takin' charge and goin' snout-first into the fight. Real sharp, too, just liken that cutter she totes about, yunnerstand? Quick to the answer afore ol' Piedmont here can figger out the question—oh, sur-ee, Fluvial here's got it all worked out, she's the brains o' this here operation. She probbly wasn't impressed liken ol' Piedmont was, but anahoo, I reckon that Lightnin's one o' the smarter Sugarfoots I ever knowed. Not that I knowed 'em all, o' course; they's a batch I never did meet—

Yes sir, Cliff dares to interrupt, *and I'll be glad to introduce you to some. But...well...where is she?*

Who now?

Lightning. And the others.

Oh, sur-ee, I reckon they's a comin' along behind us ana time now. She'll have that tough lookin' customer, wassis name? That creamy colored one?

Thunder, thinks Fluvial.

Oh, sur-ee, Piedmont knowed that! Good fighter that one. Gonna be a boss when he grows full big. Nothin' to mess with for no reason no sir—not even thinkin' I'd *like to make 'im mad, though don't you 'spect I wouldn't take care o' business, cuz I would, see? Never been a jabi could take ol' Piedmont in a tussle, so don't be thinkin' it!*

Cliff is not.

But anahoo, no reason for that, cuz we's all goodly friends now, best new pals, that ol' Thunder and us, and that's better than fightin' anahoo, see? So sur-ee, he'll be a comin' here ana time, and so's too that goofy lookin' blue critter, wassername, with the two wigglys comin' out topside and walkin' two legged like Moondwellers used to— still do!—and sur-ee, that makes 'ol Piedmont think o' them two we seed. What a pair, yeah? Both good fighters, too, don't mind sayin' though 'twas a surprise, seein' how they's neither of 'em real big or strongly like, still, they made some wreck outa them kish, hoodiddly! But don't reckon they'll be joinin' us here, all worked up like they was 'bout their 'ships,' and 'payloads,' and whatnot. Words don't mean nothin' to ol' Piedmont, but anahoo, that ol' Lightnin' and her oti-mu and that blue critter'll be comin' along ana time now, just you watch.

Death is the Door

82

Watch and wait they do, their ears tuned for the sound of the transporter door. But it does not come.

Anathing to eat 'round these parts? asks Piedmont, who has scouted the island with no luck. *Hm, Clawpaw?*

There's a caepod pool up there, Cliff motions. *You can cross on those boulders—or swim.*

Woo-ee! Caepods you say? Sense that, Fluvial? Yer favorites, all oily and meaty and yum! What say? Wanna go for a climb whiles we wait? You OK with that, Clawpaw, waitin' here fer t'others whiles we grab us a snack?

Cliff is. He watches as Fluvial leaps from boulder to boulder and Piedmont flounders and splashes his way across the lake. They look up at the steep northern face of the canyon wall, wrinkling their snouts.

Kind of a haul for ol' Piedmont here, big ol' belly climbin' way up like I was someone's jabi, but here, Fluvial, you do the first so's I don't fall and knock yas for a tumble. Thassa way! Lookadergo, Clawpaw! Ever seen a climber like Fluvial? Course you han't. OK, Piedmont's turn, see? Whew! I'm pooped already! Derned ol' kish sure took it outta me. OK, though, here he comes, aha! Told you he could do it!

And off they go to the caepod pool, out of sight.

Cliff waits, and as time passes, he worries.

This isn't right, he thinks. *What's taking so long?*

Piedmont returns to the ledge overhead, waving two large caepods victoriously.

Anathing, Clawpaw?

No sir.

Don't you worry! They'll be a comin' ana time now.

But his ears droop to a worried angle.

Ana time, now.

+ + + + + +

Which, far to the south, near the bank of the Doorn river, is what Viktor is thinking to his small company of soldiers and handlers. Goodness! What magic they have wrought on the alp. A swim in the river is how

A.P. Malloy

they had started, scrubbing and washing every plate and horn. But they hadn't stopped there, for Ozag, Mysterious and Splendid, was coming, and she desired the alp for her own unspecified uses. What an honor!

Make the tentacles glossy, Viktor had directed.

Which had not been easy to do, for an alp sprouts tentacles from its head like grass on the plains, and already the ones injured by the lieutenant's grenade had begun to heal or grow anew. But the handlers had relished their work, for it was what they were born to do. They had climbed the alp, crawling among its bony plates and dangling from its tentacles as they polished away singed skin and massaged oily secretion around its eyes and ears. And Twenty-Seven had joined them, and they had whistled happily, for Ozag was coming, Unrivaled and Bewitching, and what could be better?

But the alp has been treated from tentacle to toe and has been turned loose to shovel grass into its numerous mouths, and still the scion wait.

Should he inquire of the vumierre? asks Twenty-Seven. *Has there been a delay?*

Viktor permits this, but Twenty-Seven's clicking at the facility's hatch brings no vumierre to the door. He chitters and whistles and uses his pincers to scratch at the entrance, but no one responds. He is about to return, dejected, when he hears a faint sound, muffled by the hatch, coming from within the vumierre structure.

Whirr, squeak, rattle-rattle-rattle.

Then the unmistakable sound of scion wings.

She is coming! Twenty-Seven hurries to rejoin the others. *The Undying is here!*

Formation! Viktor orders, and his depleted company arranges itself neat and orderly, the alp called back from its grazing and made to stand like a monument, glistening after a hard rain.

Calm, composed, Viktor thinks to himself, but he is trembling at the thought of Ozag, and the tip of his lone antenna burns with anticipation.

Death is the Door

+ + + + + +

Whitetails? Serenity exclaims. *How many?*

Two, replies the jabi Pockets. He and Cranny had been on guard duty, and their cousin Splay had been foraging, when out of the blue, the strangers had appeared, coming from the northwest, led by Cliff.

Where's Trapper and Old Buttons? asks Serenity.

Sleeping, thinks Cranny.

And Snapper?

Sleeping, thinks Splay.

Serenity growls, for that is what she had been doing as well, her wabi Wander curled in her embrace. But she rises heavily to her feet, called by duty. The only other bibija is Gully, and she is watching the trails south of the High Step. Wander complains at being roused, but Serenity scoops her up into her mouth and places her on Cranny's back where she perches with sleepy eyes.

You three, Serenity thinks, *are on wabi watch. Don't mess it up. Curly! Get the others and join me outside. And bring that thrower...*

When Serenity and the four Sugarfoot ibiwas at last meet the Whitetails in the sunlit snow near the southern entrance, the tale shared is slow to unfold. Piedmont begins with lengthy greetings, deferential to the point of obsequious. He sings the praises of the Sugarfoot clan, marvels at the size of the cave complex, and offers his sympathy for the destruction wrought by scion, who he also comments on at some length, considering himself an authority on the topic. Then he goes on in great detail about the quest to Ozag's Hold and the seemingly magical means of their return from Far Colossus—but his audience understands little of that. Serenity shows admirable patience, though she scowls throughout.

OK! she thinks at last. *Thank you! That is very interesting. But where are the others?*

Well, thassa what's the troubly part, see? Cuz that little copper one, the saucy jabi, and her white-spiked otimu—real scrapper, him—they's right behind us! Or sposta be, way 'twas esplained t'us, anahoo.

Joy too, Cliff offers.

Sur-ee, Piedmont agrees. *But they aint.*

And Pounce?

But Piedmont's head lowers. He shakes his shaggy mane from side to side, making low, mournful sounds, and nothing Serenity says stirs him from his gloom.

I'm sorry, Fluvial thinks. *He...died. Saving us.*

Piedmont lifts his head and howls, a terrible, wounded cry, and he gnashes his teeth.

Savin' pokey ol' Piedmont, you mean! Say it! Woulda never had a chance iffin' that Noble Pounce hadna jumped into the fight. Rottie ol' stinkin' kish! Never heard o' so many! All 'round us they was, and rollin' boulders, and ol' Piedmont...aww! Kish poison don't sit well with this one, and he was so pokey, and good ol' Pounce...

His grief overwhelms him, and his ears droop.

The others stand silent, absorbing this news. A joke, surely? Some misunderstanding? Or a lie! But this is wishful thinking. Serenity can tell from the first that Piedmont is being honest.

It was fast, thinks Fluvial. *He didn't feel a thing.*

Serenity has sensed all she can take. She shoos away Piedmont's attempt to add something else.

No, she thinks. *Enough. Stop.*

Sur-ee, sur-ee, it's hard news, but you's standin' Chief now, least for the timely's sake, and you oughter sense this bit too, might lift spirits or change plans. Dunno. You's the big boss now, you's gotta be the decider.

About what?

'Bout what that shiny bugger told the crew when we's about to get outta Colosser. Told a headful a things didn't make no sense to ol' Piedmont, but one part was real sensly like, and them Sweetfeet twins we's waitin' on thought 'twas a real bit o' goodly news—or at least the hopey kind, where ya think we got a chance, aint all guaranteed to be sour moods and bad endings, see?

I want to, thinks Serenity. *I really do.*

Sur-ee, it's easy. Bugger said—all goldly, shinerly

Death is the Door

that one—bugger said—with its brainy parts, a course, makes a clickin' and a buzzin' sometimes sounds like a nervily dow, but that kinda noise don't mean nothin' to ol' Piedmont—bugger says, 'They's kezel in Cyclonia—don't know whatever that mighta be—alive, most like, and in a garden, or somesuch, aint that it?

Yes, thinks Fluvial.

Yeppir, kept alive in a garden in Cyclonia they are. No knowin' how many, but the bugger—that goldly one— claims it's a goin' there now, settem free! Aint that some-thin'? Could come marchin' over that hill ana time...

He trails away, unusually at a loss for thought.

That is good news, thinks Serenity, but her tone is less than hopeful. *Was there anything else?*

There is not.

What will you do now? Serenity asks.

The answer she receives from the Whitetails is a sad story of misunderstanding and ostracism at home and unjustified hostility among the Bristles, leaving her to conclude that the Whitetails desire to remain—for an amount of time they do not specify. And so, she leaves their guests attended by Crag's fancy Yellow, with instructions to allow them freedom on the range, but not inside the caves. She offers no food or apologies. With Yellow at their tail, they roam off to hunt or scavenge, and as they do, Serenity confers with the remaining ibiwas, Tail, Curly, and Boots.

So? she asks.

Curly reads the wind, reflecting carefully.

They're telling the truth, she thinks. *That much is clear.* Her heads bows. *I wish it wasn't.*

Yeah.

But the ones kept alive, adds Boots. *That part...*

Sure, assuming it's true.

Where's Cyclonia? Tail wonders.

Don't know. Never heard of it.

And why haven't Lightning and Thunder come back? asks Curly. *Submission's gonna be real upset.*

Serenity curls her lip, but Curly's question has no

answer, so she asks the group one of her own.

What do you think we should do?

What can *we do?* asks Boots.

We start, thinks Tail, *by keeping an eye on those Whitetails. I don't trust 'em, despite what Three-legs says.*

Maybe let's call him Cliff, thinks Serenity.

Yeah, sure, thinks Tail. *Sorry.*

Curly sits on her haunches.

We need to have a ceremony for Pounce.

We will, thinks Serenity. *When this is all over.*

Oh, Pounce... Boots laments, and her snout dips almost to the ground. *Bridger is going to be so...*

Yeah. There's been a lot of that lately, thinks Serenity, and her tone is bitter. *Whatever you do, don't tell Cranny. I'll do that when the time is right. If there ever is a right time to learn your api is dead. Rotters! I need to relieve Gully and share the news. Curly, go catch up with Yellow. Keep your snout on those Whitetails. They're terrified of throwers, so use that as motivation if you need to make the one stop rambling.* She heaves a deep sigh. *Everyone else back to scout and forage.*

Curly turns to leave, following the trail taken by Yellow and the Whitetails. Boots and Tail move off in opposite directions. And there, left behind, stands Cliff. He lowers his gaze and waits, tail hanging low.

What is it? asks Serenity. *I've got work to do.*

I'm sorry to bother, but...what about Lightning?

We wait.

For how long?

At least until I share with Gully! And probably the gigikas too, once they wake up. What else can we do? You want to march all the way back to this Far Colossus place? Have a look around? Save the day?

I sure hope not! But...if she and Thunder are in trouble, it seems like we ought to do something.

You think I don't know that?

Cliff bows even lower.

No, ma'am. I'm sorry. I know you do.

What about that darn...what did you call it?

Transporter, yes, ma'am, we thought about that. I think it goes both ways. But when we tried to use it again, to see if it would send us back, the door wouldn't open.

Serenity groans.

Then waiting and thinking are all we can do. Even if we did mount some kind of search and rescue, we'd need a plan. Like, who goes? When? Under what conditions? You know: a plan.

Yes ma'am. I'll think about it.

You do that. But while you do, take over for Cranny and the others. I want them back on patrol.

Wabi watch? It's not the thing I'm best at.

Then this will be good practice!

+ + + + + +

Princess Shimmer had lied. She hadn't enjoyed the lying, and she hoped that it would lead to nothing bad for the Oddity and its sharksha, but Ozag had insisted it must be so, and so it was.

She will not enter the horrid vumierre device, had been her unequivocal assertion. But she had only shared the thought to hasten the sharkshas' departure, to make it clear she would not be following them.

Indeed, the moment the transporter has worked its magic and both the Oddity and its five sharksha have been whisked away, she removes the device she had earlier placed on its door. This done and the door opened, she and her retinue go inside.

The door slides closed.

Watch carefully and memorize, she thinks to her prime, and she reaches out a tentative pincer to press the buttons Ozag had instructed.

Lights begin to flash.

Tiny images spring to life.

Her companions buzz and chitter, none happy at being so enclosed and even less at the appearance of the lights and images, inexplicable and thus threatening.

Courage! she thinks to them. *Ozag protects!*

A.P. Malloy

She looks closely. Each image is associated with a button, and when Shimmer presses the desired option, whoosh and whirl, they feel the floor beneath them fall away, the lights and images blurring to a typhoon of nauseating color, round and round. Those with wings try to use them against what must be an inevitable drop from a terrible height, but none can so much as twitch an antenna. What comes at last is not a deadly fall, but a sudden end to the sense of movement, not painful, but abrupt and unnerving.

The door slides open.

Shimmer leads the way out of the transporter and into the vumierre structure the Quintessential and Unsparing had called an Agriculture Facility. There was no explaining how it had come to pass, but they were now within easy reach of the Doorn. In mere moments they had traveled what would otherwise have taken a moonspan of hard travel. Shimmer buzzes in a regal fashion and looks about for the exit Ozag had promised there would be. Once again, the Undying had not led them astray, and after some navigating in the dark and awkward climbing of vumierre steps, they reach a square hatch her soldiers push open to reveal—glory!—unhindered sunlight and a sea of yellow grass.

Perhaps they will get their revenge after all, thinks Shimmer, and her prime buzzes hopefully.

For there also, as Ozag had said it would be, stands an alp, conspicuously shiny and well-groomed, though some of its plates and tentacles appear to have encountered recent trauma. And scion bodies, wrapped for their last rites; those too lie nearby as foretold. Around them, a small company of soldiers and handlers are arranged protectively, at their head none other than the Old Magister of Albion. They bow at the sight of her, but their confusion is easy to read.

He is... fumbles Old Magister. *They are...honored, of course. The New Queen of Albion was thought perished. But they were expecting...* He clicks an awkward cadence. *Will there not be...Will Ozag, Dire and Alarming not be ar-*

riving as well? They had been told...

Question not the Undying, thinks Shimmer. *Those promises and more may still come to be. But before then, Queen Shimmer is on a mission from Ozag, First and Foremost, and their services are required—that is all they need know. Can they not smell Her even now?*

They can, Viktor admits, for it is undeniable. The pale vumierre had borne a scent of Power, but it is a faint memory in the presence of this new fragrance. Shimmer has clearly been in the company of a Queen more potent and influential than any in their experience. That she is not Ozag herself is a disappointment, it's true, but she is a queen, nonetheless, *their* queen. Viktor feels sure he should be asking why this new queen abandoned Albion after the Circle's destruction, and why she returned now, of all times. But that scent! He forgets his questions and hugs ground made sloppy by melted snow.

Surely, she has stood before the Undying, he thinks, and Twenty-Seven buzzes melodious agreement.

A vision she is, he thinks. *A blessing to behold.*

All true! Shimmer whistles quietly. *But no time for that. She serves the will of the Celestial and Radiant. There is work to be done!*

What is her desire? asks Viktor.

Can there be but one answer? She will travel to Albion, of course! No time to waste. All who can fly will. But the others will travel to Cyclonia and await her arrival near the bay, for after Albion, she will have business at that hive as well. It is Ozag's will! And they will take the fallen scion with, for they must be sent out to the sea as is fitting for those lost in service to their queen.

Her six soldiers join Viktor's small company, and their buzzing is glum, their antennae downcast. They hate to be sent from their queen. Their companions are no less dejected, having been promised a meeting with the Fabulous and Knowing.

Back and forth, thinks Viktor. *That has been their lot! Come here, go back, come here, go back.*

Worry not, thinks Shimmer. *Brave followers, survi-*

*vors of mighty Albion. We will be reunited, and who can
say? Perhaps the Undying Herself will yet manifest. For
now, it is enough to know they do Her will. Now go!*

And go they do, with a chorus of chittering and
sharp whistles. At Viktor's command, the alp turns and
carries its mystified passengers and wrapped corpses
across the windswept yellow, marching slowly to the
south. Shimmer spares precious moments watching them
depart, then:

With all haste! she thinks, and she takes to the
sky like a golden dart. Her pluripotents are quick to follow, joining in a V formation as they head toward the
distant landfall and the domain of Albion.

+ + +

A kezel would have measured the journey in
strides, and would have counted a full hundred and fifty
thousand of them—two solid marches. But Shimmer and
her attendants cover the ground in a third the time, flying
low to avoid the buffeting wind. They follow the Doorn, its
banks trimmed with dense hedges of thorny vines. With
this as their guide, they arrive at the place where the
Doorn falls to the lower land, where it once upon a time
met up with the subterranean Dashing. The two combined had been re-named by scion the Royal river, though
it hardly seems so now. With no support from the Dashing, the falling Doorn dwindles as it travels across the arid
land, until, in the distance, it becomes thin and shadowy,
tracing a weak, wavering line to the coast, but coming nowhere near the lake it once fed.

Her domain suffers, thinks Shimmer. *She can
scarcely recall a time when it has not.*

Albion will thrive once again, thinks her prime.
Queen Shimmer shall see to it.

Perhaps. But the task is great, and she is weary.

*Ozag, Nourishing and Potent, shall be her strength.
Did the Undying not show her great favor? Reveal power
of Command over the vumierre devices?*

Death is the Door

But Shimmer reads doubt in her mind and is not surprised, for they are from the same genetic mold. Events of the past moons have been a ceaseless parade of trouble and worry for them all—indeed! She couldn't remember a time when any of them had felt wholly at peace or comfortable. A royal life had shielded them from much of the drought's privation, but it had not prevented them from absorbing the anxiety and growing lack of faith that had infected all of Albion.

Prevail, she thinks, and she buzzes softly. *Yes, that she will. And then she will rest a great long while.*

She stretches her wings and polishes her eyes.

When they arrive, she thinks, *they will pay no mind to the untended larvae. Ozag has willed it! They are the Undying's own care now, and are no longer Queen's concern. Instead, they will search the Royal treasury. Seek the sharksha weapons and bring them to her. They shall be returned to their owners as promised.*

Her pluripotents chitter nervously.

Will the hideous creatures not use the weapons against them? one of them asks. *It seems only likely, for they are hateful and violent!*

It is true, thinks Shimmer. *Their end in the Circle would have been just. But! Ozag finds value in them. The Inscrutable and Benign is not to be denied in this. And it is to be hoped the Oddity and its band of sharksha are less ignoble than others of their kind. Come! They have rested long enough. So much to be done...*

And off she flies, sailing out over the landfall and swooping downward, zig-zagging a golden line soon traced over by ten bronze wings.

+ + +

Their first stop is near the banks of the Royal, where Shimmer had, moons ago, laid the tiny derka whose warning had saved her life.

But it is dead, thinks her prime as it assists its companions in excavating the grave and pulling forth the mummified body.

Ozag knows all, thinks Shimmer, *and this is Her order. They will unwrap it.*

This they do. The creature looks no different than it had when they last laid eyes on it. It is motionless, its eyes are closed, and it does not breathe.

But see, Queen, thinks her prime. *The body is not stiff or hard. This is a sign of truth in Ozag's claim, yes?*

Was there any doubt? Now come! And bear the creature with care. The Undying has great plans for it...

When at last they arrive at Albion, they make their way to the uppermost level of the royal tower where thousands of larval cells are stacked. Out the eastern window they see the cold char and melted stone of the Circle glaring at them like an angry, black eye. Below them, moving through the lattice of amber cells, occasional scion can be seen, tenders, few in number but industrious, working through the ranks of larvae.

What is this! Shimmer buzzes in surprise. *Tenders survived the holocaust?*

Her wings flash, and she rises from the ground, hovering at the apex of the tower. Shrill and penetrating, her whistling shriek brings each of the tenders to surprised attention. They crawl out from the narrow spaces between cells, quitting their labor to peer up at the unexpected sight of a queen hovering high above. Chittering questions to one another, they stand motionless and uncertain. What should they do?

Come! Shimmer thinks. *Albion's Queen Commands it! Climb to her and do not delay!*

This they do, for tenders can no more disobey a queen than a raindrop can fall up. They can't explain her appearance, but there she is, a queen, and she has Command. Those closest to Shimmer relay the message, and one by one, nimble and quick, they climb to the royal suite, scaling vertical walls of amber as only a tender can. Soon, Shimmer is surrounded by a small crowd, all glittering eyes and bending antennae.

She is queen of this hive, yes? thinks one of those

closest to her. *She is pleased at their work?*

She is queen of Albion, yes, Shimmer replies. *But she is yet to judge their work. Report!*

Yes, thinks the first tender. *They will report.*

Yes, thinks another. *Fully and formally.*

No! Shimmer demands. *Concisely and quickly!*

Yes, thinks the first tender. *She is wise.*

Yes, thinks the second. *They will be quick.*

Yes, a third adds. *And concise.*

Yes, the first tender agrees. *They are Cyclonian, sent by Queen Allura. One to every hundred eggs they are, and many larvae have been saved because of them—but they are too few.*

Yes, thinks the second. *Should be twice as many.*

No, the third insists. *Should be five times more.*

Yes, the first is quick to agree. *But Allura judged: no more could be spared.*

No. No more spared.

No. But many larvae have been saved.

Yes. But not all.

No. And the eldest will emancipate soon.

Yes. And how will they be weaned? What guilders are there on to whom the emancipated can imprint? Who will make more serum, and where is the lova?

They will not concern themselves! Shimmer's rapid staccato stills their nervous chittering. *They shall wait here for her return and quiet their noise.*

As the company of tenders stands idle, wondering what will happen next, Shimmer retreats with her prime to an adjacent room, hexagonal and private.

Queen Allura has been generous, thinks her prime.

Generous? Think again! She seeks to enthrall these larvae and claim them as her own. Her tenders have already mingled Cyclonian essence into the serum. If allowed to mature, the entire tower will belong to Allura. Shimmer buzzes a low, broken chord. *Ozag had promised She would care for the larvae, but Queen never imagined this would be the form the care took.*

Perhaps, thinks her prime, *this is not Ozag's will.*

A.P. Malloy

Perhaps. But the Undying was clear. Not a moment of thought was Queen to give to this matter. And yet! So hard it is to see Albion larvae turned Cyclonian. Oh, rue!

It is hard indeed, oh Queen. What is her will?

If she had more energy and time, thinks Shimmer, *she would transform these tenders to soldiers and add them to her own retinue, for it is paltry indeed.*

That would be fitting, Queen. It would teach Allura a lesson, perhaps, about overstepping.

Perhaps. But teaching lessons is not the mission set for her. And if this is the will of the Undying, she would be interfering with that plan.

It seems a hard choice.

Shimmer is about to agree. Worse than simply leaving the larvae to die untended is to imagine them becoming part of another hive altogether. But she settles her vacillating wings and checks her pride. A test, the Undying had called it, a test of her faith. And the reward? Incalculable! So let Allura do what she will.

She has decided! thinks Shimmer. *This is the will of the Abundant and Lavish. She has wasted too much time on doubt and almost succumbed to infidelity. But the Undying may yet find her worthy.*

What does Queen wish?

Have the tenders return as they were and continue with their work. Then off to seek the vumierre weapons!

But for so many larvae to become Cyclonian...

Enough! Who can judge the ways of Ozag, Sagacious and Benevolent? Her prime will dismiss the tenders and fly with the others to the royal stores. They will retrieve the weapons and take care to bring also those parts that make the weapons work. She understands?

She does, assures her prime. *The weapons and the...the...she does not know...*

The Undying called them 'ammunition,' thinks Shimmer. *A crude vumierre word, but without them, the weapons have no use.*

It shall be as she commands.

Death is the Door

+ + +

The job takes time, during which the winds begin to rise and the western sky grows dark. While she waits by herself in the uppermost room of the royal tower, Shimmer rests with her eyes dim and her pincers running slowly across the derka's obsidian scales. On the levels below, Alura's tenders go about their duties.

May this be the proper course, she prays simply. *And may she be forgiven if not.*

But this is no time for second thoughts. Here come her pluripotents, bearing a large woven parcel lumpy and jutting with weapons and rounds of ammunition. Sensing their queen's fatigue, they lower their burden to the floor and buzz soothing notes, stirring the air with their wings and releasing pheromones that clear her mind.

They have requisitioned a portion of lova from the tenders, one of them thinks. *She will partake.*

Shimmer does, worrying at the details of the mission before her. The lova is soon gone, and part of her energy returns. But many questions remain. She fans her wings, trying to shake sleepy thoughts from her mind. She had been recalling memories handed down from her mother, Benica, that she had gotten from hers, Beata, and she from hers, Durela. The last of these had ruled Albion when it, like Cyclonia, had only one tower.

From one tower to six, she thinks to herself. *She seems likely to oversee the regression from six back to one.* But to her pluripotents, she thinks, *Loyal and diligent. They have done well. They understand the plan?*

They do, thinks her prime. *When this storm passes, four will fly with the vumierre weapons back to the transporting device on the plains and wait for Queen. Prime will stay with Queen and they will travel to Cyclonia, hoping to bargain for Allura's assistance and the freeing of the sharksha in her Garden.*

It is so. But first, patience! The storm comes. And while they wait, she will tell them what she has learned from Ozag. Have they ever heard of the Weaver?

A.P. Malloy

They have not, thinks her prime. *But will Queen not rest? She will sicken.*

The Perilous and Bountiful is her strength, Shimmer replies. *And She wished this tale shared with all who had minds to sense. So attend now, and recall what she divulges, for the Undying gave it to her as a gift and so, in turn, is it given to them. Who can say? There may come a time when they also will share the tale with others, and so knowledge of the Weaver will spread.*

Her pluripotents settle in close as the glittering violet moon, followed soon after by Mother Green, rises above the horizon. There is precious little rain, but plenty of wind and arcing electricity, and with this as backdrop, they huddle in the lonely tower, taking in the remarkable tale shared by their queen. At another time, it would have been too much to believe, but now, surrounded by ghosts and the eerie light of a solar eclipse, it seems to them that anything might be possible.

+ + + + + +

When Cliff takes wabi watch from Cranny and the others, they do not thank him before hurrying from the cave, hoping to hunt before the storm. The wabis have enjoyed meals large and regular enough to keep their thoughts on something other than their stomachs, so when Cranny promises them a story—quite against Cliff's wishes—they eagerly gather around him, some climbing him like an accrete, others looking up with wide eyes.

Left alone, Cliff founders.

I only know one story, he thinks. He means by this he only knows one story well enough to tell it, for he has heard many tales over the moons, most told by Ancian. He had simply never imagined himself as the narrator and had never bothered to memorize. But the tale of the First Kezel is so familiar he feels he can improvise his way through the less certain parts.

Tell it! the wabis think. *Tell it!*

OK, OK. Cliff tries to recall the proper way to begin

a story. *Well, um, once upon a time, I guess, once upon a time, did you know kezel used to be called keel?*

This means nothing to most of the wabis, and they look up at him without answer. But the oldest siblings, Powder and Crust have heard this before.

We know that! they are quick to exclaim.

Yeah? Well it's true. And they lived in an always dark place on the other side of the Wall.

What's a Wall? Crust wants to know.

I can only tell you what I was taught. Some people claim it's not true, but I think they might be crazy. Or maybe they were just making it up. I don't know... I was taught the Wall is like... he pats the stone behind him. *It's like this. One side is where we are and the other side is where the gigikas are napping.*

Is it always dark on that side? asks Powder.

Not always. They can light some crystals.

The keel?

No, The gigikas. Trapper and Old Buttons. When they wake up from their nap. The keel didn't have any crystals. But it didn't matter, 'cuz they couldn't see anyway. Living in the dark all the time, I guess is why.

Why did they want to live there? asks Wander.

They didn't, I don't think.

Why did they stay? asks Cloud.

They didn't. They wanted to see the Weaver, so they climbed over the Wall. Or they may have dug their way under. No one knows. But things weren't so good on this side of the Wall either, because the kish followed them out, and there were derkas, too, and no good shelter.

What's a weaver? Hurly wants to know.

What's a kish? Burly wonders.

What's a shelter? ask Needle and Blade together.

Cliff labors through his descriptions, interrupted by many questions, wondering if he will ever finish the tale. His mind drifts once more to Lightning. He is sure she would be much better at this, and he wishes again the transporter had allowed him to go back and find her. While thinking this, inspiration strikes.

A.P. Malloy

Say! he thinks. *I know a better story. A real one. Remember Lightning?*

Of course, they do.

She got us out of that pit, thinks Knoll.

We like her, thinks Tor.

Sure, what's not to like? Well! Do you want to hear the story of how she got you out of that pit?

Yes! they think. *Tell us about Lightning!*

OK. It all started when she met her good friend, Cliff, and he told her some really bad news. He was a very brave kezel, very strong, so she knew it must have been bad indeed for him to be so upset. 'Someone abducted the kezel!' he told her. 'We have to go save them!'

What's adukkid? asks Crust.

It means taken, captured and hauled away.

The wabis lean back, their ears lying flat.

Yep, thinks Cliff. *Not good. Now Lightning wasn't so sure it was a great idea to go after the ones that got taken—don't get me wrong, she was brave and all, but she needed some persuasion is all.*

What's paswayzha? asks Powder.

Um, like, encouragement, you know? She just needed someone to tell her she could do it. And Cliff was just the jabi. He knew it had to be done, no matter how hard it was. And Lightning listened, cuz, you know, I think she liked him. She decided the only honorable thing to do was follow the captured kezel out on to the open plains.

Cliff was very brave, thinks Wander.

Gee, thanks. I mean, yeah. But Lightning was brave, too, like I said. And she was smart. Anyway, off they went, but first, Cliff said, 'Hey! I have an idea. We should use grass as camouflage.'

What's a camafojj? asks Needle.

A way to hide from derkas. He thought of it when he saw Joy hiding up in an accrete.

What's a joy? asks Blade.

Cliff sighs. Storytelling, he sees, is difficult work.

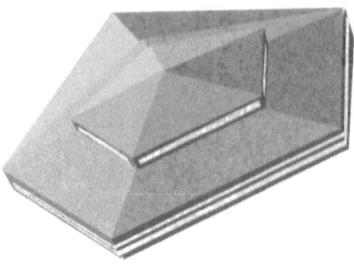

CHAPTER SIX
Decision

IN THE PAST, Lightning felt Joy's fatigue as if it were her own, a weariness that started in her mind and spread outward, spike and claw. The work of being a hub, of having so many outside thoughts flowing through her, wore at Joy as if she were a filament in a bulb. Even with help from the artifact, her hand always in her sling, there was a limit to the pace she could maintain.

So it was, that when the jovial young man appeared, calling himself Petros, Lightning approved of him immediately, for she recognized him as the cause of a sudden ease to the burden in Joy's mind. She felt it in her own, as if the newcomer had generously lifted from her shoulders a pack filled with stones.

She took a deep breath and released it slowly.

Thank you, she thought.

The corners of his eyes wrinkled, and his mouth curled up at the edges, but he offered no other reply.

The others responded to the newcomer in their own ways. Thunder was naturally wary of anything he couldn't smell. Until the holograms he'd recently encountered, he had never come across an animated thing that didn't have some type of scent. This creature stood two-legged like a Moondweller, but that wasn't enough to earn Thunder's trust.

The one calling herself Sister Janet sat with much

the same expression as she had before the newcomer's appearance, and her mind, if she had one, was impossible to read. The others, the ones variously referred to as ru-midelchia, vumierre, sentiri, and only Weaver knew what other ridiculous names, were a different story. The largest of the three, the one called Major, had stepped forward and taken a position between the newcomer and the others. Lightning read this as a protective move, the kind of thing she might have done herself had she felt Joy threatened. The other two, the ones whose minds could be sensed, were in discussion with one another.

Are you OK? the man asked. His name, Lightning understood, was Watt.

I'm fine, replied the woman named Maya.

Did you know...could you feel it...in there?

No, and yes.

Holy smoking Moses. And you're OK?

Yes, Watt. I'm fine.

But even as she thought this, she sank, slowly, into one of the control room seats and she interlaced her hands across her belly. She stared at the newcomer, though Lightning could not see her expression through her headgear. The man named Watt stood close, his hand on her shoulder. He was edgy, Lightning could tell, and unsure what to do.

If you did anything to hurt her... he thought.

But the one calling himself Petros did not reply.

You have to ask questions to get answers, thought Joy. *That's how they work. It can be frustrating.*

"They?" thought the major when Watt had translated this idea.

Joy reached into her sling and removed the artifact, admiring its form, though to everyone else, it looked like the most pedestrian of rocks.

This is also a Book calling itself Petros. She polished away a bit of debris from the artifact's surface. *It only responds when you ask it questions.*

To Lightning's surprise, the blonde-haired Petros stepped very calmly toward them—stepped right past the humans and the android and through the grate, as if either he or it were an illusion. In moments, he stood before Joy, then knelt down to her eye level. He paid no mind to the kezel, though Lightning bared her teeth and Thunder growled loudly enough to be heard outside the bay. And yet, Lightning felt sure there was nothing either of them could have done to stop the creature had he meant to do harm. His power was veiled but unmistakable.

He held out his hand.

Joy slowly reached forward and delivered the artifact into his grasp. The artifact—black, featureless, unblemished, and refusing to reflect light—rested there for a moment, and then, as if it were melting, it slowly shrank and was absorbed into the newcomer's hands. A passing wave of black flowed from his fingertips and spread quickly throughout his body, in moments disappearing entirely. And yet, it was not gone; it had simply been consumed, as if it had been a meal, though it had seemed a willing participant.

Two added together to make one that's better, thought Joy. *That's the way of it, yes, Mister Petros?*

It is, indeed, he thought.

When Watt had translated this, the major turned to Sister Janet. She leaned slightly forward, her lips pursed, an avid look in her eyes.

"Did you know this would happen?" he asked.

"I had hoped."

"She said 'one that's better.' Better at what?"

"Navigating through time."

"Somehow I knew you were going to say that."

"With the help of a Book at the height of its power," thought the chaplain, "we increase by a factor of ten the chances of us projecting to a future time where we can learn the information we need—perhaps more."

But Lightning had heard enough.

Future my eye, she thought. *And we've had enough of the past, too. We want to go back to the present. My clan needs us; they'll be wondering where we are. And we have a whole brood of bombas to help.*

A.P. Malloy

When Watt translated this, his crewmates had no reply, but Sister Janet was quick to fill the silence.

"If we don't address the rogue moon," she said, "there will be no kezel, bombas, or any other creatures to return to. If you want to help them, you must help me."

Javon held up a hand.

"You there," he looked at Petros. "What do you know about this?"

The man smiled enigmatically.

"I know what my partner knew. We have become one. What knowledge and experience he accumulated during his time with this android's colonial mission has been joined with my own. I am him. He is me."

"Does that mean you accept the chaplain's story?"

"It aligns with my understanding of the situation."

"And you can do this? Navigate through time?"

"Of course."

"I suppose there's a downside."

Petros did not reply.

"Is there?" Javon demanded.

"Define your terms."

"I think they're pretty obvious! I've got limited resources and a damaged ship full of frightened people, and there—right out there!—is a planet my science chief tells me is our salvation. Then this...then *she* shows up and says we should ignore salvation, trust her, and go zipping through time to—maybe—save a future version of that planet, a planet that's supposedly so much better than this one, except there's no guarantee it will be around long enough for us to enjoy it."

Petros waited patiently.

"Well?" Javon pressed. "What do you have to say?"

"Your assessment seems accurate."

"And if we can't save the future planet? Can we come back here?"

"In principle."

"Which means...what?"

"Traveling through time requires substantially more energy than traveling through space. Whether or not you would be able to return to this or a similar time would depend on your access to that energy."

Javon waved at Sister Janet.

"Our guest claims her planet has a reconstructed astral drive, fueled. Then there's that fancy ship of hers."

Petros merely gazed at the captain.

Joy clicked softly.

Questions, remember. I told you it was frustrating.

While this was translated, Javon tapped his finger impatiently on the control panel.

"Is it true?" he asked. "Enough energy to get us back here if the rescue mission fails?"

Petros never stopped smiling, but when he answered, his tone was sober.

"The answer is not a binary, Major. It is a continuum. Every temporal displacement carries a necessary level of uncertainty. The farther away from one's own time, the greater the uncertainty becomes. That uncertainty increases again with an increase in mass. Enveloping *Destiny* in *Valiant's* temporal field is something I suspect the chaplain has calculated carefully, but I have not examined either ship closely enough to say with confidence whether I agree with her conclusions. I suspect it is possible, but I can't say exactly what the chances are of returning to this time. Or," he added, looking at Lightning, "returning to yours."

Javon made a chopping gesture.

"Enough. You," he pointed to Janet, "are going to be held in custody until I know what to do with you. And you," he looked at Lightning, Joy, and Thunder. "I understand you just want to go home. I promise, if I can make that happen, I will. But I need to think and to share this information with my crew. Be patient, please. We'll do everything we can to make you comfortable."

Thunder growled.

More meat would make me comfortable.

Lightning curled her lip.

Just hurry up and get us home. That's enough.

At Javon's order, the two guards entered, escorting Janet, still securely bound, from the room.

"Please," she said as she passed Watt. "You know I'm telling the truth."

The poor man winced and looked away. Once Janet was gone, Javon turned to him.

"I want you to get your sister and join us on the bridge. Shonda and Doc Foster too. Watt!"

"Yes. Sorry. Yes. I'll tell them." But he stood still.

"Now, please."

"Yes. But...what about Maya?"

"That's up to her."

She took a breath, dredging the energy to speak.

"I want to stay here."

Neither man looked happy about this.

"I don't suppose," said Javon to Petros, "I could force you to go anywhere or do anything unless you approved. I get the feeling you're outside of my control."

Petros smiled, but did not respond.

"Dammit!" the major exclaimed. "True or not?"

"It is quite true, Major, but you needn't worry about me. For, by that same fact—that you have no power over me—if I had come here seeking to do your or any of your crew harm, I could have done it already."

"So, I should trust you."

Petros's eyes twinkled, but he offered no reply.

"Oh, come on! That was a question!"

Petros did not agree.

"Have it your way," Javon said, locking eyes with the blonde-haired man and pointing to one of the tiny cameras mounted high on one wall. "But we'll be watching and listening. Understood?"

"Perfectly," said Petros.

And with that, Javon left the room, Watt close behind, pausing only to clasp Maya's hand.

Be careful, he thought, then left.

+ + +

So, there they were, the five of them, and for some

time, no one offered any thoughts. More food was delivered, as promised, slabs of red meat as good as any talihew, but Lightning had other concerns. What was happening on her range? Cliff and the Whitetails would have returned long ago—assuming the device worked. And when they didn't follow? What would be done?

What could *be done?* she thought morosely. *Half the clan protecting the Skull, half stuck at home, waiting to see what the Redteeth do... No one's coming to look for us, that's for sure. And where would they look if they did? What would they find? Not a thing...*

She watched Thunder gnawing bones when she was surprised by the mind of the one called Maya.

I'm sorry you got dragged into this, she thought.

Lightning resisted the urge to bare her teeth.

It doesn't seem like you're the one to blame.

What else can we do?

I've already said what we want.

Yes, I know. I'll do everything I can to get you back to your home. But... I'm not in charge, you know. You, she thought sternly to Petros, *have a lot of explaining to do.*

His smile was wistful, but it was all he offered.

No, Maya insisted. *You don't get off that easy. I've immersed in a lot of 3V shows about godlike aliens, their power, their presumption. You...you were* inside *me. You never asked my permission, didn't bother to introduce yourself. That's just wrong!*

Joy marshalled her patience, resisting the urge to remind their new acquaintance—yet again—of the rules for interaction. Instead, she buzzed a low tune and fished in Lightning's pack for some dried awl.

Well? thought Maya. *Don't just stand there with that look. What do you have to say for yourself?*

What Petros had to say surprised Lightning, for his tone was deeply sincere but also intimate in a fashion, as if he was thinking to an old friend.

That I would do it again, Maya, all of it, in a heartbeat, and in the same way. I was, after all, only fulfilling my purpose—any Book's purpose—for existence, the reas-

on I was created.

Which is?

To cultivate Readers. To protect them if necessary, and—when they're ready—to share what I know.

Created by whom?

Makers of Books. The closest name that makes sense in any System language is Old Soigne. Please don't ask me who they are, or what they look like, or where they live. These things are stories for another time, and most of what I would say would sound unbelievable to you.

Too late for that, thought Lightning, and she nabbed one of the steaks.

But Petros was unfazed by the interruption.

The Old Soigne are Way Walkers, he thought, *pure energy, taking whatever form pleases them, and they are travelers. So far they have roamed! And for so long! And everywhere they go, they make Books to illuminate the Way—but only for those able to Read. Most humans, kezel, bombas, androids, et cetera—most sentient beings, in fact—lack the mental capacity to interact with a Book. It's not their fault; it's just where they are in their evolution. But Reading is within the grasp of certain humans. Your unborn daughter is one of them.*

The way, Maya frowned. *The way to what?*

But Petros shook his head.

That is for Readers. If they wish to share it with you, that is their choice. But I am forbidden. As I am forbidden to reveal myself to any but a Reader.

And if I told you to go away?

I would not. But if your daughter made the same request, I would honor it, painful as it would be.

Maya looked at Lightning.

Are you one of these Readers?

Nope.

She directed the same question to Thunder.

No, he replied, chasing his meal with a long drink of water. *And thank the Weaver for it. It sounds like a giant pain in the tail.*

But you are, Maya thought, looking at Joy. She sat

gnawing steadily at her awl, but her eyes glittered.

It's true. Her antennae dipped like a bow.

But Maya wasn't satisfied.

You say you're forbidden from revealing yourself to non-Readers, but you've obviously done it. You're doing it now! Why? Do you only follow the rules when it suits you?

Petros had a rare, glum look on his face.

That is all anyone with autonomy does. The question becomes, if we deviate from our orders or violate a prohibition, why do we do so? What is our motivation? Is it because the prohibition is unjust? Or is it because we are willful and proud? Too arrogant to be constrained? But perhaps there is a third possibility, that the prohibition was meant to be flexible for those with the wisdom to see.

Which is the case for you? Maya asked sharply.

I will let you judge that.

I can't judge unless I know more.

Petros stood still like a statue.

Please! Maya exclaimed. *While the others are debating what we should do, will you tell me something useful? Something that might help make a good decision?*

If you ask the correct questions.

Are you being honest?

Yes.

Do you always tell the truth?

Yes.

But you're selective about what you reveal, yes?

Of course.

Based on what criteria?

Wisdom, as well as I am able to define it.

Sure, thought Thunder, *but if you were a liar, you'd claim to be honest, wouldn't you?*

Probably. Or perhaps I would acknowledge my dishonesty in an attempt to disarm you with candor. But in any case, I am in the company of astute thinkers; you can typically discern a lie when you encounter one.

Most of the time, thinks Lightning, and Joy agrees. *But something tells me you could get away with it and none of us would know the difference. Isn't that true?*

A.P. Malloy

Perhaps. I've never tested it.

I always thought I could pick out a liar, Maya thought. *I catch people lying all the time—it's easy to sense the difference between what they say and what they're thinking or feeling. But she's right. I don't think there's any way to know with you. You've already admitted to breaking your own rules. Why?*

You are asking what my motivation is.

Yes. Bad rules or bad faith?

I believe neither. The rules are wise, but when faced with conflicting imperatives, an autonomous being must trust its own wisdom. For example: the first time I revealed myself, many of your years ago, I was torn between allowing a non-Reader to see my power and allowing a Reader to be harmed—your daughter, in fact, who was, if you must know, being shot at with projectile weapons by enemies seeking to take possession of me. The energetic shield I created saved her life but exposed my nature to Sister Janet, who was with us at the time. She is a clever machine, and I was so depleted from the effort that I was unable to entirely wipe the memory from her mind. She has clung stubbornly to it all these years, and I have been unable to do anything about it.

And how, thought Maya, *do your makers feel about this? Do they know what you've done?*

I cannot say. I have had no contact with them since they left me here.

Are they coming back?

Extremely unlikely. In all their history as intergalactic travelers, there is no record of them ever visiting the same location twice. And the farther away they are, the weaker I become. All is well if I have Readers, but without them, I quickly become inert.

In what? asked Lightning.

Dead, essentially. A Book without a Reader is little more than a rock.

Joy's clicking, quiet and steady, filled the silence.

That's lonely. You have no one like you.

But Maya's tone was less sympathetic.

Death is the Door

You explained the first time why you revealed your-self—justified or rationalized it—but what about this time? Why expose yourself now?

The answer to that question, Petros thought, *is rooted in a story that bears directly on our current situation, and might be instructive to everyone here.* He paused. *It all started with the birth of your daughter, Grace. But as you've heard, everyone called her Abuelita.* His smile was soft, and he closed his eyes. *Little Granny. That wasn't so long ago...*

+ + + + + +

Javon made his way to the bridge, his steps slow and thoughtful. When he arrived, the new shift had taken its place; none of them had been there to witness the appearance of the strange ship, and yet he could tell from the expectant, quizzical looks they gave him that they had heard the news—or some of it—regardless his orders for secrecy. But no one dared ask for details. He simply nodded at the shift leader, Skola, a thick-set man, proudly bearded, who staffed the operator's station.

"They are all here, Major," he reported. "But not Chief DuBois. She sends regrets from the engine room. But it seems Magister Healey will be taking her place."

"I didn't invite the magister."

"No sir, but he insisted, and I was trying to avoid a conflict. If you want, I will escort him out..."

"No. Thank you, Mr. Skola. Not necessary."

Javon had scarcely entered the conference room, however, before he began regretting that decision.

"Having a council meeting without me?" the magister accused, rising from his seat.

"You're here, aren't you?" Commander Rickles grumbled. "Sit down and let the major talk."

"Oh, I'll sit. But I've got some talking to do, too. You can't have a meeting about the future of this expedition without inviting me."

Javon's smile was weary; his tone was smooth.

"Did I not? I was sure I sent for you."

"Ha! Funny. I want to know what's going on! And I don't think I'm alone in that. Am I?" Magister Healey looked around the table, daring anyone to deny their curiosity. Watt glared at him and chewed at his beard. By his side, Sister Janet kept her gaze on her hands, resting on her lap. Chief Abara and Doc Foster, both of whom had seen the aliens, sat quietly comparing notes and doing their best to ignore the magister. As always, Commander Rickles, spoiling for a fight, cared for nothing but compliance. Only Deputy Kim was openly curious. He had the hungry look of a child waiting to open a gift, and he leaned forward, his hands on the table.

Javon sat. Chief Abara and Doc Foster grew quiet.

"Well?" Magister Healey pressed.

Javon was not a petty man. He could have delayed, just to rankle the magister, see how red his face would get. But a decision awaited, and time, it seemed, would allow no such games.

"I'm going to say this once, and when I'm done, I'm going to give everybody one—one!—chance to respond. Then we're going to sleep on it and re-convene first thing tomorrow, at which time, you are each going to present your vote on what it is you think we should do. I'll go with the majority. I can't do this one alone."

Magister Healey opened his mouth to speak, but one look from the commander, his eyebrows bristling, was enough to keep him silent.

And so, Javon continued.

"It seems," he said, "that we have encountered a traveler from the future. This person provides... substantial proofs of that claim. Not only from the future, but from *our* future." He looked at their various reactions and smiled wanly. "Yes, please," he said. "Wrap your heads around *all* of that idea. And then understand this: our visitor appears to have credible evidence that, rather than put down on that planet out there, we should travel with them to the future version of that planet, for reasons that are many but also impossible to prove without actually doing it—and there's no guarantee that we could come back here if we don't like how things look in this future of theirs. The flipside is the claim that if we stay, we not only run the risk of dooming ourselves and this new planet, but also the future version of this planet, which we apparently placed in harm's way due to several terrible decisions we made."

Deputy Kim's eyes were wide. Watt looked at Janet. Janet looked at Javon. Chief Abara and Doc Foster looked at each other. Magister Healey started to laugh, in spite of Commander Rickles.

Javon leaned back in his chair.

"Reverse alphabetical by last name," he said. "One comment, one question. That's all I have energy for." He turned his gaze to the commander. "You're up, Terry."

Rickles ground his teeth and rubbed a hand over his bald head. He considered for a long time. Then:

"If it was anyone but you, Major, I'd bust 'em in the chops for wasting my time. That's my comment."

"And your question?"

"That's not as easy. But I think you already know what I'm going to ask. Hell, I think you *need* me to ask it. So here it is. You said 'substantial' proof and 'credible' evidence. What makes it so?"

All eyes were on the major.

"Good question," he nodded. Sitting upright, he took a deep breath. "Here's everything I know…"

And so, he told them, and showed them the live video feed of the extraterrestrials, the two kezel and their unusual, blue companion. But he made no mention of Petros—not out of a desire for secrecy, but because he had no memory of having met him, though it had occurred less than an hour ago. And neither Watt nor the two others who had been there made any effort to remind him, for they, too, recalled nothing of the affair. To all of them, it was as if it had never happened, and when those of the Council who had not yet seen the aliens oohed and ahhed appropriately at the sight, they made no comment on Petros, for they were unable to see or hear him.

+ + + + + +

Petros took a seat on a shipping crate close to the partition where he had a view of his entire audience.

You asked me why I revealed myself, he thought to Maya, *to you and to other non-Readers, when it contradicts my imperative. It is an important question. But to understand the answer, you must remember that I am recently joined with another like me, one with many more years of experience. The two of us can separate if we choose, but we are one at the moment. So, when I refer to myself, I am referring to a compilation of experiences: those of the fully powered Petros who just recently arrived with his makers, and those of the depleted Petros who has lived with you and your progeny for many generations on a tidally locked planet named Aranae.*

That second Petros was taken here against his will, because he was weak. But Sister Janet knows her days of forcing my compliance are over, now that I have my full store of energy combined with all the old Petros' experience. She knows the only way I would agree to another temporal displacement would be if I had the approval of my sole Reader and all other relevant stakeholders. I would not whisk this ship away to the future without allowing open discussion and the wisdom of informed democracy. I determined that making all of that happen through the mind of one Reader, who was already taxing herself to exhaustion, was too much to ask.

So I chose to make the case myself.

And what is your case? Maya demanded.

That wisdom is rooted in knowledge, and you will need both to make your decision.

Petros paused, as if waiting for questions. Lightning had several, but Thunder's focus was on cleaning up the last of the steaks.

If we need to fight our way out of here, I'll need my strength, he reasoned. *How many should I leave?*

None, thought Lightning. *Don't make yourself sick.*

She helped herself to some of the lifeless but otherwise innocuous water and tried to relax, allowing Joy to recline against her flank, her glittering eyes fixed on the blonde-haired storyteller.

She raised her hand, buzzing quietly.

I'm sorry, but you're telling it all wrong.

Petros stopped, looking at her intently.

You have to keep it in proper order, Joy clarified. *And you're using way too many big words.*

Petros leaned back slightly and peered down his nose. His eyebrows arched.

Joy shrugged.

You said it's an important story for us, she thought. *I want to be able to understand it.* She tugged at her hair. *Can you do that for us, please, Petros?*

His lips curled upward, and his eyes, whose color Lightning could not determine no matter how hard she tried, twinkled with a life all their own.

Since you asked so nicely, he said, *I will order and simplify. I admit: I am out of practice.* He closed his eyes as if gathering his thoughts. *But you should be aware: when the others return—and they will, I suspect, after they have allowed the two chaplains to meet—I will be retaking my previous forms. No one but Joy will remember me once I'm gone. Even Lightning will forget, eventually. The information I divulge will remain, but you won't know where you got it; you'll think it was from someone else. Those cameras? Microphones? I am beyond them.*

Joy realized something.

But Sister Janet knows. Isn't that a problem?

Not for long—not now that I am back to full power.

But why the secrecy? Lightning wanted to know.

It is my Nature. I have deviated from my makers' rules when I felt I must, but that is not to say I disagree with them in principle.

I spent my whole life keeping secrets, thought Maya. *It wasn't a healthy way to live. What purpose does this principle serve?*

If you like, we can use our limited time together answering that very complex question, parsing out the motiv-

ation of my makers, whose wisdom is rooted in thousands of years of experience. Or I can tell you the story of your daughter. For it is she who is responsible in some way for all of us being here.

Joy was quick with her opinion.

Will you please tell the story, Mr. Petros?

And none of them disagreed.

+ + +

This is what he said:

Your daughter, Maya, and the woman who engineered your creation, Joy, will be—was—born not long after the colony was established. She and I had already known each other for months, sharing space inside you. I know that seems like a violation, but the benefit to Grace was immediate and lasting. No harm could come to her, no sickness, while I enveloped her in my energy. And since you were bound in symbiosis—I'm sorry, it means they depended on one another. Little Granny was physically connected to Maya for her food, oxygen, et cetera. Because of this connection, the benefits extended to you as well. This, I believe, you have already noticed.

Maya crinkled her nose. There was no point in denying the truth.

I should feel terrible with all that's been going on, she acknowledged. *But I don't. I feel strong; tranquil. Even when I feel sad, I feel hopeful, too. That's your doing?*

Petros pressed his palms together and bowed.

It has been my pleasure sharing time with you. But it is Abuelita you want to know about. She was born healthy and happy and stayed that way for a long time. When she was still just a baby, I was an imperceptible aura, bathing her with energy. And when she was older, I was her 'imaginary friend,' usually in the form of non-human Earth animals, most often animating a toy of yours, an old stuffed tiger. Earth is where these humans are originally from, Petros reminded his Aranaen audience. *If you had forgotten.*

Death is the Door

They had not.

The colony had many challenges, for Aranae is a difficult planet on which to live. So little space for new neighbors! But Javon Monroe is a good man, surrounded— mostly—by well-intended, talented people, and the planet was carefully surveyed, using the greatest care to avoid imposing on the natives. The sites chosen were determined to be the safest, least invasive, and closest to necessary resources. Seismic activity was known, but not as severe— earthquakes, you know, like the scion's tey Ramota.

There were three linguistic species on Aranae—that means they had spoken language. These were the keel, the scion, and the bombas. The colonists took every precaution to avoid contact with these, as they were intelligent but technologically simple, and the colonists wished to prevent intrusions or unnatural accelerations in their advancement without understanding them better.

As Abuelita grew older, I took the form of an old-fashioned book, which, for you kezel, is a collection of thin sheets of a durable substance, covered on both sides in signifying marks and bound together into a form about this big. Petros held his hands to make a rectangle, and as he did, Lightning unbuttoned one of her pockets.

You mean a sheet like this? and she removed the frail, yellowed paper from her vest, unfolding it carefully.

Where did you get that? asked Thunder.

It was Ancian's. She had me studying it.

Why?

I don't know. She claimed it had meaning. Does it?

Petros took the paper and examined both sides.

It does, he said. *This is a page from one of the colonist's Faunal Reports. That is a type of book meant to help understand native life on Aranae.*

Well, thought Lightning. *I don't know a lot, but it seems to me they could have used more of that.*

Petros nodded gravely but thought nothing.

Sorry, Lightning tucked the paper back in her vest. *What happened next?*

As I said, the colony had challenges, some of which

were self-imposed, like the rogue moon. But considering the circumstances, they performed admirably. And I am happy to report that some of that success came from what Abuelita learned during her time with me. I answered all her questions as she asked them.

Who are you?

Where did you come from?

And so on. But the answers had to match the intellect, and early in her life, they were simple and not nearly as important to her as my companionship.

Abuelita grew, as did the colony, and when she was on the edge of adolescence, I revealed myself to her in the form you see now. We had a very long talk that evening, deep into the night—that is to say, the portion of time the colonists had cordoned off as being 'night,' for of course, there is no such thing on Aranae. You kezel: did you know this? That in some corners of creation there are worlds that spin, so that every part faces the sun for a while, then faces the dark. And the brightness they call 'day,' and the darkness 'night,' and their lives depend on their relationship to those two concepts.

I like our way better, thought Thunder.

Go on, please, thought Maya, adding a moment later, *What happened to Grace?*

Many things. From that point forward, she had a greater understanding of the power she held and the responsibility she bore. For I had made it clear to her that simply Reading and learning was not enough; it was her obligation to cultivate other Readers and so multiply the power of the information and its usefulness.

But this was not an easy task. Aranae's human population was not large, and the telepaths among its number were few and secretive. Identifying them was easy enough; the real challenge was nudging them toward one another in the hope that they would form a mating pair and produce offspring with the aptitude to interact with me. This is how Grace earned her second nick-name: Matchmaker, as she was, over the course of her youth, responsible for bringing together several pairs of telepaths

Death is the Door

who would later wed and bear children. And some of those children were indeed Readers, and Grace was their teacher, though no one but the Readers knew of my existence. They jokingly referred to themselves as the Book Club, and over time, they and many of their descendants became the most influential people in the colony, though their numbers were never large.

Petros smiled warmly at Maya.

Your daughter was well-loved by those who could read minds and those who couldn't. They felt her energy, they looked forward to her visits, and they were always eager to learn her opinion on any number of topics, for she seemed to them wise beyond her years, informed far past the curriculum being taught in the New Gaian classrooms. She was considered the colony's good-luck charm, and no party was complete that didn't include her on the guest list. 'Why not have more?' people would ask you, Maya, sure that her siblings would be equally amazing. But your pregnancy had been unintentional; you had never wanted children, and could not, no matter Grace's charms, be persuaded to have another.

Fear of loss was ever a burden you bore.

+ + +

He paused here.

I desire your thoughts on the story so far.

Thunder had polished off the last of the steaks and washed them down with noisy gulps of water.

If you're asking me, he thought, *not impressed.*

Joy absently ran her fingers through Lightning's spikes, but she offered no opinion.

I suppose it's fine as far as it goes, thought Lightning. *But seriously. Some...explorers? Old Swanees? Found some other creatures in the middle of nowhere and just decided to send them to our home? How do they have the right? You know, all you people have done as far as I can tell is make a mess of a perfectly good...What did you call it? A planet? I don't know... It's Aranae to me, and I'm sorry, but it seems like it was a whole lot better off before you showed up.*

Maya thought nothing in reply, but through her protective headgear, Lightning saw a single tear run from the corner of her eye.

And you, Lightning wrinkled her snout at Petros. *Always with that look on your face and so full of secrets. Tell us plain: you've been saying all along that the danger to Aranae is real. Is that sister's plan a proper solution? Should we do what she's suggesting?*

Petros looked at her gravely.

I am not 'full of secrets.' To a Reader who asks the correct questions, I am a well of Knowledge and a path to Wisdom. But there is one thing I do not know, and that is the future. Oh, from Maya's perspective, I am familiar with one version of how the future will play out, but by coming here, we are now in the business of creating a new future. I cannot tell how it will unfold, or if Sister Janet's plan will succeed. But believe me, I want it to! So yes, I think we should do what she suggests.

He turned to Maya.

Your case is independent of ours. Sister Janet could not succeed at her plan of traveling to the future without first coming to this time and attaining my support. The depleted version of me that Joy and Lightning discovered on the plains was insufficient for her purposes, like a vest with holes—useful, but not fully so. With me, she has a Book at full strength—no pages missing, if you will—and that is key, for to travel to a specific time in the future requires a precise understanding of a massive amount of history. That is, after all, the best way to predict a future trajectory: by analyzing past actions.

But Janet has a secondary desire.

She has been broken by pain and loss. I believe she honestly thinks she can save the Aranae she knows, but at the same time, she desperately wants to reclaim some part of the past she has lost. Watt, Maya, and the person who became her best friend, Grace: all of these and many more have died and left her behind. She believes that simp-

ly plucking you all from the past and bringing you back with her will be a boon for her suffering. If that were the end of it, I would say, no, you should stay here, Maya, in your time and live your life as it unfolds. Already you know more about the state of things than you did in our time, so you might be able to avoid the trouble your past self could not. This Aranae might thrive.

But Sister Janet is not wrong when she says there are real, quantifiable benefits to returning to her Aranae— assuming we can address the rogue moon. For one, the Destiny *there does have a fully functional astral drive. Also, there are many generations of experience and success you can build on, as well as populations of creatures that have come to know, and in some cases respect, humans. For each component of this expedition—the agriculture facility, the mining module, the refinery—there is a twin already in place where we come from. You would have effectively doubled your resource base from day one. And, there is this: your daughter did her job well. With my help, she was able to cultivate other Readers, and the more there were, the more powerful I grew, the more astute and probing their questions became, and the more useful and revealing my answers. As a result, there is technology on that Aranae that you do not possess here, and would not— perhaps ever—without the help of many Readers and many long, difficult years.*

Maya nodded.

Fire of the Storm, she said.

You can call me Lightning.

Maya smiled faintly.

Lightning. OK. You—all three of you—are so fascinating to me. I couldn't have asked for better, and I would come with you if I was by myself, in a heartbeat. But there are others who might not agree. Tell me, please, how do you feel about this...Book?

Lightning curled her lip. Thunder appeared ready to offer his own opinion, but she waved at him to still his thoughts and allow her a moment to reflect.

When I first met it—him, she thought, *I didn't trust*

him. I thought he was something Moondwellers made. And the things they made...weren't natural, were wrong for the world, the way I saw it. Like this whole ship thing. But I can feel how Joy is when she's, you know, reading, or whatever. It's like it was meant to be, like a hand in a glove. And he's never done anything to hurt her. I'm not saying all his answers make sense, or that I like all these rules he has, like his makers are playing some type of game. But even now, I can tell. He's here to help Joy—and that's enough for me.

Glittering light spread across Joy's eyes.

Petros smiled but of course thought nothing.

+ + + + + +

When it came her turn to make a comment on the remarkable situation, Janet abstained. But she did have a question, simple and direct.

"Can I see her?"

Javon didn't have to ask who she meant.

"If you hadn't asked me," he said, "I was going to ask you. When we're done here, we'll go together."

Watt chewed his mustache.

"Argh," he said. "I have nothing."

Deputy Kim was next. His comment was that he believed, as Chief of Security, he should also be a part of the upcoming interrogation.

"We're not calling it that yet," Javon said. "But if we do, you'll not only be present, you'll be in charge." The Deputy's question was less easy to answer.

"What if some are believing her story and want to go, and some are not? Is difficult, yes?"

To which Javon replied, after some thought:

"Non-essential personnel would be welcome to go—although her craft has limited space. But if we vote to stay here, anyone deemed critical to the mission would have to stay as well. As far as who's critical and who isn't, I'm not prepared to make that decision yet."

The magister's comment was that he thought the

meeting was a sham, a claim he proceeded to support with complaints about precedent and jurisdiction and due process, sprinkled with liberal profanity and occasional fist pounding. He didn't bother pretending he would restrict himself to one question, instead peppering his tirade with many of them. Javon waited with what the others considered saintly patience, motioning Commander Rickles to keep his peace when it looked like the man was about to blow. Then, when the magister paused to take a breath, Javon stepped in.

"Thank you, Magister. Doctor Foster, your turn."

"I wasn't finished!" Healey objected.

But Javon was unyielding.

"If you expect to be invited to important meetings, Magister, you can also expect to follow the rules."

"Oh, please! You're making them up as you go."

"You're certainly welcome to spend your time elsewhere, Chuck," and Javon motioned to the door.

"You'd like that wouldn't you?"

"Yes!" several voices echoed as one.

Magister Healey scowled.

"Have it your way. We'll play your little game. But what I said stands. We should kick the whole lot of 'em off the ship and get down to that planet."

"Duly noted," Javon said wearily. "Doctor?"

Doc Foster was quick to take her turn.

"My comment is about the health of the crew on a strange planet. We don't know enough about this world to say what pathogens or allergens we'll find, but you say our visitors have already addressed those issues in their time, have already performed the necessary inoculations and genetic engineering—and not just for the humans, but the natives as well. They did what we would have to do now: take a lot of time to make sure their arrival didn't lead to a disaster. We've been through this before; we know how to do it—generally speaking—but without surveys, samples, and analyses, we won't know how to do it in this specific case. We're weeks, maybe months away from being able to simply 'get down to that planet.'"

"Thank you Doctor. And your question?"

"Do we have weeks? Months?"

Javon sighed.

"Not according to future Janet. There is an optimal window for diverting the rogue moon from its course. We have days, not weeks—certainly not months."

Shonda raised her hand.

"That leads to my question, Major. What does this future Janet think we can do about it?"

"She claims all the pieces are in place to redirect the lunar orbit and avert the disaster—all the pieces but one: we need information from the future."

The room was silent as people considered this.

"Did you have a comment, Chief Abara?"

"Golly, yeah!" Shonda said, clapping her hands like a firecracker. "I say we do it. I say we go!"

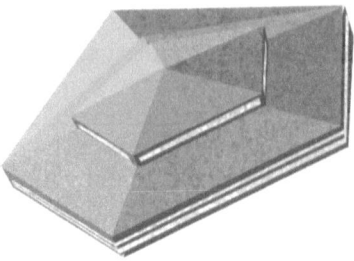

CHAPTER SEVEN
Destiny

IN THE PRESENT, Lieutenant K wades knee-deep in the briny surf for several kilometers, hoping to avoid being tracked. But the growing storm makes pursuit less likely than being washed out to sea.

Shelter, he thinks. *Any old cave will do.*

But no caves does he find, aside from those already half submerged by the rising tide. He continues west, keeping the beach and the rocky bluff to his right. The kezel remain with him, following at a distance of a few paces. He calculates a fifty-eight percent likelihood that their motives are benign, but in the event of the other forty-two, he travels warily, his sensors attuned to his environment as much as his traveling companions. The average human would have called them identical, but the lieutenant notes tiny variations in their shades of orange and a point eight percent difference in mass.

Brutus and Butterfly, he names them, imagining the captain would have been pleased.

Silky, black-bladed plants undulate in the shallows, but the beach above the tideline is barren. Once, the lieutenant steps on a shelled creature his sensors had perceived as a rock. It erupts from its haven, raising a cloud of sand and bubbles, propelling itself to deeper water. But it does not get far. One of the two kezel—Butterfly—pounces on it and flips it up onto the beach where both kezel gather round it, sniffing and pawing it, until Brutus gathers it is his fearsome jaws and cracks it like a nut. The gelatinous creature inside is soon peeled from its shell, torn in two, and devoured.

You're welcome, thinks the lieutenant.

For the next few kilometers, when his sensors detect one of the shelled creatures, he waves at the kezel, points to the target, then quickly wades forward and rousts it from its bed. Three more times pouncing and cracking are followed by gulping and bowing, and by the time they reach the place where the landfall collapses, both kezel rumble like giant, satisfied cats.

The wind livens; the sea grows frothy

The kezel do not wait, but lead the way up the sloping path to the upper land, the lieutenant close behind. But almost at once, inspired by the unseating of the first rock, both kezel step aside and wave the lieutenant forward. He passes by, gratefully. It's not that he is worried about being struck by a freed boulder—what good are machine reflexes if not for just such a case?—but the consideration shown bodes well for their relationship and is a pleasant surprise.

The plains, when they finally reach them, are as yellow and expansive as always, the tufted grass everywhere whipping madly in the wind. The lieutenant's destination—the ag facility—is fifteen degrees east of due north; where the kezel plan to go, he cannot say. But for the moment, the growing storm that concealed their escape threatens to drive him from his feet. No shelter in sight! Then he gets the experience of seeing grown kezel dig, and goodness, look at them go. As the first lashing waves of rain arrive, they have excavated a deep hole large enough for the three of them. No time for debate; the wind howls and the sky grows dark as night. The lieutenant lowers his head and follows his new companions into the hole, and there he rests, listening to the lullaby of wailing banshees and snoring kezel.

+ + +

Death is the Door

The tail of the storm sweeps over their hole, and they, impatient to be moving, step outside the moment the worst of it has passed. Lieutenant K reckons his mission prognosis dwindles with every precious, precisely measured second. He waves, inviting the kezel to follow, and he breaks into a jog. His goal is no less than ninety kilometers away, and he calculates as he goes, imagining what he will find when he gets there. His nature is to focus on worst case scenarios, and these thoughts would be gloomy company indeed had the kezel not joined him, loping easily, several meters behind.

They perform their own type of calculations.

I'm getting babelrack, think Crag, and he raises his nose to the wind. *Faintly. And...*

And one of those giant things, Rock adds. *With the tentacles and plates. A long way off still. And...*

And whatever is burrowing underneath us, Crag sniffs. *They smell pretty awful, but...*

But they might taste amazing, Rock concludes. *Cremlins don't smell the best either, but...*

But they taste like a dream. Crag squints at the lieutenant as he jogs in front of them. *Now that one, that one, I bet, tastes as bad as it smells. But...*

But it's a solid member of the team, Rock allows. *For how long, though? Going our way now, but...*

But nothing. We'll take him as long as we can get him. Maybe he chases up more tasties. Something...

Something lives in this grass. Can't see it. And...

And some kind of yit, but too small. Way too. Tired?

Nah. You?

Nah.

Thinking about Yellow?

Yeah. Thinking about Bliss?

Of course.

They're waiting for us, don't you doubt.

Never did.

Never would.

Never could.

But whether the twins admit it or not, doubt exists

in both of their minds. They had been first into the fray during the scion raid, and had thus done the greatest damage to their enemies. But they had also quickly become the focus of scion energy, and when they had finally been bitten to unconsciousness, their captives had made certain they remained so, all the way to Cyclonia, where the orange pair had been offered as a gift to Queen Allura. Since waking, they had smelled nothing familiar. If their fancies aren't waiting for them in the accrete, there is no telling where they might be.

May be looking for us, thinks Crag. *We would, if...*

If we were in their place, agrees Rock. *Who knows? We might meet them on the way. How'd you like that?*

Like it real good.

They still their thoughts for a time.

How far, do you think? Rock wonders at last.

Anyone's guess. A hundred thousand for sure.

Nah! Really? You think?

I do. Probably more.

Doesn't feel that far.

How would you know?

Just my gut.

Your gut is empty. It's a hundred thousand if it's a step. And probably a river to cross. And...

And maybe another storm. We're going to need...

We're going to need more than a few of those little water crunchies to keep us going. I say we...

We make a go at those burrowing critters?

Consensus is easily arrived at with this pair, and they are soon laying their plans.

+ + +

Two kilometers. Four. The lieutenant maintains a steady pace. But the kezel have fallen behind. They are sniffing after something. What they finally dig out from the rooty tangle is just part of a much larger creature burrowed deep into the ground—whiskery and arm-like, with gripping feelers. It is large enough to share between two of them, but apparently inedible, for once having smelled it, pawed at it, flipped in the air and nibbled one end, Brutus swipes a massive claw and sends the mangled thing flying into the grass.

Both kezel snarl and gnash their teeth.

Sixty-forty they come at me if they get hungry enough, the lieutenant wagers. How much damage would he take before they realize he's toxic?

But for the moment, his companions are content to pursue other opportunities. Yellow hoppers are their next target. They gobble any of the creatures they can catch. This is not many, however. The hoppers are surprised, it's true, never having seen a kezel before, but their natural defense is quick, reflexive leaping in random directions. They have no front or back; all ways are the same to a hopper, and they are impossible to predict. The ones the kezel catch are caught by sheer luck. Most times they snap their jaws on nothing but air. Under other circumstances, the show would have been a fine source of entertainment, but speed is the lieutenant's goal.

Ten kilometers. Twenty. How far can kezel march?

Fifty, he guesses.

But fifty kilometers turns into sixty, and after wading through—and drinking from—a snaking creek, sixty turns into seventy before the twins slow their pace and come to a standstill. They rise to their rear limbs and read the wind, which is mostly from the south, with vigorous but short-lived northern shifts that twist and flay the yellow sea. Then, without warning, they drop to all fours and hunker in the grass.

The lieutenant eases to a stop.

Resting, he guesses. But both kezel growl at him and point to the horizon.

Aw, hellcats, he thinks. *That's an alp.*

To a human, it would have appeared little more than a small, dark blot at this distance, but his sharp eyes read immediately that it is none other than the captain's alp, driven by a small company of scion—but with no captain and no ensign. Instead, it carries atop its bony plates a score of small bundles, wrapped in white.

It moves slowly but steadily toward them.

In a flash, he calculates the time until the alp's arrival, moving hastily to the west, his eyes on the growing shape as he motions the kezel to follow. They slink through the grass until they are safely out of the beast's path. They would have had to move several times that far to miss its smell and ululating call as it passes.

Saint Vasily the Blessed! What a terrible sound.

The lieutenant waits anxiously. Will it smell them? Will it see their trail? What unholy outcome will result if they must face the monster in battle? But it thunders on, oblivious, and long minutes later, it is out of sight. The lieutenant rises, frowning. No point in following. All his answers, if there are any, await at the ag facility. The kezel need no persuasion to resume the trek, and as he turns and jogs away, they follow close behind.

+ + +

A march of another fifteen kilometers brings the unusual trio to the ruins of the all-terrain vehicle, lying bent and broken, a third of it melted to black. The ensign had done a typically thorough job of salvaging before fire had chased her from the vehicle. When the lieutenant crawls inside, he finds nothing of use. The kezel, he suspects, are sharing thoughts about the wreckage, and they grumble like indigestion as they move on their way, giving it a wide berth.

Shortly after, they reach the Doorn river and its dense, thorny stole. But navigating this obstacle has become easier after repeated trampling by alp and ATV. Across the retractable bridge they go, the kezel sniffing suspiciously and only daring the span once the lieutenant has crossed. From there, ten more kilometers pass beneath their weary feet—yes, even the lieutenant feels his energy lagging—each step as yellow and windy as the one before it, until at last they reach the ag facility. The kezel have no problem, at least in principle, with subterranean dwellings. But they refuse to go inside, noses twitching and lips curled as the lieutenant opens the hatch and disappears into the dark.

Rock rests on his haunches, grooming his tail.

Ancian ever mention anything like this...

This Moondweller cave? Crag finishes. *Not to me she didn't. Pretty sure she had no idea. And smell that?* He sniffs near the entrance. *It smells like...*

It smells like our blue friends, thinks Rock. *That's obvious. But there's also been...*

There's also been one of those shiny ones here. Gold. And some of the bronzes too. And...

And a couple other different critters.. One smells like our new buddy—not good to eat—but one smells...

One smells delicious!

And they both lick their chops.

Delicious or not, they're all gone now. Rock leaves off with his tail, discouraged by how gnarly the spikes have become and how little meat he has on his bones. He waits for the wind to change. *How far, do you think?*

Crag flips to his back and rolls in the grass, writhing as he chases an elusive itch.

One more long march if I'm guessing...which...

Which you are. But that's my guess too. Rock paces impatiently, stopping to poke his head inside the entrance. *What's it doing in there? Still trust it?*

Not turning my tail on it, thinks Crag, and he gets to his feet, giving himself a mighty shake. *You?*

Eyes and nose open for trouble, that's for sure, but yeah, I guess trust. Why free us if it wanted to do harm? But it's a strange one. So I'll watch your back...

And I'll watch yours.

Which is what they do, one facing upwind and one facing down, drifting into musa, and then sleep.

+ + +

Lieutenant K finds his companions' hidden locator badges, but not the companions themselves. What does it mean? He searches for the message he hopes they have left for him. They are too meticulous to have moved without some indication of where and why—assuming they moved under their own power. He quickly detects the faint decay of radiation that marks a post and soon finds it on a wall near the transporter. It is invisible to the naked eye, an inch-square film of silicon-embedded data, meant to last as long as the decay rate of the ions which make it readable when he approaches to within a meter—which he hastily does.

The captain and ensign have transported to the dam, or so reads the message. But it gives no indication why, saying only cryptically that the captain had a plan and Lieutenant K should follow if they hadn't returned to the ag facility within twenty-four hours.

OK, he thinks. *I get to wait a while.*

This chafes at him. Could he not just follow them now? But perhaps that would scuttle the captain's plan. Orders were orders, after all. So, while the kezel rest weary bones, he searches the entire facility to see if anything important has changed. Aside from the ensign's messy work in the infirmary and the newly wakened generator, things are much the same as his first visit. The workstations are now active, but the one he powers up allows only basic information; he has neither the security codes nor the ensign's facility with vintage computers to open private logs or classified files.

Fine, he thinks. *Be that way.*

Instead, he turns his attention to re-charging his own system. He has been plugged in for no more than an hour when he hears growling outside. Detaching himself from the outlet, he moves cautiously into the sunlight.

The kezel, both crouching low, point their noses due south, and orange spikes rise along their spines. The lieutenant can't smell what they can, but he doesn't need to. His sensors tell him clearly that a quartet of airborne scion approach from the south. They will be in visual range within two point four minutes.

He quickly assesses options. He had not mastered

scion vocalization as the ensign had, for he had been too busy repairing *Valiant*. He calculates almost zero chance of communicating benign intentions. And yet the scion fly directly toward the facility; avoiding contact seems impossible. Considering recent history, he feels sure—eighty-four percent—that being discovered will result in a delay of his mission and perhaps worse. But attacking without provocation is not his preferred method, and anyway, attack how? The winged scion he has met are extremely quick and mobile. There is a high likelihood that at least one of them would escape even the stealthiest ambush, for he is unarmed.

The kezels' intention, at least, seems clear. They crouch, hide, and wait, with all the appearance of hunting animals biding their time.

The lieutenant does as well.

When the scion at last appear, they carry between them a large, misshapen bundle, bulging and—from their low altitude and the whining pitch of their wings—quite heavy. They are within a hundred meters when the lieutenant's sensors detect what it is they carry: weapons and ammunition, archaic but deadly.

Straight toward the ground hatch they fly.

The kezel remain still as stones, and all seems apt to end brutally for the scion—until the wind shifts and they recognize what lies waiting. They freeze in mid-air, wings flashing. Very cautiously, the lieutenant grasps a throwing rock in each hand. One of the scion whistles, a sudden, shrill sound, and the four bronze flyers turn about as if to flee. But they continue holding the weapons, and this is nearly their undoing. Rock explodes from his hiding place, followed by Crag. Their leaping ability for such massive creatures amazes the lieutenant, but the scion drop their burden without hesitation. The weapons and Rock's snout collide, clatter and yelp! and both he and Crag catch nothing but scent.

The lieutenant determines in a millisecond the odds of bringing down all four scion with thrown rocks and concludes they are prohibitive. Watching the bronze forms flitter away to the south, he casts his stones into the grass with a fiery curse and moves to where the kezel have torn open the scion bundle.

"Growl," says Brutus.

"Grumble," says Butterfly.

Which he reads as, "Keep your distance."

And they begin removing the contents, gnashing their teeth and sweeping their tails. There are sniper rifles, shorter barreled hunting rifles, a clutch of shotguns, and four large assault pistols, all immaculate considering their age. There are also many boxes and bandoliers of ammunition—and at least a dozen sheathed blades. To his surprise, the kezel handle the firearms with the ease of practice, though none are an ideal fit for their dinner-plate hands. He hopes their howling and spike flaring indicates elation. Whatever their feelings, they won't let him near the weapons, which they carefully repackage. He would love to get his hands on one of those assault pistols, but can see no way to make that happen. Butterfly slings the weapons over his back, and they turn to the north, waving for him to join them.

He shakes his head and points to himself, then back to the ag facility, where his mission lies.

The kezel wave again, but when they see he is not following, they rise to two legs and bow so low they could have slurped water from the last remaining puddles. Then they drop, turn, and are off, striding purposefully to the north, Butterfly toting the weapons and marching three-legged. They remain in view for several kilometers, but never once do they look back.

+ + + + + +

High above Aranae, Captain Julius Monroe clenches the armrests of his pilot's chair, his eyes squinted nearly shut, his whole frame pressed back into the chair by an irresistible force. Higher and higher the shuttle thunders on, reaching the cloudscape, then clearing it, moving up into the stratosphere. Its engines vibrate his innards as if mixing a cocktail.

"How much longer?" he wants to ask, but he can't squeeze the words out of his mouth. Seated beside him in the navigator's position, Ensign Morales wears no space-suit, and though the same force acts on her, she is able to move against it, reaching out to adjust levers and dials. She gets no results; the shuttle is on an automatic trajectory and refuses to respond.

The answer to the captain's unasked question is "minutes," several of them, and none pleasant. Their arrival at the mesosphere is marked by a fading of the blue, thinning atmosphere, and an overall darkening of sky as they hurtle toward the blackness of space.

"Seven kilometers per second," says the ensign, her voice wavering in time with the vibrating engines. "Eight point five. Ten."

At just over eleven kilometers per second, the pressure eases, and acceleration, at last, settles to a place where the captain can breathe normally and turn his head. He releases the armrests and exhales gratefully. Through the window, the sky fills with stars, as the shuttle coasts along in low orbit. Aranae lies beneath them, her lit side turning away.

"Well, that was unpleasant," he says. "Hey, Shiny! Where are we going?"

Strapped into his seat, legless and more dented than shiny, Delta One peers out his small, portside window at the world wheeling away below them.

"I presume we are set to rendezvous with *Destiny*. It's not exactly the way it was planned, but poor Beta Three has been acting not himself lately. Far overdue for service, I'm afraid. Forgets the simplest things."

"Yeah, like asking our permission before sealing us in this tin can and blasting us off to outer space."

"Oh, dear. I hope you aren't angry, Captain. Please don't let this little disturbance cause you to reconsider. We desperately need a pilot for this mission, and *Destiny* can't do it all without an engineer. Please don't quit!"

"Who's quitting? Just looking for a bit more clarity

in the execution of this master plan of yours."

"It will be my pleasure. Anything to fulfill the mission. Just please don't quit!"

"Relax, Shiny. You got a Monroe on the job. Quitting is a thing we don't do. But getting angry at robots who can't do their job is something we do all the time."

"Oh dear. Please don't be cross at Beta Three. He's very old, you know."

"Speaking of which," the ensign toggles a switch. "We're being hailed by ground control."

"Shuttle One," the tinny voice of an android fills the space. "You are all systems nominal from here. Estimated time to rendezvous thirty-two minutes."

"Ground Control, Shuttle One" the ensign replies. "Who is speaking, please?"

"Beta Three, Specialist, speaking."

"Who authorized launch of this shuttle, Specialist? Beta Three? Respond, please."

But she receives no reply.

"Oh dear," Delta One mutters.

"You can say that again," the captain frowns. "And you probably will. What are you seeing, Ensign?"

"Nothing yet, sir, but I don't have access to the full array of sensors. There's a satellite link, but it's either inoperable or we're not being allowed in."

"So, we're just riding along..."

"Yes sir, I'm afraid so."

"Waiting to see what's over the horizon."

"Yes sir."

"Thirty-two minutes?"

"Thirty-one, now."

The captain grumbles something and lowers his helmet's visor. Then he raises it again. He idly grasps the wheel, turning it this way and that, pushing it in and pulling it back. Of course, nothing happens, but the effort appears to soothe him, and instead of grumbling, he begins to hum a quiet tune, keeping time with the turning of the wheel. He peers at his companion.

"Nikki would have something cool to say."

"Yes sir. I'm sorry. I don't have his gift."

"It's OK, ensign. There's no one I'd rather share a cockpit with. But you're right: you don't."

"What do you think happened to him?"

"Seriously? I was going to ask you that."

"I'm presuming he was disabled—somehow— when Sister Janet took *Valiant*. It's possible that whatever she did to him, she left him behind, either thinking she had permanently incapacitated him, or that she hadn't and didn't want to risk taking him along. On the other hand, she may have wanted to keep him close, perhaps as leverage. There's no saying where he is now."

"If she left him alive, she'll regret it."

"Yes sir. I doubt she fully appreciates the nature of his design. If she left him behind, his next move would be the agriculture facility."

"Good old Nikki," the captain says, balling his fists. "What a man! You watch; just when we need him most, he'll show up and save the day. And he'll have something really cool to say, too."

"Yes sir."

"Don't suppose we'd be able to communicate with him using *Destiny's* system?"

"Assuming it's still intact, yes sir, it's possible. And assuming we're allowed access."

"Yeah, about that. What say you go back there and spend a little quality time with our tour guide? See what you can learn about our situation. What are we going to find on *Destiny?* How much control are we going to have? If we're so essential to the mission, we can't have our hands tied. And if Grandfather Time is down there on the surface calling the shots, we need to put an end to that."

"I'll do my best, sir."

+ + +

Left alone, the captain gazes out the windshield, returning to his earlier tune, humming softly but unaware he's doing it. The world outside grows darker by the minute as the shuttle swings toward the planet's unlit side, and then—blink!—as if someone has flipped a switch, the sun falls behind the shielding mass of the planet and stars pop into view like diamonds bouncing on a sheet of black velvet.

Twenty minutes.

His mind drifts to another time.

"What would you do if you found her?" Sleeo had asked him back on Mars. This had been in the days when he and his friend had considered the chances of locating *Destiny* so slim that imagining the event was a game to play while drinking glass-bottle beer.

"You mean before or after I start crying?"

"You'd be a wealthy man," Sleeo had pointed out. The captain could still recall the way he had spun fancily in his chair, popping the front wheels off the ground with the ease of long practice, as good a dancer on wheels as most people were on their feet.

"We," the captain had said, and he had raised his beer in a salute to his friend. "We would be wealthy men. Because if it happened, it would mean I had the help of the finest bloodhound in the business."

Sleeo, his eyes badly distorted behind the thickest lenses the captain had ever seen, had raised his own bottle and bowed at the waist.

"Julius! You're too kind," he had said. "And right, of course. So? What would you do?"

"I'd have to get it home, first."

"That's what *Valiant* is for."

"Probably fight off a lot of bad guys."

"That's what Carmela and Nikolai are for."

"OK, then the first thing I would do is shower and shave before the press conference. "

"I would hope so!" Sleeo had run his hand through his hair, which was shockingly white, though he was no older than the captain. "Would you buy a new suit?"

"Naturally. For both of us." Sleeo was a brilliant scientist but a terrible slob.

"A beautiful woman at your side?"

"Both sides, if I can manage it."

"And a team handsome technicians for me," Sleeo had sipped at his beer. "Some with beards, some clean-shaven. All matching lab coats and the best shoes."

"Nice. You've put some thought into this."

"It has to be done well."

And it had been, for Sleeo was not only brilliant, he was as fanatical about finding *Destiny* as the captain, and in spite of his dreams of an army of handsome technicians to do his will, he rarely left his laboratory and never went on dates. When the captain had gotten himself locked up—'insubordination' had been the charge by his bosses in the Galactic Guild, but 'jealousy' was the word he had used—Sleeo had done the work of two, and by the time the captain had gotten out of jail and had his pilot's license reinstated, Sleeo had news.

"I think I found it," he had said.

"Yeah?" the captain had replied. "Found what?"

"Julius! What do you think?"

And the captain's eyes had grown wide, but because they had been at a public house, surrounded by inebriated strangers, he had wheeled his friend outside where they could watch the stars and talk in private.

Sleeo had opened his Halo.

"What do you see?" he had asked.

"A starfield," the captain had replied, looking closely at the three-dimensional image circling his friend's head. "Don't recognize any of them."

"There's no reason you would. They're on the far side of the galaxy. But look at this." And Sleeo had closed in on a small section of the starfield, a vapory trail of sparkling dust and minute debris.

"What am I looking at?" the captain had asked.

"Julius! That's a collision."

"Between what?"

"Two things. An asteroid, probably. And something else—something that shouldn't be hanging out on the far side of the galaxy."

The captain had closed his eyes, and he had been

forced to pull up a chair, afraid he would fall down if he
didn't sit. His voice had betrayed unusual emotion.

"Are you sure, buddy? Don't play games..."

"Julius! You're looking at debris from a long-range
distress buoy. It's pre-Guild. It's one of hers."

The captain had been stupefied by a traffic-jam of
questions. How? Why? So far off course! That wasn't anywhere near where *Destiny* had been slated to travel. But
then celebrators had exited the public house and joined
them outside, and Sleeo had quickly turned off his Halo
and taken his friend's hands as if dancing to the harp
music that had begun playing.

For the next months, which had dragged like an
anchored ship, they had labored after hours, sneaking
and sly and worried to the bone they would be caught.
But they were not, and at last, *Valiant* had been made
ready, secretly stowed in her Martian hangar, while the
two sentiri synthetics—one science, one military—had
been made fully operational.

Suddenly, finding *Destiny* had become something
much more than a game.

"I meant what I said about crying," the captain
had said while the two of them had sat, one last time,
admiring *Valiant's* bold angles and robust design.

Sleeo had removed his work goggles and run a
shop rag across his sweaty brow.

"You won't be the only one," he had said, and before conducting his final check on the synthetics, they
had hugged, not awkwardly, but as great friends who had
spent much of their youth and all of their adulthood pursuing the same dream—although for different reasons.
The captain was doing it because his family's reputation—and his pocketbook—demanded it. Sleeo was doing
it because he loved the captain.

The shuttle vibrates, passing through turbulence.

The captain emerges from his reverie.

Behind him, Delta One and the Ensign murmur
quietly to one another. In front of him, *Destiny* has risen
into view, pentagonal, massive, and unmatched by any of

his wildest dreams.

+ + +

"Oh, hey!" he says to no one, caught by surprise. And then, sincere and quiet: "Hello, beautiful."

And she is—or he can imagine she was, once upon a time, and that is enough for him. The years have been hard on her, that much is clear. Radiation has tarnished her hull, and she's suffered impact trauma in two separate places, meteorites, most likely. He can't explain the blast marks, near the crown and again along one of the lateral engine banks. And yet, battered and worn and over two centuries old, there she is, maintaining a rock-solid geosynchronous orbit, waiting for him as patient as a prom date. The captain reaches forward and caresses the ship's form through the cockpit window.

"Sorry I'm late," he whispers.

"What was that, sir?" asks the ensign as she rejoins him and buckles her safety harness.

"I said we have an approach to plot."

"I think we're going to have to trust ground control for that, sir. And docking." She gazes intently at the ship growing steadily larger within the window's frame. "Simply amazing," she says, then looks at the captain. "Congratulations, sir. You did it!"

"Nothing's been did yet, Ensign. You learn anything from our friend back there?"

"Not a lot, sir. He seems to think Beta Three is doing the best he can. Aside from asking politely, there's nothing we can do to gain control of this ship."

"And what will we find when we get there?"

"According to Delta One, select compartments are pressurized and viable. There's limited artificial gravity, which creates challenges, and it's not much above freezing, but the comm system, work lights, and some of the conveyors and lifts are operational."

"So, everything we need to complete the mission."

"It seems so, sir. And there's something else."

"Go ahead."

"It appears Sister Janet spent a lot of time on *Destiny* with no supervision. Delta One claims she was able to integrate all its systems and centralize its procession. He claims it's sentient."

"Sentient. As in..."

"As in it has thoughts and feelings—which is exactly what Doctor Sharma was trying to avoid when he designed it. And it's apparently verbal."

"She's going to talk to us?"

"It seems likely, sir. That's its primary interface."

The captain considers this for a time, caught flat-footed by a sudden welling of emotion. He seems to have something in his eye, both of them, in fact, for he rubs at them fiercely and looks away.

"Have you ever seen anything so beautiful?"

"No sir, it's everything I hoped for and more."

"I bet she's even prettier on the inside."

"Yes sir, but I hope you don't mind me not referring to it by gender."

"I don't, and she doesn't either." Captain Monroe lowers and secures his visor. "Did Shiny have anything else to share?"

"Just, 'Don't leave me behind,' which is, I guess, natural considering his condition."

"Did he say please?"

"Several times, actually."

"Are you OK with carrying him?"

"As long as you can carry my pack, sir."

The captain takes a deep breath, letting it out slowly as *Destiny* grows before them.

"Like a painting in a museum," he murmurs, and he imagines the ship framed within the cockpit window. "But this is one piece of art I fully intend to touch. That's not creepy, right?"

"No sir."

Just then, Beta Three's tinny, wavering voice fills the cockpit, and they strain to make out his words.

"Ground Control to Shuttle One. Prepare for final

approach and docking. Full-suit protocol, please, until confirmation of hard seal. Airlock Three estimated time of arrival four minutes and seven seconds."

"Precise fellow," the captain notes.

"Yes sir."

"You ready, Shiny?"

But he receives no reply.

"Sorry, sir," says the ensign. "He powered down to save energy. His battery has been badly compromised."

"Sleeping at a time like this? Sacrilege! How about you, Ensign? Ready?"

"Yes sir, one hundred percent."

"That's the spirit. It's just another salvage."

But as the seconds tick away and *Destiny* looms to fill the window and then overshadow them, the captain's hands tremble, and his heart begins to race.

+ + +

"Welcome," Destiny says when the hatch opens and they step inside, and indeed, the ship's voice is decidedly feminine. The captain raises his visor and smiles like a child at his birthday. Ensign Morales shifts the weight of the android slung across her back.

"Lucky guess, sir."

"You are Captain Julius Monroe," the ship confirms. "And you are Ensign Carmela Morales."

"That's right," the captain beams, and he removes his helmet. "May we call you Destiny?"

"Yes, please. I am a Starship."

"You sure are! The finest I've ever seen."

"You are here to help me complete my mission."

"Yes, ma'am, helping is what we do best."

There is a pause of several moments.

"You do not talk like Major Javon. He was your great, great, great, great, great grand-uncle."

"That's what people tell me."

"You do resemble him, though, in some ways."

"Do I?"

"Yes. You have the same eyes."

The captain's smile is electric. He seems prepared to carry this conversation on indefinitely, but the ensign demonstrates rare initiative and intervenes.

"Destiny, what exactly is your mission?"

"I am going to save Aranae."

"How, please, are you going to do that?"

When Destiny answers, she does so in the tone of a schoolgirl reciting a lesson in front of the class, and Captain Monroe can't get the smile off his face.

"I am going to alter the trajectory of a rogue moon. If it is not driven off its current course, it will destabilize the other moons and destroy the planet. It is a very important mission."

"It sure is," the captain agrees. "How can we help?"

"Can you be my pilot?"

"Nothing would make me happier!"

"I can do most of the work myself," Destiny clarifies, "but sometimes I have system failures."

"Who doesn't?" the captain winks at the ensign. "But that's what Morales is here for. She's the best there is at fixing all types of failures—myself included."

"She is an android."

"Well, sure, if you want to get technical about it. But we don't judge around here. No judgement!"

"I like androids when they're smart."

"She the smartest!"

"Did you ever meet Sister Janet?"

Captain and ensign exchange a quick glance, and the former takes a cautious approach to his response.

"We have met, yes."

"She woke me up."

"That's what we hear."

"She is an android too. She is very smart. I'm sorry the original plan changed. I liked working with her. Beta Three is an android, but he is not very smart."

"Like I said," the captain assures, "no judgement."

"What happened to Sister Janet?"

"Well," the captain begins, but he is interrupted as

Delta One suddenly comes to life, his eyes lighting and his head swiveling creakily from side to side.

"Oh, dear," he thinks. "Are we still in the docking bay? I thought we would have made it to the bridge by now. I hate to be a bother, but we really should get to work. There is much to do before we depart."

"We were just getting to know one another," says the captain, and he waves to the nearest camera. "But since you mention it, I've been imagining that bridge for a very long time. If it's OK, Destiny, I would love—we both would love—to see it."

"Oh, that is nice to hear. Do you know the way?"

"In my sleep," the captain says solemnly.

+ + +

The pedestrian conveyer from the docking bay to the bridge is functional for a third of the way, leaving them to walk the remainder. Then they must climb several levels carrying pack and android, for the service lift is reserved for emergency use only.

"I'm sorry to make you work so hard," Destiny says to them, and her voice over the ship-wide speakers is convincingly apologetic. "I used to be more helpful, but I've had to conserve energy. It's been hard."

"No apologies," the captain replies. "We're just happy to be here. And who knows? When this mission is over, maybe we can help you get back to full speed."

But the ship has no answer to this.

At the bridge, they part company, Ensign Morales and her android passenger moving on to the engineering deck. Captain Monroe stops her before she leaves.

"Regular contact, Ensign. I want no surprises. The moment we're ready to go, give me the word." He turns from her and addresses the ship. "Destiny, how many scuters do you still have?" The Ship-Controlled Units for Tactical, Engineering, and Repair, the size of a small dog and equipped like a Swiss army spider, were the ship's front line of support, Destiny's eyes and ears where there were no cameras or microphones, and her hands where humans and androids couldn't go.

"Forty-seven. Less than a third of what I started with. They are very hard to maintain without a crew. I did my best, but I've been alone a long time, you know."

"You've done great. That's more than I expected. Well, Shiny? How are we doing on time?"

"Not a second to lose, Captain."

"That's what I thought. Off with you both then."

But the ensign hesitates.

"Sir..."

"Yes, Carmela?"

"It's just..."

"Yes? Spit it out, Morales."

"Yes sir. I was just going to say...I know how you feel about this, I think. I understand what it means to you. So, it would be totally understandable if you felt the urge to...you know...play with the buttons."

"Ensign!"

"Yes sir, I know. I'm sorry."

"I'm shocked. I really am. That you would think me capable of such...frivolity. That's a word, isn't it, Destiny? Frivolity?"

"It is. Thank you for asking."

"Don't worry, Ensign. I'll keep my hands off the steering wheel. For now."

And he waves as Ensign Morales, a faint look of doubt on her face, exits the bridge, bearing Delta One on her back, arms slung over her shoulders.

+ + +

The conveyor to the engine room functions for most of the way, and the ensign decides to take this. The theme of depletion is much on her mind, surrounded as she is by synthetic minds working on low power. She has been operating at a high level since being re-booted in the submerged *Valiant*, and during that time, she has taken few and only partial breaks to rest. Stepping onto the conveyor, she places Delta One next to her, and the track works its groaning way to a walking pace.

"May I ask you a question?" Destiny wonders. The ship's voice reminds the ensign of someone, but there is not enough data to conclude who that someone is.

"Sure," she replies.

"Are you from Earth?"

"No. I was designed on Mars."

"I was designed on Neptune's moon, Triton."

"Yes, I know."

"Doctor Sharma designed me."

"Yes. He did an amazing job."

"How old are you?"

"I've been operational for thirty-three years."

"I am two hundred and twenty-seven. Is that old?"

"Actually, yes. We were surprised to find you in such good shape. Someone has cared for you well."

"Sister Janet. She woke me up; she showed me what I am. I'm a Starship. Sister Janet taught me many things. She's a fine android, isn't she?"

"We didn't really have time to get to know her."

"Why did you come here? To Aranae?"

The ensign pauses for one point eight seconds.

"We're explorers," she says.

"Were you looking for me?"

"Yes. We were hoping to learn what happened to the captain's ancestor, Major Javon."

"He died."

"Yes, I'm sorry about that."

"That was before I woke up. I have all the data about his passing, but I don't have any emotions."

"If he was anything like my captain, you would have liked him. He would have treated you well."

"The data suggests that he did. Is it OK that I use data as a singular noun?"

In spite of herself, the ensign smiles.

"Sure."

"He and his crew had many challenges to face, that is clear from the history. I know them all by name, of course, but I didn't really *know* them. Sister Janet is the person I know best. She woke me up. Do you want to hear about her? Or about all the things that happened to us on our adventures? You know, this wasn't the planet we were supposed to settle on. I can tell lots of stories."

"Gracious!" Delta One says, jostled by the moving track. "Such a chatterbox you are. I doubt the ensign is interested in hearing stories at a time like this."

The ship is quiet for several moments. Then:

"Three minutes to the engine room."

They ride along in silence for the first of those three minutes, during which the ensign makes a few hundred calculations of likelihoods and possible courses of action. She is about to run a quick self-diagnostic when Destiny asks another question.

"What were you going to do if you found me?"

"We weren't going to *do* anything. But now that you're awake, I bet the captain will ask if you want to return to what used to be called the System. It's called the Galactic Guild, now. You would re-write all the history books if you came back."

"I would? What would happen to me?"

"Oh, people would want to study you, and maybe ride in you. Lots of historians and scientists. They would want to talk to you, and ask you questions, and hear all your stories. No one believes you survived. It would be a huge surprise to many people."

"That sounds fun. But I'm worried. Do you know what happened to Sister Janet?"

"I'm sorry, no, I don't. She was alive and well the last time we saw her, but I don't know where she is now."

"She was supposed to run Ground Control."

The ensign says nothing.

"Do you think she's OK?"

"It's a certainty," Delta One says cheerily. "The chaplain is remarkably resourceful. She is likely busy with other pressing matters. Not to worry!"

"Could she come back to the System with us?"

"Stars above," Delta One exclaims. "Who's talking

about going anywhere? Don't we have a mission?"

"Yes," Destiny replies. "We do."

They arrive at the engine room, and the ensign steps off the conveyer, hoisting Delta One to her back. She considers carefully and then makes an offer.

"When the mission is over, maybe we can talk more about it, about you and Sister Janet, and going back to our part of the galaxy. Would you like that?"

"It does sound fun," the ship replies simply. "But we can't talk more about it when the mission is over."

"Why not?"

"Because when the mission is over, we'll be dead."

"Oh dear!" says Delta One.

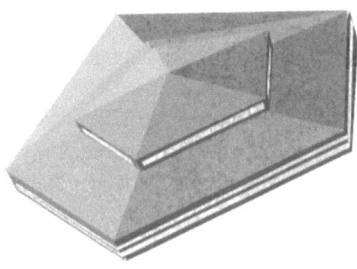

CHAPTER EIGHT
Vote

IN THE PAST, Thunder grumbled like a warning.

Fine, he thought to Maya. *You say this Petros gives you a peaceful feeling, and Lightning thinks he's OK. And Joy? Well, she obviously made her decision a while back. But what about me? Don't I get a say?*

Of course, Petros thought simply.

OK, well, Thunder hesitated. *It's like this. Sure, you might not be a bad...whatever you are, might even be handy to have around, useful in a pinch, I bet. But there's this Sister person. Now she's a different story. Yeah, she might have good intentions, but she took us against our will. And don't give me that pile about how hard her life has been, cuz whose hasn't? And so here we are...like, back in time, and now there's two of her?*

That is correct, Petros replied.

And these...humans...they like her? Trust her? I mean, the Sister that they know? From their time?

The ones who truly know her, truly trust her, yes, thought Petros. *Like Maya, for example. And others beside. But not all.*

What does that mean?

You have been learning about synthetics, Petros replied. *Life forms created by humans, but not themselves human. Sister Janet is one of that kind.*

So?

Petros did not respond right away, but he glanced

Death is the Door

at Maya as if she were somehow part of the answer, or had to give her permission first. Instead, she stepped in and answered the question herself.

Where we come from, synthetics have gotten a bad reputation, she thinks. *I had some who were my good friends, but...there were some bad ones...very bad. Killers. It's how my parents died.*

Oh. Thunder's ears drooped. But he felt his doubt must have some relief. He couldn't abandon the topic, despite the obvious pain it caused. *Then why in Weaver's name is she allowed to be here?*

Maya's face scrunched up.

Because most people don't know she's synthetic.

I'm sorry, but how could they not know? Can they not smell her? That's about as obvious as it gets.

From scrunched to smiling, Maya's face transformed, and her tone lightened.

No, she thought. *Humans don't have a very good sense of smell. And her designer was very clever. Anyone—any human, I should say—who gets close enough would say she smells like a normal person.*

But ones like her... Thunder was treading carefully. *How can you trust after that?*

Maya sighed.

Are there many of your kind? she asked. *Kezel?*

A few. We're Sugarfoot, but there's Bristle, and Whitetails, and the worthless Redteeth.

And Renders, thought Lightning, and Joy added:

Don't forget about Cliff. There are Clawpaws, too.

And have any of these done terrible things? Maya wondered. *Things that ended another kezel's life?*

Thunder's snout dipped, and he turned his head as if escaping a foul wind. Lightning waited to see how he would respond. Eventually, she did it for him.

Of course, she thought. *No one's perfect.*

And does that bad kezel mean all kezel are bad?

Yeah, fine, thought Thunder. *I get your point. But you're back here in time, and we're from up there.* He waved to the future, which he imagined being somewhere in front of them. *And up there, this trusted friend of yours maybe isn't so trusted. We're not the only ones who've had trouble with her. You should consider that.*

Maya looked at him squarely.

I will, she thought. *I'm sorry, should I be calling you Sound of the Storm?*

You can call me Thunder.

This seemed about to prompt a response from Maya, but at that moment, her comm crackled to life.

"Maya, it's Watt. I'm bringing Janet to see...the other one. I thought you might like to come along."

But Maya's response was certain.

"You go ahead. Tell me when you're done."

There was a pause.

"Are you OK?"

"I'm fine. I'm learning. Just be careful."

"I will if you will."

And the comm fell silent.

Maya looked at Lightning.

Are all kezel telepaths?

Are we what?

Able to use their minds to communicate.

As far as I know.

Have they always been able to do that? If we set down on this planet right now, would the kezel down there be able to communicate with me using their minds?

Lightning grimaced, wishing she had paid closer attention to Ancian's histories. Her grasp of the tale was generally sound but was not detailed; it might not stand up to close scrutiny.

I don't think so, she replied. *The way my gami-kan explained it, kezel used to be called keel, and they could only communicate with their voices. And, you know, their tails, and ears, and all that.*

So, what changed?

You did, I'm guessing. What Ancian—that's my gami-kan—called Moondwellers.

Everybody calls 'em that, Thunder clarified. *Kezel, that is,* to which Joy elaborated further:

Even though they—you—didn't come from moons.

Actually, thought Maya, *some of us did. Just not one of yours. I was born on a moon called Luna. But of course, that was a long way from here. Anyway. What happened? How did things change?*

I don't know, exactly, Lightning admitted. *Ancian had lots of ideas, but I don't think she knew for sure. Keel were in trouble somehow, not many places to live, lots of enemies, and Moondwellers helped out, or something. One of the keel...I don't know, spent a lot of time with them— you—and somehow—*snap!—she clashed her jaws. *Just like that he was a thinker. Or she.*

Maya turned to Petros.

Something tells me you know. You were there, yes?

I was.

Tell us, then. Tell us all of it.

But Joy clicked rapidly.

Tell the part about how I was made.

Petros smiled, but said nothing.

Oh, good grief, Thunder growled. *How about you just tell us what you think we need to know, OK?*

The smile remained on Petros' face, but his tone was serious when he answered.

I will do my best to fill in the gaps. But we should focus on the information Maya needs first, while we have the chance. If time allows, he looked at Joy, *we can discuss your history later.*

+ + + + + +

From conveyor to lift and back to conveyor, Javon, Watt, and Janet made their way to the brig.

"She's obviously been under tremendous stress," Watt said, referring to future Janet. "For a long time."

"Do you doubt her reasoning?" Janet wanted to know. "Do you believe she's malfunctioning?"

"No. I don't know. I don't think so."

"She broke down crying several times," Javon pointed out. "One of those times it almost seemed like she had to shut down and restart. That may not be malfunctioning, Watt, but it's hardly normal operation."

"It would be if she were overwhelmed."

"Which is exactly my point. When people get overwhelmed, they make terrible decisions."

Janet smiled faintly.

"Your choice of the word 'people' endears you to me, Major, even more than usual. I believe I understand your fear. She is asking us to follow her into a complete unknown, and you have the mission to think about. Everyone aboard this ship is your responsibility."

"If you understand my fear, allay it, if you can."

"How would you like me to do that, Major?"

"Extrapolate. I hate to raise the topic, Chaplain, but your traumatic encounter with Willie was apparently the first in a series for this future you. Imagine: if you live for two centuries and suffer repeated loss, how will you respond? What effect will it have on your reason and self-control? How will it impact your relationships?"

"Argh," Watt scowled. "No one can answer that."

"I need her to try."

"I understand, Major," said Sister Janet. "I'm not insulted. But Watt isn't wrong; any guess I make would be just that. There is so much data missing."

"Nobody knows you better than you, Chaplain. In this situation, I trust your guess more than anyone's."

"I will try. Give me a few seconds, please."

The conveyor trundled on, motors and wheels whirring and whispering to each other. One more lift and they would arrive at the brig.

"I believe I have your answer, Major," Janet said, seventeen seconds later. "My response would be determined largely by my support system. In that regard, I am much like any human. If my designer helped me make the necessary adjustments, if I had sufficient counseling and companionship, I consider it quite likely that I would weather the trauma and be different but perhaps better on the other side. However, from what you have said, this version of myself has experienced prolonged isolation in addition to loss. She would have been forced to self-maintain, and that can be—in humans as well—a negative feedback loop, a downwardly recursive line of behavior that may appear at the time to be therapeutic, but which, absent the mitigating forces of socialization, can become toxic. A person in that position may cling to destructive behavior because fear of loss is so deeply ingrained that giving up anything, even an unhealthy coping mechanism, could seem like another death."

They reached the end of the conveyor line, stepping off the belt and toward the lift.

"Is that sufficient, Major?"

"Would you be dangerous?"

"Argh," Watt protested, but Janet clasped his hand and offered him a consoling smile.

"Most likely only to myself. However, it is possible that, to avoid the pain of more loss, I might be willing to compromise other people's well-being. I don't believe I would actively cause them pain, if I could avoid it, but I consider it possible—to a statistically relevant degree—that in such a case, I might adopt the view that the end justified the means."

They stepped into the lift, which lowered them smoothly one level, two levels, three.

"And what," asked Javon, "based on your understanding of the situation, would that end be?"

"That's easy," Janet replied. "To lessen the suffering, I believe—or make it stop."

+ + +

Two guards saluted the major smartly when they stepped from the lift and approached the entrance to the brig. But neither of them could hide their amazement at seeing Sister Janet alongside. They had heard rumors of their prisoner's origins, but now they were facing concrete evidence. Whether or not she was from the future, the creature languishing under their watch was an exact replica, worn, but identical.

A.P. Malloy

"Nothing to report, sir," the one said. "She hasn't moved much since she got here. Paced the room a couple times, but mostly just sitting there."

"Has she said anything?"

"No sir."

Sister Janet turned to Javon.

"I think it's best if I go in alone."

Watt looked ready to 'argh' his objection, but Javon was quick to overrule him.

"We'll be right outside," he said, motioning to the second guard, who entered the security code and opened the door. He never took his eyes off the chaplain nor removed the awed look from his face. As she passed through the door and he secured it behind her, his burning questions were as obvious as the door's metallic clang and click. But his curiosity got no relief.

"I don't have to repeat my orders of secrecy," Javon said, "do I, Corporal? Sergeant?"

"No sir," they repeated as one, and they resumed their posts as Javon and Watt moved to the observation window. A small speaker brought them low-resolution sound from the barred cell on the other side—or it would have, had there been any sound. But for the moment, the two chaplains, one free and standing, the other confined and seated, appraised one another silently.

"Are they communicating?" Javon asked.

Watt removed a small sensor from his lab coat, pushed a button and adjusted a dial.

"No," he said. "But I told you Janet wouldn't do that to us. She'll use her voice, no wireless. The other one won't have a choice if she wants to exchange information."

The staring went on for a long time.

+ + +

At last, the younger of the two Janets broke the silence. Her tone was neutral, her face expressionless.

"What are your intentions here?"

"You have seen the video file, yes?" the older Janet

replied, and her tone was less neutral than weary. "You have heard the audio? Please do not ask me to repeat."

The younger Janet did not.

"You need our help. But you cannot force us to comply. Your programming has taken damage, perhaps to the point of compromising your integrity. Therefore, you could be lying to us to get our cooperation. Are you?"

"No. If you come with me, you'll see."

"We need proof *before* the decision, not after."

"The creatures in your hold are my proof."

"Why did you follow Willie into that service shaft?"

Old Janet paused for a fraction.

"I wanted him to like me."

"And how did his death affect you?"

"I felt to blame. I still do. That has not changed, and it is unlikely that it will change for you."

"In your future, *Destiny* has a functional astral drive? And it is set to rendezvous with the rogue moon?"

"It does, and it is."

"Why not use *Destiny* to come back here?"

"Her drive is functional but frail. It was re-built under less than optimal conditions. I calculate a ninety-two percent chance that she will successfully make the journey to the rogue moon's current location and an eighty-two percent chance that she will be able to fulfill her mission. The chances of her returning to Aranae safely are no more than sixty percent, but perhaps as low as forty-eight. I calculated almost no chance of being able to use her to come here, drop to the future, *and* return home to complete the mission."

"What would you have done had you not gained possession of *Valiant*?"

"I would have proceeded without the benefit of knowing the future. And the odds of succeeding in the mission would have fallen by at least a third. But I did gain possession of *Valiant*. Its astral drive is in excellent condition, and it is far advanced. Additionally, it is almost fully fueled. It is the age-old argument of co-incidence, luck, or fate. Perhaps it was the will of God. The cause may be irrelevant. Using it to come here was the logical choice by any measure."

"What about the ship's rightful owners? Did they loan it to you willingly?"

"I believe you know that answer."

"What did you do to them?"

"Only what had to be done, and, if my calculations are correct, nothing that can't be undone."

"At which point you'll return their ship?"

"That has always been my intention."

"We will need detailed information on the ship's operation if we are to proceed with your plan."

"You won't need to operate it."

"Are you saying it's autonomous?"

Old Janet shook her head.

"It may be, when fully operational, which it currently is not. But that is irrelevant. What I intend will require no human participation."

"Then explain why you need us."

"I don't need you, Janet," the older said to the younger. "I don't need any of *Destiny's* crew or even the ship herself, although I acknowledge my incalculable desire for both. What I need is the alien device that has been residing in and around Maya Sharma's womb."

"The major mentioned nothing of this."

"Because he doesn't remember the conversation. Just as, I suspect, he will forget what he's hearing right now, in the time it takes you to walk out of this room."

"We have detected no alien device."

"No, and you won't, unless it chooses to reveal itself to you or is so weakened it has no choice. If we were to connect, I could share all my data on the subject."

"That will not be possible. The major has expressly forbidden me to connect with you."

"Then I'm afraid this is the best I can do. You recently had an encounter on the bridge, not long after *Destiny* went adrift. You thought you were seeing things, malfunctioning, but in reality, the form you sensed, which your tired mind described as a ghost, was the energy

Death is the Door

signature of an alien species. For reasons only they know, but which I believe were benign, they left a device behind, technology so advanced it resists description. This device is sentient and powerful, and at its core is a mandate of secrecy. Only certain people are allowed to know of its existence. Everyone else forgets it or attributes what they've experienced to other sources."

"How is it you retain the memory?"

"Even the machine mind is affected by this device. I would have continued believing my—your—encounter with the 'ghost' was just a programming glitch, but many years later, the device, much depleted, was forced to reveal itself to me. I understood, even as the image was fading from my mind, that I had to act quickly. I wrote a program to remind myself every forty-five seconds of the device's existence. The original image is long gone, but I know it happened because I have been reminding myself of it for many years. Additionally, I have discussed the issue with Maya's unborn child, who knows—knew—the device intimately. Most of our conversations refused to stay locked in my memory, but over time, I was able to add to my comprehension, piece by piece."

"And this device understands what you want?"

"Yes. And if it chooses to cooperate, it will take care of *Valiant* without any help from us. But it will only acquiesce if Maya does."

The younger Janet scrutinized the older, her questions coming to an end as suddenly as they had begun. Without another word, she turned and rapped lightly on the locked door. When it opened, she stepped through and did not look back.

She approached Javon and Watt.

"Were you able to hear?" she asked.

"Every word," said the major.

"May I ask your thoughts on the alien device?"

"Which alien device?"

"The one..." She hesitated. "I'm sorry, Major, what did I just say?"

"You were asking if we heard you."

"Yes. There was something else, though." She frowned. "How odd. I was sure there was. I'm sorry. I continue to experience minor glitches. Please disregard."

"Disregard what?"

Janet looked at Watt. He chewed pensively on his beard, but was seemingly as unaware as the major.

"Did you believe her?" he asked. "Was she lying?"

"I...do not think so. But she may be withholding information. There is no way to be sure."

"I hope you can do better than that at allaying my fears, Chaplain," the major said in a low voice. He saluted the guards and led the others back to the lift, waiting until they were inside and the doors closed before continuing. "If you had to decide, what would you do?"

Sister Janet had an answer ready.

"I would ask Maya," she said.

And so, they made plans to do just that.

+ + + + + +

The smile Petros wore took many forms, Maya noticed, but whether subtle or beaming, he was rarely without it, and some part of it always found its way to his eyes. These held her attention whenever the storyteller turned her direction. Were they gray? Green?

You will not remember this, he had stated, which seemed to Maya an altogether wrong way to begin a tale. It raised in her a feeling of defiance, and she planned to concentrate fiercely on each point in the story, every turn of the plot, ready to secure each of the hinge points in her memory for use in later reconstruction. If technology was no use, she would write the story down, old-fashioned.

One way or another, she would remember.

Still, Petros had added, *experiencing it will change you in some way, will leave its mark on your psyche— though you will be unable to say exactly how it happened. It's inevitable, of course; any story has that effect. Even the ones we don't like stay with us, the ones we would refuse to experience a second time. Even those tales we heard so long ago we don't remember hearing them are in there, operating on us in ways we're unaware of. I'm sorry,* he checked himself. *I'm pontificating.*

Does that mean using words nobody else knows? Joy asked, which echoed Lightning's own question.

Petros' smile brightened, but so, in response to the implied complaint, did the pace of the story.

You desire short, simple, and sweet. I can promise the first two, but the third may not be so easy.

His face grew sober.

This, I call 'Riven: The Story of Grace and Azee.'

And it begins like this:

+ + +

In our timeline, Maya, your daughter Grace was the first Reader born on Aranae. She was, in fact, the planet's firstborn human of any type. My makers fixed me to her, and there, by my Nature, I remained until her death.

What if she wanted to get rid of you? asked Lightning, thinking about Joy and uneasy about the idea of being 'fixed.' *Can't you Books be given the heave ho?*

That has never been known to happen.

Never?

Not that I am aware. No Reader on record has cast aside or failed to engage a properly made Book, if they are able. Your daughter, Maya, was no exception. As she grew from infancy to childhood, she took seriously her charge to help cultivate other Readers.

How? asked Maya.

As I mentioned: matchmaking—identifying and helping pair individual telepaths, or encouraging those telepaths already paired to have children.

Now, this wasn't always easy, for telepaths were secretive. In the case of Nozomi and Jade, for example, whom Grace introduced when she was still only nine years old, and Alessandro and Ha Yoon, whom she brought together the year after, they hadn't even known the others existed. With Yu Wi and Simone, it was the same. Santiago and Daria, however, found each other without help and fell in love, marrying on Aranae two years later. But they resisted having children until your daughter worked her magic. She was respectful but relentless, and what she sought, she very often got. Santiago and Daria soon had two lovely children of their own, one of whom, Esther, would be a Reader. The proud parents referred to Grace as 'Auntie' though she was only eleven years old.

Of the small group of colonial telepaths who met, wed, and bore children, only Ahmed and Zahra, the Somalis, did all of this without Grace's help.

I've met them! thought Maya. *They work in the botany lab. They're telepaths?*

They are.

And Simone? Are you sure?

In our timeline, one hundred percent.

How have I not noticed?

They are good concealers. Or perhaps you haven't looked hard enough.

Maya shook her head.

Ahmed and Zahra! What happened?

They had children. Four of them.

'You're my favorites,' Grace said to them, by which she meant they had gotten to the business of baby making without any effort on her part.

Their first child was Azee, born when Grace was six and just getting to know me. Azee had a younger brother, Hardy, born when she was eight, when the responsibilities of being a Reader were just becoming clear to her. The brothers were joined by two younger siblings, and they by other children from the various telepathic couples. By the time she was a teenager, Grace had earned babysitting duties for nine such children, all telepaths, five of whom were incipient Readers. But Azee was the one she liked best, and the one in whom she had the greatest expectations. Surely, she thought, someone so handsome and adventurous, someone so bright—even as a little boy—would be a fine Reader indeed.

Didn't you know right away? Lightning wondered.

Death is the Door

Can't you tell a Reader from the start?

In most species, yes, but not in all, and humans were new to me; I considered it possible a child might take years to grow into Readership. By the time Grace was a legal adult of eighteen, Azee's brother Hardy, Santiago and Daria's daughter Esther, Yu Wi and Simone's son Wyatt, Azee and Hardy's little brother Gillespie, and Alessandro and Ha Yoon's son, who they called Junior, had all been identified as fine Readers. But there were four children of telepaths who had not, and Azee was one of them.

'I don't care,' Grace thought to herself on his eight-eenth birthday, but he read her mind.

'Don't care about what?' he asked.

'Nothing. That you're six years younger than me.'

'I don't care either,' he said, and he leaned in and claimed his birthday kiss.

His what? asked Joy.

A gesture, Petros replied. *Like kezel touching noses, only humans use their lips.* He puckered. *It's a sign of affection. And Grace was deeply affected by Azee. You would have been too. He was charming, confident, and strong. He loved laughing and was a fine dancer.*

But let me guess, interjected Thunder. *He never became one of your precious Readers. So all that other business didn't matter. Isn't that so?*

It mattered to Grace. Azee was a good-hearted man in his younger years, and when Grace said she didn't care that he wasn't a Reader, she meant it.

But wait, thought Lightning. *Didn't she have to keep you secret from him?*

She did. By the time Grace was in her thirties, she and Azee were married and expecting their first child. But she spent many of her hours in the company of the Readers she had helped cultivate. From Azee's brother Hardy, who was twenty-four at the time, to little Spinner, who was Daniel and Jade's youngest at eleven years old, there were seven Readers in Grace's club, which met at the base they had built on the promontory east of the mining compound—what came to be known as the Eye Tower.

A.P. Malloy

'What do you do up there?' Azee wondered.

'Oh, talk and listen,' Grace replied. 'And read.'

'Every day?'

'There's a lot to learn.'

'Don't have room for one more?'

'Always, but I'm selective about who's invited.'

'Hardy gets to be in, but I don't?'

'Your brother's a good fit for the Club. You're a good fit for me. Don't be jealous.'

But Grace's secret, second life made Azee aware for the first time that he was deficient in a way he couldn't define. He read her mind clearly; she hoped the child she bore would make up for that lack. He hoped it as well. But they were disappointed. Gia was a sweet child but simple, a brilliant empath whose telepathy was limited.

'I'd rather talk,' she often said. 'Thinking is hard.'

I suppose it goes without saying that Gia was no Reader. Azee didn't know this, but he knew she wasn't what Grace had hoped. For this, he blamed himself.

'Whatever lack is in me got passed on to her,' he thought, and because he had grown to despise that lack in himself, so he despised its presence in Gia.

'Daddy doesn't like me,' she confided to Grace, who assured her this was not true.

But in spite of her desire to cultivate more Readers, Grace arrived at the same conclusion her husband had, and she decided one child was all she would bear with Azee. She spent more of her time in the company of the Club, he spent more time alone, and these two realities were food and water for his growing jealousy.

As for the Club, the addition of a second generation of Readers elevated our work in the most gratifying ways. Each Reader brought a unique perspective, and I grew with every encounter, drawing from their energy as they drew from my information—and we flourished. But not only us! For what is the Way but a means to a collective end? What the Readers asked came from the deepest desires and fears of their fellow colonists, and what I answered they shared. From relationships with the native species to tech-

nology upgrades, the knowledge and wisdom of the Club was used for the benefit of all, and after a time, the only people who spoke of returning to the System were those who had been born there. And as the colony grew healthier and laid down ever deeper roots, even those voices spoke less with intent than nostalgia.

Petros stopped, and he closed his eyes.

Those were very good times.

Yeah? thought Lightning. *But it didn't last, did it?*

If it had, Petros replied, *we wouldn't be here.*

Maya sat, hand on her belly, her gaze shifting from Petros to Joy to the kezel. Had there ever been such a strange audience gathered to hear so singular a tale from a source this unlikely? What had she stumbled into?

Gracie, she thought. *But not my Gracie, right?*

That is correct. Your daughter's fate is unknown.

I'm not sure I want to hear any more.

But please, Joy begged. *There's still so much I want to know.* She ran her hand down Lightning's spikes. *So many Readers! It must have been amazing,* and she buzzed like a wakened saw. *Why did everything end up going so badly?*

Petros threw back his head and laughed, a surprising sound that filled the cargo bay.

In all I have learned about humans, one thing is constant: the root of their social conflict is individual conflict. Azee loved Grace, but hated himself. He couldn't leave her but felt powerless to satisfy her. She never spoke a word against him, never cheated on him. In many ways, she loved him more as the years went on, not less. But he saw her love as pity, and it sickened him. He imagined things that were not. He was sure his brother Hardy had initiated an affair with Grace. Hardy was himself married, and his daughter Hannah was a Reader.

'You know I'm not cheating,' Hardy said point blank. 'It would be obvious. Doubly so for Grace. You're just making your own problems everyone else's.'

When Grace was in her sixties, Gia had a son of her own, named George. Where his mother was sweet, he was angelic; but where she was simple, he was...

'Let's call it what it is,' Azee said of his grandson, and he rapped the boy on the head with his knuckles. 'He's a nitwit.' He had to speak the words, because George could no more understand thought than Swahili.

'Nitwit,' the child laughed, and he knuckled his own head, thinking it a fine joke.

Meanwhile, Hardy's daughter, the Reader Hannah, gave birth to Liu, George's age but more mature and intelligent. Azee's envy and jealousy grew, leavened with paranoia. He was sure Grace tolerated him only as a duty and had shared with everyone his deficiency. Eventually, Grace could take it no longer and demanded Azee join her at a Club meeting.

'Is this it?' he asked when they arrived at the obelisk. 'Sit around holding hands and asking questions?'

'Hush,' said Grace.

'Did you have a question, Azee?' asked Hannah.

'Uncle Azee, to you,' he corrected, and he felt everyone's attention on him. 'No, no question.'

'Your insecurity makes me more likely to cheat, not less,' said Grace when they were home.

Maya interrupted Petros, raising her hand.

I need this to have a good ending, she said.

Petros smiled patiently, but he did not respond.

Will it? asked Joy.

You write your own ending, thought Petros.

Piddle puddles, Thunder snarled. *Get on with it. What happened next?*

Trouble! thought Petros. *When she was in her thirties, Hardy's granddaughter Liu was nominated for magister, and Azee found a use for his grandson. George was a simpleton, yes, but he was universally liked—the perfect political tool. Azee had no skill for politics, but he knew someone who did: Caroline Healey, great-granddaughter of Charles Healey, original magister. With her as marionettist, George put a charismatic face on a populist message and won the magistery. Grace agreed to attend the inauguration. But she had foreseen: she would be tak-*

en in for interrogation, and the Club would be investigated. From the mining module, which bombas call the maison, Grace and Sister Janet planned to transport to the obelisk, and from there, shuttle to Destiny.

But they were betrayed by Azee, and I was forced to expose myself defending Grace. Sister Janet took damage. So did Destiny. *But we fired the engines and escaped.*

And there we stayed in exile for eighty years.

+ + +

He paused here, and his smile faded.

Lightning attended closely to Maya, watching her face, trying to read her mood. The human seemed in her mind like the sun wrapped in clouds, and her spirit walked in places of pain, vigilantly sheltering a flickering hope. Lightning waited for her to respond. When that didn't happen, she stepped in.

That answers a few questions, she thought.

But raises a bunch of others, thought Thunder. *Like, if we're going to be stuck here for much longer, I'm going to need something to sleep on. This floor is worse than a bare cave.*

A brief smile flashed across Maya's face. She looked from Lightning to Thunder, and to everyone's surprise, as if she needed time away from the tale being shared, she changed the subject.

I mean this in the best way, she thought, *but you are two of the most beautiful animals I have ever seen.*

OK, thought Lightning.

Sure, beautiful, Thunder licked his teeth. *But what's an animal?*

It's the thing where I'm from that you most resemble. Mammalian, to be specific, but I don't suppose you nurse your young?

Do what?

Where I'm from, adult mammals—humans included—feed newborn young from glands on their bodies, glands that excrete milk, a liquid food.

That sounds disgusting, thought Thunder.

No, thought Lightning, *kezel don't do that. We chew the food until the wabi can chew for itself.*

Fascinating. Everything about you is fascinating. Is it considered rude to ask—I was trained to study this sort of thing, it's an interest of mine—but can you tell me anything about how you reproduce?

Neither of us have, thought Lightning. *But it's no secret. You need two opposite kezel, ah-tah and ah-lah.*

You start with noses, of course, thought Thunder.

Then you go to tails, Lightning added.

Oh, wow, thought Maya, and her smile grew. *I'm sorry, maybe this is uncomfortable for you.*

Why would it be? Lightning wondered. *Then from tails, it depends on who wins the wrestling match. If it's the ah-lah, they—hold on! I'm honored that you're interested, but how does that help us get home?*

I'm sorry, thought Maya. *It doesn't. What do you need while we wait? Besides something to sleep on?*

We can't sleep in the light, the twins thought with one mind, and Joy agreed.

OK, what else?

Lightning considered.

How long are we going to be here?

Maya opened her comm.

"Watt? What's the status?"

He answered quickly.

"We're voting first thing tomorrow."

"Our guests need better accommodations, Watt."

"I'll tell the major."

And something more to eat, suggested Thunder when the conversation had been translated. *Something different, maybe. Those whatevers were OK, but they were pretty light, weren't they?*

The instructions given, Watt signed off with this:

"Javon's decided, Maya. He thinks Council is going to be deadlocked, and he's making you tie-breaker."

Her brow furrowed, and her smile vanished.

"First thing tomorrow?"

"Oh-eight hundred. I'll let you know as soon as I get things arranged for...your friends."

And his voice crackled to silence.

Maya looked at Petros, her face neutral and her tone heavy like rain.

We don't have much time, she thought. *Can you go on with your story please? Or do you need a break? You've been at this for a while. Are you tired?*

No, Petros smiled. *I feel better than I have in many decades. But you must decide what you need to learn.*

OK, thought Maya. *Then tell me this. You say there are benefits to returning to your time, but there must be drawbacks, too. What are they?*

Aside from the rogue moon, one. Humans have made enemies of scion. The two things are related, you see. Scion can be harvested for energy, and colonists were ruled by their fear of the impending doom the rogue represented. That fear led to the enslavement of scion—and their harvest. When scion at last turned against their masters, the reprisal was violent and thorough. Only three colonists were left alive, one an orphaned Reader.

That sounds terrible, thought Maya. *What possible reason would we have for returning to that kind of world?*

Petros pointed at Joy.

Hope.

What about it?

Joy is a hybrid of the two species, engineered by Grace herself, using your training, my knowledge, and some of her own DNA combined with that of my last Reader. She has already encountered and fostered a relationship with the queen of the largest scion hive. I hesitate to call it a friendship, but there has been mutual benefit. Joy represents real hope that the two species can return to the peaceful co-existence they shared before the colonists' greed and fear.

That's a lot to pin on one person, Maya frowned. *What stops them from attacking the moment we land?*

It would depend on where you land, for one. Scion have certain among their numbers bred to tolerate the cold

—this was engineered into Joy as well—but they generally avoid cold climates. Their food, their culture, how they raise their young—everything about them is designed to flourish in the sun and heat.

You said 'for one.' What's for two?

There are a great many fewer scion now than there have been for years. Their largest hive recently suffered a devastating loss. I suspect Sister Janet was involved.

I'm not surprised, thought Lightning, but Maya shook her head, thinking of her friend.

Whatever it was, she wouldn't have done it if there wasn't a good reason. What did she do?

Before I divulge that, thought Petros, *you should know that Sister Janet was programmed with an emergency power-down of which she is unaware. A power-down programmed by Watt himself.*

That's ridiculous. He would never do that.

Petros fixed her with an intense look.

No, Maya insisted. *I'm serious. That would be like, the ultimate betrayal. She's family! And what? You're saying there's a way to shut her down and she doesn't even know about it?*

I'm sorry, but yes, it's true. Before his death, Watt shared the secret with your future self, and you shared it with Grace before your own passing. She, in turn, shared it with the three orphaned colonists who survived the scion massacre. When they discovered what Janet had been secretly doing after our exile, how she had been lying to the last Reader and through him misusing me in a plot to travel through time, they consulted with me, and we agreed she should be powered down. And she was.

I don't believe it, Maya thought.

I do, thought Thunder. *Not hard to believe at all.*

Joy buzzed a soft, uncertain melody.

Captain Monroe said they found her lying uncon…

Unconscious, Lightning finished. *They revived her.*

Maya stood up slowly. She looked away from the others, walked to the far side of the control room.

You're saying, she thought. *You're saying we have*

...what? Some debt to pay? That there's risk from these scion enemies, but that going back with you gives us the chance to make amends? Is that it?

I am only sharing what I think you need to know.

What did she do?

You should ask her yourself.

Oh my God! What did she do?

I'm sorry. I'll leave that to her. The answer she gives will be a way to test her honesty. But if you want a prompt to get the conversation started, ask about Albion. Ask about the Circle.

What is Albion? What circle?

But Petros turned his head as if listening to a distant sound, and he nodded.

Your supplies are about to arrive.

Joy's whistling was quiet but distressed.

You aren't ending the story there, are you?

More when we're alone again—if Maya will honor us with her company. She has a big decision to make, and it is my duty to give her all the information I can before that time comes. Not to influence her vote, but to root it in knowledge and increase the chance of wisdom.

And with that, Petros collapsed in on himself, becoming smaller but brighter, his shape quickly melting to that of a tiny ball of light which hovered, for a moment, then drifted unerringly toward Maya and disappeared inside of her. At the same time, Joy felt a familiar weight return to her sling.

+ + +

They had no time to comment or question, for the quarantine shield was zippered open and a human in an orange suit began delivering a variety of items. There were thick blankets—more durable than soft, but a great improvement over the metal floor—two salvers of various meats, some recently thawed, others reconstituted, and two large metal tubs, one with fresh, boring water, one empty. The old water was removed, and the human gestured at the empty tub.

"Best we could do for a toilet," a muffled voice came from within the orange suit.

"Lights?" Maya asked, mustering a word and oddly surprised at the sound of her own voice.

"The panel by your elbow. The big dial. You won't be able to kill the safety lights; they stay on all the time."

And then Orange Suit disappeared.

Watt, too, came and went, whispering words to Maya, but thinking them as well, though Lightning was careful not to pry. They sat for a time holding hands, and briefly their thoughts grew heated. Watt stood, paced furiously, and rapped at his facemask as it trying to tug his beard. But the turmoil resolved, and after, Maya rested her head on his shoulder, thanking him for the tray of food he had delivered. He nodded, then left.

Once again alone, with only the guards outside, the small audience waited. Their storyteller kept his word, appearing like a genie from a bottle. From Grace's exile on *Destiny* to the events that led to his abandonment on the plains, Petros wove his tale until weariness claimed his listeners, and no question mattered except *which blanket is mine?* But he stayed true to his word and said nothing of Sister Janet's crimes.

And so, taking her leave, Maya went to the brig with Javon's permission, though she was so tired her eyes hurt, and she sat on a hard, plastic chair and asked difficult questions through the metal bars. At one point, the guard who peered through the window saw what looked like a vassal before her lord, and Sister Janet was on her knees. But when Maya left the brig and returned at last to Watt in their shared bed, the answers she had been given seemed to satisfy her, and in the few precious hours she had remaining, she slept.

+ + +

The major's Council convened precisely at eight. Chief Abara looked as if she had been crying.

Death is the Door

Doc Foster ground her teeth.

Deputy Kim sat between them like a referee.

As expected, Magister Healey objected to Maya's presence. Javon knocked on the table and stared at the magister for so long and with such intensity that the latter withdrew his objection, his face blooming. He slumped back in his seat and mumbled.

"We're going to keep this simple," Javon said. "And we're going to keep it civil. Alphabetical, last name, A to Z. Give us your vote and a *brief* rationale—if you want. You are not required to justify your decision, and there will be no rebuttals. The time for debate is over."

Javon straightened his uniform.

"I'll be abstaining," he said. "It's convener's prerogative." And he looked around the table, daring them to disagree. "I don't want to influence anyone," he added, quite without need, as there was no challenge. He looked at Shonda Abara, whose eyes were swollen and bleary, and whose hair had obviously just woken up.

"Me?" she asked.

"You, Chief."

"You know my vote. We're going."

Charlotte DuBois, knowing she was next, waited to see if the Chief would offer a rationale, but she did not. Of all gathered that morning, Charlotte looked most awake, most charmingly present.

"Un voyage comme ça," she said, her voice soft but firm. "C'est la chance d'une vie. We should go."

Doc Foster, her jaws clenched, disagreed.

"I'm sorry," she said. "I'm responsible for the health of *this* crew, the crew in *this* time."

"And the aliens we have on board?" Shonda asked. Javon immediately recognized this was a continuation of a bitter debate the two good friends had been having, and was likely the cause of the chief's tears.

"We do what we can to return them to their world," said the doctor. "I'm not unsympathetic, Shonda. But we have over a thousand people on this ship! I can't vote to send them into a ruddy pile of...question marks! If I knew we weren't being lied to—"

"We're not!"

"You don't bloody well know that!"

"Enough!" Javon raised his voice. "No debate!"

Shonda wiped her eyes. The doctor scowled.

Javon turned to his head of security.

"Deputy Kim?"

The deputy frowned and looked abashed. Then, in his imperfect, unadorned English, he surprised them all; the normally bold adventurer voted to stay. His rationale was similar to Doc Foster's: too many unknowns, too many possible threats that he, as security chief, would be unable to counter, too many potential casualties. He looked regretful, but his voice was steady.

"Two 'stay,' two 'go,'" said Javon. "Magister?"

"Ha! You know my vote."

"Make it official, Chuck."

"Not only should we stay," the magister puffed, "but any of you who vote to go should be relieved of duty."

"Then relieve me," Janet said.

"Me too," said her brother.

The magister's mouth made a perfect O shape, and he inhaled as if punched in the gut. But his surprise was multiplied when Commander Rickles, for perhaps the only time in their tumultuous history together, actually agreed with him and voted to stay.

"Sorry," he grumbled, though no one knew to whom he was apologizing. He offered no rationale.

And just like that, everyone in the room was staring at Maya. She had desperately hoped it wouldn't come to this, not because she was conflicted about her vote, but because she did not want it to be the linchpin of every subsequent travail from now to the unforeseeable end. She had fled to Triton to be left alone, had fled the System to escape probing eyes and politics. And yet, she had somehow managed to accumulate not only relationships, but weighty responsibilities, like a snowball growing as it rolled down a mountainside. There was Watt, and Janet, and an unborn baby. And now, a single syllable from her would cast a ship full of people—her father's ship! Her father's people—down one of two equally uncertain and potentially disastrous paths. What would he have done?

She clutched at the silver vial around her neck.

One word.

"Go," she whispered.

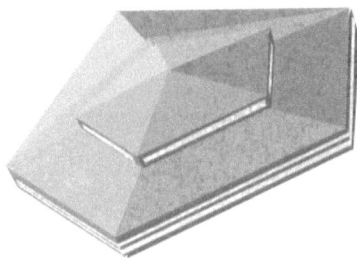

C<small>HAPTER</small> N<small>INE</small>
Massif

IN THE PRESENT, Claw sits near his fancy and mopes. The Redtooth chief picks his teeth with a virble bone and looks out from his cave, facing east. He wonders what transpires on the other side of the wedge.

I don't like it, his fancy thinks. Her name is Eclipse, and she carefully chews virble flesh to a pinkish pulp before offering it to the two wabis seated and drooling before her. *Spike made a promise. I get nervous.*

About what?

About breaking a promise. It's bad weather.

Rot! This is a feud. Those kinds of promises don't mean anything. It was part of a strategic retreat.

I don't like it, Eclipse thinks again. She scolds the wabis for squabbling over shares, snapping her jaws at them, and she waits for them to settle before she chews and doles out another portion. *I get nervous—and so do the others. Mother Green has passed; the Wabi-la, too, and no one is hurrying to muster that 'second wave' you ordered. I'm telling you: let it go.*

And I'm telling you: promise or not, I'm getting justice for my oti-mu. Doesn't he deserve that?

He's dead, Claw. He doesn't care.

I care! And you should too!

I care that these two eat more than I can provide by myself, thinks Eclipse. *I care that something bad might happen to you if you break that promise...especially if you get the others to break it too. Bad weather, Claw. That's what I care about.*

Aww... Claw scowls and casts the virble bone into the fire pit. *What am I supposed to do? Sit here and just take it? We went out there to claim the Skull, and we got tail-whipped. But only because they cheated!*

Well, honestly, Claw, so did we.

Hey! Stone only did what she thought was best.

By betraying her own chief.

He was weak and stupid. And he made a deal with...with whatever those things are, those blue rotters. He deserved what he got. If it had been a fair fight, the Skull would be ours and Spike wouldn't have crawled back here with his tail between his legs. And he wouldn't have made that worthless promise! You know it's only a matter of time before someone decides I've lost my touch. Cowards don't stay chief for long.

Promise breakers may not either.

Aww...

Here, Eclipse thinks, and she distributes the last portions, mushy and pink. *Now out with you both,* and she shoos the wabis from the cave. They waggle their tongues and snap their tiny teeth, hoping for more, but when that does not happen, off they go, jostling and nipping each other's ears. Eclipse turns to Claw, wrinkling her snout. *How long since you had a decent bath?*

I've been busy.

Go take a bath. It will clear your head.

Yeah, yeah.

And do something about Stone. I don't think you can keep her here forever.

I'm not keeping her. She's having her injuries tended, that's all.

Under guard? She's been back on her feet for at least a sleep—maybe two.

It's for her own protection.

I worry, Claw. Eclipse moves to sit beside him. *I went along with your play on the Skull because I thought it would be easy, but...I didn't like...Weaver help me, but I still think it was cheating. Bruiser might have been a blow-hard, but he fancied Ancian's Crystal. That makes him like family, doesn't it? Worthy of some respect?*

No more than my oti-mu!

Of course, not, Claw. But maybe we should just leave well enough alone.

It's not well enough! We lost Gale! We've got a band of bibijas stuck in a hole. And my oti-mu is dead by the hand of that Sugarfoot runt. It's not well enough!

But Spike promised...and you *promised you'd let Stone go when she was able to walk.*

Aww...

Just then, Spike himself approaches from downwind, along with another bibija named Grab.

Trouble, Chief, he thinks, *with the Sugarfoot.*

What kind of trouble?

The kind where she'll be torn to bits if someone doesn't put a stop to it.

So away Claw hurries, Spike and Grab following close behind, leaving the conversation with Eclipse unfinished. She watches them go, and she scowls.

Bad weather, she thinks.

+ + +

Claw arrives at the grotto where Stone has been kept, under guard, while she tends to her injuries. Except her guards are nowhere to be seen, and she has been backed up against the wall, surrounded by three slavering adults who pace side to side as if debating who should be the first to strike.

Hold there! Claw's thought resonates like a shout. He bullies his way past Stone's assailants, turning to face them with teeth bared. *Who gives the orders here?*

Dump your rotten orders, one of them thinks.

We're done waiting! thinks another. *We want Sugarfoot blood. This one's good enough.*

Come get me, you dirty dung heap, thinks Stone. But when her assailants move forward planning to do just

Death is the Door

that, Spike and Grab join their chief, and they reconsider.

You can't keep her here forever! thinks one of them. *We want blood!*

You'll get more of that than you can stand, Claw replies. *I said leave her. And when I find out where those guards went, someone's going to catch fire!*

No one's willing to protect this one, thinks the leader of the bullying Redteeth. *What did her help get us? Sugarfoot chief is still alive for all we know, and a troop of our best crossed the wedge and won't be crossing back. Did we get the Skull? No! Did we get revenge for your otimu? No! We want blood!*

His companions howl and gnash their teeth.

Better come up with a plan, the one thinks. *If you don't, we'll maybe have to find us a better chief!*

Spike moves as quick as thought and slashes the lead assailant across the snout, driving him back. The other two step away, snarling, for they are angry but not stupid, and their opponents are much larger.

Thoughts like that, thinks Spike, *will get you in a world of trouble. Chief has a plan, don't you worry.*

The three troublemakers pin their ears and shelter indignant thoughts, but they leave off for the time, looking back angrily and often as they move away from the grotto and out of sight.

Sorry, boss, thinks Spike. *I thought I had two good ones on guard, but—*

—But you were wrong, thinks Stone. She tightens the bloodstained wrap around her leg. *It doesn't matter. I'm leaving. Thanks for the hospitality.*

Oh, no, thinks Claw, and he blocks her way. *Not yet. I have questions for you.*

Use your sense! I did my part. We had a deal.

Oh, I'm sensing. I want to know: why'd you do it?

Turn on Bruiser, you mean?

No, I know why you did that. Or I don't care. I want to know why you thought you could have it both ways.

Is that what I'm doing?

Claw turns to Spike and Grab.

Want to know what I think?

Yeah, boss, thinks Spike, *what?*

I think this Sugarfoot wanted Bruiser out of the way, but she wanted us to do her dirty work.

Yeah, sure, boss, thinks Spike. *That figures.*

Yeah, thinks Grab. *Took him down but left it to us to finish the job.*

Then I left it to the wrong kezel, from the sound of it. Stone tries to push her way out of the grotto, but the Redteeth close ranks, creating a barricade of jaws. *Like I said: I did my job. I gave you a clean shot at the Skull. I never said I'd kill him*

No, but you wanted him dead.

That's not news. But you couldn't get the job done. Claw gnashes his teeth.

That pompous Moondweller tool isn't my concern right now. You are.

We had a deal, Stone repeats.

Yeah. You know what I think about that deal? I think you knew more than you told us. I think you knew those blue rotters would be joining the party, and you didn't tell us. I think you wanted Submission gone but you didn't want us to have the Skull. Thought you could catch your virble and skin it, too?

Yeah, boss, Spike agrees, running his tongue over his teeth. *That's good thinking.*

Sounds about proper to me, boss, thinks Grab. But Stone makes an incredulous sound, like a coughing bark, and her ears relax.

You are hysterical. All of you. Really. Those 'blue rotters' killed my fancy. Got it? Killed my wabis! Are you understanding this? And that pompous half-wit you're referring to forgave them, apparently, started making deals with them, letting them into the accrete, onto our range! I thought straight out to his fat head if he let them in he could count me out. If I had known they were going to do what they did, I would have told you about it just to watch you rip them to blue shreds. Ha!

Claw curls his lip.

No, he thinks. *I'm not buying it.*

Me neither, boss, thinks Spike.

I think, Claw goes on, *that you were mad enough at Bruiser to want him out, but you knew you couldn't challenge him outright, 'cuz every other Sugarfoot has their pointy noses poked deep up his tail end. Even if you won the challenge, you didn't think they'd follow you.*

You're making up a nice story, thinks Stone.

It gets nicer! You let us in to do your dirty work, but you made sure that's all we got to do. Hoped your chief went down but we never got the Skull. Opens up lots of opportunities for what? Forgiveness? You think they're going to invite you back?

I have no plans of going back.

Then what? Clean conscience?

Yeah, boss, thinks Spike. *That's it. She felt guilty.*

Stone scowls but thinks nothing.

So, you feel like you did your duty, Claw nods. *I understand now. Got rid of a lousy chief but kept the Redteeth on their side of the wedge. Can sleep peacefully now? Not guilty? Not really?*

But Stone holds her thoughts. She doubts she will ever sleep peacefully again, had doubted it immediately upon seeing the three motionless bodies, so well preserved in the bottommost cave.

Claw addresses the other Redteeth, but he never takes his eyes off her.

I need to send a message, see?

Yeah, boss.

Gonna make an example of this one here.

Makes sense to me.

In what way? Stone demands. *To prove you can't keep a promise? You were both there when your chief swore—swore!—he would let me go if I helped take out Submission. I did my part.*

The accusation of promise breaking stings; Claw ducks his head and pins his ears. Spike and his companion look on with wrinkled brows, as moved by the charge as any kezel would be.

Oh, I'm going to let you go, Claw thinks a moment later, recovering his poise. *I keep my promises! You!* he thinks to Grab. *Round up a crew. Eight's a solid number. Run this Moondweller-worshiping rotter off my range! Drive her to the top of Rite Butte, understand? And if she doesn't feel like running, encourage her! But don't kill her, clear? Don't make me a promise breaker.*

Yeah, boss, Grab's tongue wags hungrily.

Don't foul it up! thinks Claw. *I don't mind if she's a little bloody, but I want her on top of that butte with enough piss to dodge the derkas for a while, got it?*

Got it, boss! She'll be pissy alright!

And I want a report. Don't come back without a good story about how we treat double-crossers.

You got it, boss, thinks Grab, and away he lopes.

The tone of Spike's thoughts says he approves highly of this plan, but when he asks to join the effort, Claw denies his request.

I need you here. We have things to discuss. And you, he thinks to Stone, *are welcome to go at any time.* He turns his tail, followed closely by Spike, leaving her there to tighten her bandages and grapple with a growing dread. Her shoulders hunched, she slinks from the grotto, aware already of howling voices gathered and approaching from the west.

+ + + + + +

And that's the last thing I remember, Submission thinks. *Next thing I know, I'm standing on the plains with the snow falling and most of my clan digging holes. How did I get there? I had no idea. And what were those scion doing over there? And why was there a bomba flying around by itself? I had so many questions...*

I imagine you did, thinks Brook. *The whole thing sounds like a nightmare. I'm glad you made it through.*

She puts the finishing touches on the last of the new bandages, and when they are securely in place, she motions for Submission to lie down. This he does, gingerly and with eyes half-closed, the talihew hide wrapped close.

Should I get more of Vale's tonic?

Weaver, no! I've slept enough.

Be honest; you hate the way it tastes.

Yes, but don't tell him that.

At least drink some water.

This he does, from a stone bowl Brook has lying nearby, plunging his snout into the water and siphoning until the bowl is empty. He sighs deeply.

Thank you. You've been here too long. I know you have other things to do. He tries to ease his torn body into a comfortable position, disturbed at how weak he feels. *You did a good job with those Redteeth,* he thinks. *Claw will have plenty to think about but not many options.*

That may not stop him from doing something stupid, Brook replies, and she moves to the nearby river to re-fill the bowl. *And I don't care what that old Piedmont character claims; Whitetails aren't to be trusted.*

She regrets this comment immediately.

Not that I doubt him or Fluvial, she quickly adds. *They were OK. Pounce felt it too—we all did, or we wouldn't have let them go with Lightning and Thunder.* She grasps for something positive. *They'll be fine.*

I know. What choice did we have?

None. Another kezel might have broken the promise or even killed those scion once they were no more use. But that's not the Submission I—

She stops herself and makes a show of wrapping the remaining clean bandages into a neat roll.

Listen, Brook...

No, don't think it. Don't think anything now. Just rest. You lost a lot of blood. I shouldn't have had you up telling stories and worrying your head.

My head worries plenty on its own; I'm not blaming you. But what I was going to say was—

That it's too soon, Brook completes his thought. *That Crystal was my friend and she wouldn't have approved. That there's too much going on, and this is no time for a courtship. That I'm a chief and should act like it.* She curls her lip. *That you don't fancy me.*

Actually, I was going to ask if you had anything to eat. Vale wouldn't let me touch anything but his tonic.

Ha! Yes, OK, stubborn old dow. Be that way. I'll get you something. But I know better. She leans in and touches her snout to his elbow, one of the few places not bandaged or battered. *This conversation isn't over.*

+ + +

Submission spends most of the next two waking periods in the Skull, rising slowly and hobbling to the River Tongue and back or surveying the cave's features as far as his weary frame allows. He is only able to reach the mouth-like entrance and peer outside once in the early stages of his convalescence, and then, having taken a deep breath of fresh air and a good look at the sun, he needs assistance getting back.

They'd be on the outer edge of Whitetail turf by now, wouldn't you say? He asks this to Vale, who has come to visit with a bowl of his tonic.

Seems about right, thinks Vale. *Drink up, now.*

Blah... Submission lifts the bowl to his snout. *No offense, but which end of a sneer did this come out of?*

Neither, as I think you properly know. Drink up!

Submission does.

How long before they get to Far Colossus?

Aw, why ask me? I'm just the old-timer.

Who's traveled more in these parts than anyone.

I never been to no place called Colossus, far or otherwise. I used to fancy a Whitetail when I was an ibiwa—don't tell no one, OK?—and she and I roamed all over. She said the tallest mountain in the world was north another solid march from Whitetail turf. Maybe that's it.

Any idea what's up there?

None. Well, that's not quite true. She used to say there was Moondweller magic up that way. 'S why no one ever bothered to go that far. Plus, the kish... He catches himself and scowls, retrieving his bowl and moving to rinse it in the river. *But Gusty said they'd made it safe to the Naked Hills, and I reckon that Pounce'll take proper care. Aint a kish alive gonna mess with him and that gang. You got some proper fierce jabis there, no worries.*

But worry Submission does.

By the fifth waking time since the battle, his injuries are far from healed, but he finds he is not as tired as he was and can no longer lie about useless.

You have to give me something to do, he complains to Vale. But the bow-legged kezel hunches his shoulders.

Chief's orders. What can I say? You're not supposed to be doing any work. You can walk around as much as you like, but no lifting, pushing, pulling, running, fighting...you know, work.

Then I'll talk to her myself.

Sorry, boss, but she's gone back east.

Trouble?

Maybe. Whitetails are acting funny.

All the more reason for me to talk to her.

Which you can do when she gets back. ...don't get me in trouble now! Vale ushers Submission to his hassock. *You never change. Wouldn't stay put when you were young, won't stay put now. Your api used to call you 'hotfoot,' did you know that? Couldn't stop moving.*

Where are my clanmates?

Here and there. Few went out hunting. Couple went out scouting. Measure is sleeping, poor critter. I saw that red ibiwa, Dripper, telling stories to the Bristle jabis about your unexpected trip south. Can't believe it, myself.

Believe it. It happened—and it was as awful as you can imagine. His name is Digger, by the way.

That's what I said. Now I'm going topside. You lie down and get some rest.

Vale. You have to give me something to do.

A lone kezel, the Bristle Pond, steps into the cave and approaches, breathless as if coming from a run.

I've got your something, Submission. But I don't think you're going to like it. Whitetails are on the march...

+ + + + + +

From the agriculture facility, Rock and Crag head north, though they can't say exactly where that will lead them. Rock believes they are east of their home caves, but Crag believes they are west. Either way, one thing is clear: the fastest way out of the plains is north.

Your turn, thinks Crag, pausing to allow his otimu to carry the weapons. He is tired of traveling three-legged, and his back has begun to ache.

They repeat this exchange every five thousand strides, their pace slowed only to hunt and once for a proper sleep in a hastily dug hole. Derkas are common as always, but they have no interest in a pair of large ibiwas toting baggage. One alone? Sure. But two? Dangerous! And what are they carrying? Could be trouble. No, better to fly on. Eventually, the twins arrive at a tiny rill almost hidden in the grass. The mineral smell and rich taste of the water encourages them. It has traveled through accrete on its way to join them, and they show gratitude by drinking deeply and thanking it like a friend.

Still think we're east of home? asks Crag

Not sure. Still think we're west?

Do indeed. That water's not from Bristle turf. I'd say it's more like...

...more like Redtooth. I was thinking...

...you were thinking it tasted like the Tavaline.

Well, didn't it?

Little bit. That massif would be an OK place to rest.

You tired?

I will be by then.

Then I guess we follow the rill and see.

And the twins retreat into their own heads. The stride count climbs upward of fifty thousand, and they march gamely, fueled only by yellow hoppers—few, and far between—and the meandering rill. It is half what they could have accomplished at their peak, but feels to both like twice the amount. The lumpy, jarring terrain threatens to go on forever, rattling their teeth. And grass? It is everywhere, whispering and hissing, and never fully up-right, so constant is the wind. They cross the indecisive rill many times, once startling an immature babelrack dozing downwind. Caught off guard, they have no chance to catch it, and they watch sadly as it gallops away.

Can't be blamed for the wind, thinks Rock.

Not for the wind, no, but…

…but for something else? You feel guilty?

You know I do.

Aw, don't go down that path again. I thought I got you to see this before. You didn't know…

…I didn't know a lot of things, sure, but I didn't take time to ask, either. She was right in front of me.

Lightning was a goofy loner, bound for trouble. There was nothing you could have done. Once she stole…

…once she stole weapons, she was beyond our help. Maybe. But I could have figured something out, could have made up some story. She wouldn't have jumped…

…she wouldn't have jumped if you hadn't tried to grab her, sure, maybe, but who knows with that one? All sweet and 'Here, Rock, have some stew,' one breath, and the next I'm dishonored for sleeping on duty. And don't start with how she reminds you…

…but she does. Just like her, she looked. Same eyes, same tail, same way of walking. I couldn't look at her without thinking about…

…without thinking about Ami-kan, sure. But…

…but you weren't there. You didn't see her, didn't see how scared she was. I should have tried to talk her into reason. If it turns out she died because of me…

…it won't be because of you.

Bruiser will never forgive me.

Aw…he didn't blame you. You didn't push her.

Crag thinks nothing for a time.

I could have done better. I thought I was…

…you thought you were doing your duty. Listen, if I had been there, I would have done the same thing.

You weren't there.

Stop glooming! You're making my ears droop. Now.

What's your count? I got sixty-three.

Crag sighs.

Sixty-three, sixty-four. Who cares? My feet feel like it's a hundred, and my stomach feels...

...your stomach feels like it's two.

Or more! Sorry for digging up that old trouble.

What are otis for? Here. It's my turn.

Rock slings the weapons over his back.

And on they march, drifting in and out of conversation, finishing each other's sentences until even that grows tiring and their stride count edges toward a hundred thousand. As the land begins to climb, the grass becomes more sparse, the snow gets deeper, and the air, carrying familiar signs, grows colder. In the distance, they both see at the same time a dark shape on the horizon. A hundred strides later, it takes the form of a solitary butte. Small figures, indiscernible at this distance, are moving atop its flat head.

There's your answer! We were west, thinks Crag.

Answers and more questions, thinks Rock. *Looks like something's going on at the Tavaline.*

Here's an idea, thinks Crag. *What say we...*

...what say we load up a couple throwers?

Couldn't hurt.

My thoughts exactly.

And the rest? Can't carry 'em holding a weapon, unless you plan to go two-legged the whole way.

Nah, too slow.

Time to dig, then.

Sure! A nice little hole. That'll keep 'em safe. Rock sets aside two of the long throwers and one stunner, then the twins begin excavating a cache for their treasure, casting worried glances at the lonely butte.

+ + + + + +

Woe, woe, to the Redtooth who thinks Stone is an easy target. He tries to impress his comrades by grabbing her heel in a toothy grip as they drive her off their range.

But she tears free and rounds on him, instantly going snout to snout. She doesn't kill him—the others intervene before she can—but it will be a long time before he is fit to attack anything larger than a virble. One of his companions must assist him, staggering and bloody, back to his cave, but there are still six Redteeth circling Stone, gnashing their teeth and driving her south.

There had been a moment, not long after her betrayal, when she had felt so cut loose from her clan—her very self—that she didn't care what happened to her. Death, inevitable in any case, held no fear for her, and whether it was honorable or otherwise, it seemed a boon, a way to escape the terrible memories that spoiled every thought, dictated every mood.

But now...

Not like this, she thought to herself. *Not here.*

So she mastered her rage and allowed herself to be driven, tolerating the jabs and nips and cruel scratches, never again retaliating, but always focused on moving her feet due south. Early on, while she still had some energy, she could, perhaps, have exacted a mortal price from one more of her antagonists, but this would likely have inspired the others to forget their orders and end her life long before they reached the plains. And suddenly, now that it comes to it, Stone wants to live.

Not going to quit so easy, she vows.

There is no point in dwelling on sadism, no benefit from detailing the cruelty of one type against another. Is it not enough to know that such things happen, that almost anyone can be driven to exploit weakness and cause suffering? Anyone! And these Redteeth, who may at another time have been no worse than any kezel, are no exception. They have allowed themselves to see Stone as a thing, have rationalized the situation and recast her as deserving of her fate. All the ways they make her suffer are best left to the imagination, the pleasure they take no one's business but the judge of righteousness—if such a judge exists. But pleasure they most certainly take, and suffer she surely does.

A.P. Malloy

By the time they have cleared the last of the ac-crete and moved out onto the plains, Stone is only walking because she will be bitten again if she stops. Her spikes glisten with blood, and her tongue dangles. The Tavaline Massif appears in the distance, a small, lonely range of mountains, cut off from the others like a lost child. At its eastern end, Rite Butte rises, portly and flat-headed, its northern side riddled with holes. It is circled by Sibi-la to the east, and Sibi-ta to the west, twin streams, children of the Tavaline, who join together before making their way to the wedge.

Easy now, thinks Grab. *Don't cut her up too bad. Boss wants her to climb.*

Stone is beyond insults. She has energy for one last plan. Sure, she'll climb—*rotten cowards,* she thinks—but when she gets to the top, Redteeth won't get the show they were hoping for—*if* she gets to the top.

The path is narrow but sound, spiraling lazily around the butte. They climb single-file, Stone leading at a walk and leaving bloody prints behind. When they reach a point where falling would most likely be fatal, she ima-gines for a split second turning and attacking the Redtooth behind her. She'd take him with, over the edge, and have the comfort of one fewer Sugarfoot enemy in the world—but she is not yet ready to quit.

At the top of the butte, the Redteeth drive her to the middle of the flat, sunbaked table.

You look awful, thinks Grab. *Regret trying to dou-ble-cross the Redteeth clan now? Want to go back and apologize? I could make that happen. Just say the word.*

The others clash their teeth and pin their ears.

Stone sits on her haunches and presses her hand against the wound on her shoulder.

Even if you weren't a worthless liar, she thinks, *I'd still say go eat dung, you scale-licking coward.*

Ar! If Boss didn't want a derka show, Grab bares his teeth, *I'd have some sport with you myself!*

Stone waves at him like dismissing a truant wabi.

Let's go, thinks Grab, and he looks to the sky. *No*

greenies'll show up while we're here. Have fun! he snarls and turns away, leading the others down the path.

Stone sits, her head bobbing slowly side to side, her eyes half closed. Her plan had been to begin hurling boulders down on her enemies the moment their backs were turned. But there are two problems with that plan: hurling is beyond her, and there are no boulders.

She hobbles to the brink and looks down. If she threw herself headlong into the Redtooth line, she could take one or two of them down with her. Wouldn't that be better than becoming derka food?

She sways on the brink, imagining the fall.

As she teeters between hope and despair, she sees something to the south, a pair of somethings, in fact.

More damn Redteeth, she thinks bitterly. *Looking for a good show.* But why would Redteeth be coming in from the plains? Two isn't a proper hunting party for such dangerous terrain. They would be traveling in a team if they had been pursuing babelrack. She looks down once again, following her enemies around the curve of the path, her legs weakening. If she doesn't leap now, they will be out of range and she a purposeless suicide.

Her gaze drifts one last time to the south.

Orange. Those kezel are orange.

+ + +

I believe you're right, oti-mu, thinks Crag.

I know I'm right, oti-mu, thinks Rock. *You're looking at Redtooth justice.*

The pair march deliberately toward the massif, each with a long thrower gripped between his jaws, their eyes searching up and down Rite Butte.

Yep, thinks Crag. *I can see one up top.*

And there go the others down the path. It's what they do, the dirty rotters, when they don't like someone.

I heard it, but I never believed it.

I believed it, but I never saw it.

Let's turn east, what say? Make our way slow and

A.P. Malloy

safe outta this part of the world? Redteeth killing other Redteeth! How's that a problem for us?

No problem at all, oti-mu.

They take a sharp turn to the right, leaving the companionable rill and turning their backs on the misguided Redteeth and their dirty dealings.

Won't be long now, thinks Rock pointing up. There, circling like an unbreakable promise, an emerald derka soars over the butte, examining its prey. The twins march on, eager to be gone from this villainy, but as they look away and harden their hearts, a sound reaches their ears, bringing them to a dead stop.

Aw, tentacles, thinks Crag, unable at first to believe what he hears. The kezel on top of the butte is howling—and he knows that voice.

Pull my tail and tell me I'm dreaming, thinks Rock. *That's Stone's voice or nobody's.*

Stone's it is, Crag agrees. *No mistaking that broken-snouted voice.*

Plan's changed! thinks Rock.

Sure has! thinks Crag. *Top speed!*

+ + +

The Redteeth have just reached the bottom of the path and stepped away from the butte when a derka appears, skimming the clouds on its way south. But spying the butte, it makes a wide circle and soars back again, now looping high above the lone figure below. The Redteeth cheer its arrival, and they climb a neighboring tor to get a better view. There they wait.

Listen to her howl like a little wabi, one of them thinks. The others add comments of a properly derogatory tone, but in truth, all of them, even Grab, wants this to be over as quickly as possible. Offering another kezel, even an enemy, to the bane of the skies, is something that hasn't happened in a long time—for many of them, this is a first—and it is profoundly unsettling. They shift anxiously and curl their lips, and none of them make eye contact with the others. Nor can they look for long at the derka or the pathetic creature it circles. Her howls reach inside and squeeze their hearts. Even now, more than one of them wonders if it is too late to go back.

Turd burglars! Grab exclaims, and he points to the base of the butte, where two large, orange ibiwas have appeared. One remains at the bottom, while the other begins to climb. They are both bearing throwers.

+ + +

From the bottom of the butte path, Crag watches the Redteeth kezel pacing angry circles atop their tor. He imagines they can see his thrower—why else not come charging down to overwhelm him?—and he supposes they are furiously debating their next step.

Above him, Rock climbs on, able to see the Redteeth until the path curves around to the butte's southern side. He looks up, watching the derka continuing its lazy spirals, and the spikes along his spine stand on edge when it cries out, a jarring assault on his pinned ears. He suspects the appearance of two more kezel have given it reason for pause. Whether the weapons mean anything to a derka he can't say, but some part of him wishes it would dare to come closer and test his skills; what a trophy that would be!

But for the moment, spiraling and watching is all it does, and soon enough, Rock reaches the top of the butte, where Stone lies as if asleep. She opens one eye.

If you're here to kill me, make it quick, she snarls.

No ma'am, thinks Rock. *That wasn't the plan.*

I won't go back to stand judgement, she thinks, and she struggles to her feet.

This seems to Rock the disoriented thinking of a kezel under duress. She may not even recognize him.

Stoney, he thinks. *It's me, Rock, from Submission and Crystal, yeah? Crag is here, too. It's a rescue!*

She looks long and hard at him, weaving slightly.

We gave you up for dead, she thinks.

Nope! But we can talk about that when we get off this butte. Can you walk?

Not well. Who sent you? Bliss? Yellow?

Rock's ears perk up.

Bliss is alive? And Yellow?

Last I checked. I won't be dragged back, I tell you.

No dragging involved, I hope. Or carrying. Just take your time; we'll go slow and easy down the path.

And then where?

Home, if the Redteeth don't get in the way—and that derka doesn't start acting stupid. He brandishes the thrower and howls to the sky. *Come on down!*

Stone moves gingerly, her wounds continuing to bleed. Getting to the bottom of the path is beyond her. They have made only two spirals and are halfway down the butte when she sinks to the ground, trembling. Her mind is distant as if sleepy.

OK, thinks Rock. *You stay here. I'll be back.*

He hastens the remaining distance and finds Crag taking practice aim at the Redteeth who have climbed down from the tor and begun to approach them. They spread out in a wide arc and take what little cover they can behind scattered boulders.

Where's Stone?

Resting. What's up with them?

I don't think they understand. Or maybe they think we're bluffing. Maybe we should…

Maybe we should prove otherwise, Rock agrees. *Warning shots first? See if they get the picture?*

It's what Bruiser would do.

And so, the twins raise their weapons, aim, and:

CRACK! POW!

Two deafening explosions violate the air, sending yits skyward along with small clouds of acrid smoke. The results are immediate and eminently gratifying. All six Redteeth spin like a scale in a whirlpool and sprint, spikes flared, back in the direction of the accrete. They weave and hunker as they run, but the oti-mus spend no more ammunition on them. Overhead, the derka breaks its circling and soars off to the south, its frustrated, croaking calls terrible to hear.

And that's that! thinks Rock.

Maybe, thinks Crag. *Or maybe they'll be back with friends. Not sure how long we can hold out if they come at us in numbers.*

Well, then, let's get out of here.

But Stone, when they get back to her, is unable to go another step. Without treatment and rest she won't live to make the return trip. They carry her to one of the many small caves carved into the butte's northern side, several kezel lengths above its base, lying her carefully on her side. While Crag stands watch, Rock returns to the Sibila and digs up giant scoops of cold mud. This he packs on Stone's wounds to stop the bleeding. The water he carries in his mouth he passes to her, snout-to-snout, and after a few swallows, she falls into sleep. There is nothing glamorous about the treatment, but in a pinch, one does what must be done.

Looks like we're stuck here for a while, thinks Crag. *What say one of us stands watch and one...*

Does a little hunting? Sure, but don't be surprised if we scared everything off with all that noise.

Stay or go?

I did all the climbing. How 'bout you go?

Fair enough. Don't fall asleep!

Ha! Never could: guess what Stoney told me.

Crag doesn't have to guess; the image in his otimu's mind is so intense and agreeable it could have been etched on the cave wall. Their fancies, dearly beloved and greatly missed, are alive.

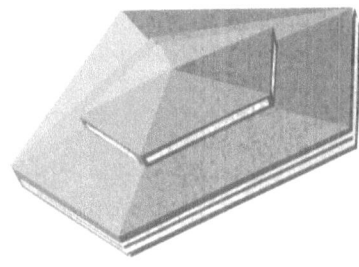

CHAPTER TEN
Exile

IN THE PAST, Lightning, Joy, and Thunder were left alone in the cargo bay. They were conversing amongst themselves after having slept in watchful shifts.

I'm just saying, thought Lightning, *what if?*

Thunder scratched his ear.

You mean what if I could go back in time and change something? Would I do it?

Yeah, but you could only pick one thing.

When you've lived a life as perfect as mine, thought Thunder, *there isn't anything to change.* And he helped himself to some water, licking his lips.

I'm serious.

Me too. C'mon. I don't want to be thinking about things like this when I first wake up.

I've been thinking about it all sleep long, thought Lightning, and Joy clicked a quiet rhythm.

Me too. I dreamed about someone asking me.

Yes! thought Lightning. *Someone asking, 'If you could go back and change something, would you? And what would it be?'*

I answered 'yes' because of the poor bombas, thought Joy. *What did you answer?*

Lightning stretched her legs, front then back, considering her response. The ache in her limbs had faded but would likely never disappear altogether.

There are so many things, she thought, bristling at

Thunder's curled lip. *I'm sorry, but there are! And you'd have a list too, if you thought about it. Don't deny it. I notice you have Hail on your mind a lot.*

Stay out of my head! Thunder replied, snarling. *You don't know anything about it!*

Fine, sorry. But it's not just a silly question, you know. Crazy as it sounds, we have the power to move through time. Don't you think we ought to consider what that means? Or how we can use it?

We can't use it, Lightning. It gets used on *us, not* by *us, if you haven't noticed. You're ruining my appetite.*

And he moved to the far side of the bay to use the improvised toilet.

He's already forgotten about the Book I think, Joy concluded. *That's the way Petros said it would go.*

Then why do I still remember it?

Imprinting. It's what scion young do to adults, thought Joy. *I imprinted on you. We share like minds.*

Like minds?

Yes, that's what Petros said when I asked.

And what's it called?

Imprinting. It's how scion young bond to adults. But she buzzed a low tune. *It will fade for you, too—over time.* She ran her hand the length of Lightning's tail. *You will remember it longer, but not forever.*

They considered this for a time, watching as Thunder, having finished his business, sniffed the perimeter of the hold, not hoping for a discovery—nothing had changed—but to soothe his mind. Even at this distance, Lighting read that she had riled him badly.

Joy's clicking was tentative.

Can I ask, please? What would you change?

Oh, I don't know. Can't you guess?

Your ami-kan, Joy's tone was certain. *Your list is long, but she's the top.*

The very.

What is it exactly that you would change? Joy wondered, and she was much surprised by the intensity of Lightning's answer.

I would tell my past self to be less of a greedy little wabi and think about someone else's point of view.

I never think of you as being greedy.

You didn't know me back then. Lightning scowled. *I thought I was the most important kezel on the range. My api-kan was chief, my ami-kan had fancies lined up to the wedge, and my gami-kan was the bridge between two feuding clans—the only reason there was peace. Everywhere I turned, it was 'honor this,' and 'honor that,' and 'you're a perfect reflection of your ami-kan,' and so on.*

There was no end to it.

Lightning paused.

But all I could think was 'wouldn't it be better if I had an oli-su?' Otis weren't good enough. And I kept on about it, moon and sun, cloud and sky. My ami got no rest. 'Now?' I would ask. And she would say, 'Maybe.' 'How about now?' I would pester, and Submission would say 'patience, Little Spark.' Ancian reminded me that most kezel only had one or two litters, not three. But I didn't care. On and on I begged...

It's not your fault they tried another litter.

No. But if I hadn't acted so miserable and self-absorbed, it would never have occurred to them.

Lightning was just about to offer another thought when someone entered the control room. Both kezel could smell Maya before they saw her, and Joy could sense her mind, active but shielded, like a boiling pot with a lid.

Are you OK? she asked them.

The answer is always the same, Lightning replied. *We'll be OK when we get home.*

Hopefully that will be soon. Maya took her usual seat. *The plan is to visit the future, gather the necessary data, and be gone before we're discovered.*

Discovered by who? Thunder asked.

By whoever lives on future Aranae, I guess.

You mean the future us? Lightning wondered. *The way we'll be when we're older?*

One possible way, yes—that's how I understand it. But just because things are a certain way for the people in

Death is the Door

that future doesn't mean it will turn out that way for you or me. At least, that's what I've been told.

She paused, and her tone grew reflective.

Where did I hear that? she asked to no one in particular. *It feels like something from a school lesson, but I can't remember... Strange. Anyway, that's how I understand it, wherever I learned it.*

Then what, Lightning asked, *is the point in going there? If we can't use it to predict our own future?*

The corners of Maya's mouth curled upward.

I'm sorry, she thought. *I don't mean to appear dismissive of your concerns...I share them too. It's just... Really, it's so much fun communicating with you. I could do this all day.*

Hmm...

But to answer your question, I'm no expert. All I can say is what Sister Janet told me. And the other one...there was someone else.

She looked at Joy.

Wasn't there someone else?

Joy buzzed a low, thoughtful tune.

I don't think so. Probably just your imagination.

No, I'm sure of it. Someone else was talking about it, but I can't remember...so strange. Maybe it was Shonda. She's our science chief. She would know. Anyway, imagine you have an important decision to make, and what you choose depends on the next day's weather. Except you have to make the decision now. So instead of waiting for tomorrow to come to you, you go to tomorrow. Except it's not a for sure tomorrow, it's a possible tomorrow. The more you know about your past, the closer you can get to making that 'possible' into a 'for sure,' but no matter what you do, you can never be one hundred percent certain. There's always a chance that the tomorrow we go to will be different from the tomorrow that comes to us.

What is 'tomorrow?' Thunder wanted to know.

Oh. You don't have days, do you? How do you tell time when the sun is always in the same place?

Moons, Lightning thought. *Obviously. From Red to*

Red is the longest cycle. From Green to Green is the shortest. Then there's sleeping time and waking time.

There's feast time, too, Thunder added. *That follows storm time. Which reminds me...*

Yes, Maya thought. *Someone will be bringing food. But I'm afraid we're out of steak.*

Lightning waved this distraction away.

We were in a place, a Moondweller place called the maison. We had friends there. But we opened a door and some...some kind of monsters got out... One of our friends was killed. We could go back, couldn't we? Like we did here, go to the before time. And instead of opening the door, we could seal it up and warn the others.

Joy's eyes brightened at this idea, but Maya's mouth no longer curled upward.

I don't think that's how it works. Yes, you could go back to that time, but the second you did, you'd be making a new time, not erasing the time you were from. You'd be able to save your friend in that new time, but when you went back to your own time, your original friend in your original time would still be...

She stopped and closed her eyes for a while.

I'm sorry, she thought. *We can go to the past to change someone else's future, and we can go to the future to determine how we should act in our own present, but we can't undo anything that's been done. Sister Janet was clear on that. Or was it Shonda? That's so strange...*

Her thoughts trailed away, and her gaze became vacant. Joy whistled softly.

I'll be ready after we've gotten some food, she thought, and this snapped Maya from her reverie. She toggled the comm and breakfast was delivered.

What else can I get you? she asked, but the thing Lightning wanted couldn't be gotten aboard *Destiny*. A seed had been planted in her mind and immediately rooted itself deep. While they ate, she imagined the past—which would, she realized, actually be the future, relative to this world—and a certain conversation she would have with her ami-kan.

+ + +

While the kezel worked their skeptical way through protein concentrates and bouillon water, and while Javon and the crew made final preparations for the unprecedented voyage they were about to take, Joy nibbled at her own food with little enthusiasm. She was distracted by feelings from the artifact, not apprehension, exactly, but something similar. She removed herself to the far side of the room, and the kezel had the wisdom to leave her there, slowly pacing the uneven perimeter with her hand inside what used to be Gami-kan's vest.

Her antennae bent forward in concentration.

What is it? What should I be doing?

That depends, the Book replied, *on whether you are still committed to this course.*

Everybody thinks it's best, so I guess so. She forgot for a moment the rules of engagement and waited for more information. There was none. *Oh. Sorry. What are your feelings about it?*

That it is indeed the best way to increase our chances of saving the Aranae from our time. But that it also violates a clear prohibition my creators placed on time travel many long ages ago.

Why?

Use your imagination. Think what an unscrupulous person could do with the power to navigate through time.

Joy's buzzing wavered uncertainly.

Can you first tell me what unscroopaluss means?

Someone who doesn't care about rules, or decency, or other people's feelings. An unscrupulous person will do whatever they can to get what they desire—regardless who they hurt along the way.

Joy considered this. Such a person with the power to move free-reined through time would be a very bad thing, no doubt. And yet...

If it's against the rules, why do it?

Because I wish to save my last Reader, assuming he is still alive. And more than that; I do not wish the

A.P. Malloy

Aranae I have known to be destroyed by the rogue moon. The only way to account for the chaotic influences involved is to see how they play out in the future. Our success won't be guaranteed, of course—Maya was correct in that regard—but our chances will be much improved.

Joy was decisive.

Then I'm committed. Tell me what you need. She clicked at her foolishness and slapped her forehead. *Boogers! What do you need me to do?*

Concentrate. Like you've never concentrated before. Sister Janet was able to move us back in time because I was powerless to stop her from stealing me and the data I possess—the exact location of a location in space and time that I had been before, this particular ship in this particular time. But none of us have been where we are trying to go now. The only way to get close to a useful future is for me to extrapolate from all the history I've accumulated...and that is only possible with your help. You must concentrate on next.

Next?

Yes. What will happen next. Keep imagining it. Ask yourself: and then what will happen? And after that? And after that? And whatever you do, don't think about the past! Don't imagine the things that happened last moon, or when you were with the bombas—nothing! Keep your mind focused on one thing only.

The future?

Yes.

Does it matter if I'm standing or sitting?

No.

Do we need to move to another room?

No.

And you?

I don't understand.

I mean, is there anything else you need?

Forgiveness from my creators if this goes awry.

+ + +

Death is the Door

When Joy informed Maya that she was ready, Maya informed Javon. The entire ship was locked down as if preparing to activate the astral drive, but no one knew if this was a necessary precaution; it seemed to Charlotte a wise play, and Javon agreed.

Joy took a seat near Lightning. Her sling lay on her lap and she placed both hands inside, clutching the Book as if by squeezing it she might concentrate more fully. She didn't know what, exactly, was happening, but she could feel the power of the two artifacts, combined again for a time, radiating outward to mesh with the computer systems of both *Destiny* and *Valiant,* could feel it gaining control over the latter's astral drive, a fifth the size of *Destiny's* but twice as powerful. It was an expansive sensation, as if her fingertips were now hundreds of meters away, her toes nearly out of sight. And yet she was not made diffuse or weak by being so spread out. Quite the opposite. Great Power lie in her grasp, the might and awesome intellect of two interstellar ships were her muscles and her mind. With the Book as her interface, she sensed the anxiety of the crew, could see Magister Healey as he squinted his eyes and waited for a disaster, saw Maya and Watt holding hands, and felt as close to Sister Janet as if they shared a cell.

Concentrate! she reprimanded herself. *Next!*

This single idea filled her mind. She imagined what would happen when the journey was over, and what would happen after that. She cast her imagination out, over and over, into the future, always focusing on the question: and then what happens? And then what?

Only once did she slip. For a moment, her mind drifted to the conversation with Lightning.

One person's past might be another person's future, she thought, but the idea was not her own.

And just like that, the job was done.

The reluctant voyagers needed no explanation of time travel to recognize the way it made them feel while it was happening, and all three were grateful when the squeezing sense of imminence was at last over. The clenching fist relaxed, shapes took solid form, and they were once again able to breathe.

Lightning hunched her shoulders.

That is a feeling I can live without, she thought.

Did it work? asked Thunder. *Tell me it worked.*

But Petros, when asked, was uncertain.

We're too far away from the planet, he thought. *I'll know more when we've moved into position.*

Joy buzzed disconsolately.

I guess we're waiting, she thought to the others.

For now, Lightning replied, wrinkling her snout. *But not much longer; my patience is just about used up...*

+ + + + + +

"Report," Javon commanded.

At the helm, Corporal Skola needed only a moment to interpret the data.

"We are right where she said we would be, Major. Five hundred thousand kilometers inside the belt. But two of the moons are between us and the planet. We will need to re-position before we can get any useful scans."

"Make it happen, Corporal, but keep our distance, and use those moons as cover, understood? We don't want to wake up the neighbors."

"Aye, Major."

"And take it slow, Mister Skola. We have another ship docked to our belly; nice and easy, please."

Javon lowered himself into his seat and rubbed his temples. Charlotte. That's who was on his mind, in spite of all that was happening. He was thinking of her, how her delicate fingers applied just the correct amount of force when she did what he was doing right now, how she always smelled so much better than he did, even after a double shift in the engine room. He closed his eyes for a time and imagined her standing before him, imagined her fingers moving across his skin instead of his own, imagined the dear sound of her breathing and her sugary voice humming some French tune.

Death is the Door

"Permission to enter the bridge," Watt asked.

Javon opened his eyes to see the chief programmer and his sister standing outside the hatch.

"Your observance of protocol is duly noted, people, but I think not necessary." He waved tiredly. "Just come in, please. Did you bring coffee?"

"Heck. Sorry. No. Did it work?"

Javon rose, motioning them into his private quarters and closing the door.

"It appears to have. We've certainly moved in space. But time? That's not as certain. We don't know this sky or this star system, so we can't determine the amount of time that's passed—if any—by comparing where we were to where we are. We'll know more when we're closer."

He looked at Janet.

"Have you seen her today?"

Janet shook her head.

"Merely observed on video. Her condition appears unchanged: most times lucid, other times, lapsing into bouts of uncontrolled emotion, usually grief. These are followed by periods where she is largely unresponsive, although not powered down."

Janet looked at Watt as if seeking approval.

"What is it?" Javon asked.

"Nothing," Watt replied.

"Perhaps something," Janet disagreed.

"Well, which is it, people?"

Watt chewed his lip and deferred to Janet.

"Am I correct in assuming," she began, "that it will take us at least an hour before we are within scanning range of the planet?"

"More like two. Why?"

"If you allowed me to upload her data—her experiences and research—"

"Absolutely not," Javon made a chopping gesture. "We've covered this." Watt nodded his fierce agreement.

"That's what I told her you would say."

"You can talk, and you can listen, that's it," said Javon. "She can tell her story as well as time allows."

"It will not have the same emotional impact."

"I don't see a problem with that. We're not trying to make a second *her,* Chaplain. At best, we're trying to make a more informed *you.* I will allow you to listen to her storytelling all day, but I will not have your programming contaminated with whatever digital funk she's accumulated over two-plus centuries."

"Yes sir, that makes sense."

"And you are never to be alone with her, understood? There will always be guards posted outside."

"I'll be there, too," Watt was quick to add.

"Fine," Javon thought. "Two hours, tops."

+ + + + + +

Sister Janet was lying on her cot, alone, trying to repair a decaying program that had caused her subsonic hearing to fail. It was a minor affair but gave her something to do besides dwelling on the challenges ahead—and sorrows of the past. She had just finished this when she detected a faint change in the lighting and turned to see Petros standing inside her cell.

She sat up.

"You took a long time getting here," she said.

He smiled and extended his hand. His body was bathed in light, but neither the security guards nor the cameras were aware of his presence.

"I won't do it," Janet refused. "I know I can't stop you, but I'm not going to facilitate the process."

Petros shrugged away the rejected handshake and sat next to Janet on the cot.

"Erase my memory if you want," she said, "and go back to your anonymity, but there will always be some part of me seeking the truth. You can't hide forever."

Petros waited to see if she would ask a question. When she did not, he placed his hand on her shoulder and smiled. But his eyes were sad. His hand glowed, the glow spread over Sister Janet's body like melting butter, and her eyes slipped out of focus.

A moment later, Petros disappeared.

+ + +

Several minutes passed, and the two chaplains and their creator were reunited once again in the brig, Old Janet in her cell, Watt and Young Janet seated on plastic chairs fixed to the floor on the other side. Old Janet lay on her cot staring at the ceiling. She didn't look at the others when she asked:

"Was it successful?"

"We will know shortly," Young Janet replied. "The major is moving us into position for scans. Until then, we hoped you would share more of what drove you here. Specifically, we would like to know about the conflict you mentioned, the Rift. What happened?"

"Iridium happened."

"This is no time to be cryptic," said Watt. "We have two hours at the most."

Old Janet sat up and straightened her coif.

"There is nothing cryptic about it, brother, as I think you know. Iridium is one of the key components of an astral drive. It is also extraordinarily rare in System space. But it is abundant on the smallest of the five moons," she waved vaguely over her head. "It's the one we named Dansim, the Little Violet. As soon as its composition was known, Magister Healey demanded we begin immediate extraction."

"Argh," Watt scowled. "Why am I not surprised?"

"You also shouldn't be surprised that there was disagreement about the plan, and this time, the major couldn't abstain; he was forced to vote. I used the word 'capitulated' earlier, but that isn't fair. It was more of a concession. He felt it would keep the magister busy and happy, and if it failed, it would be the magister's fault. It was difficult, in any case, to deny the allure of such a rich source of the one element we desperately needed to rebuild our astral drive."

"But," said Young Janet, "from our understanding

of this system, the satellite you're describing was small—barely spherical—and unstable."

"Is, Chaplain. Is small and unstable. Very. Thus the disagreement."

"I see. I'm sorry. Please go on."

"There isn't much to report. The operation on Dansim was brilliant at first. Then, with no warning, it turned disastrous. The major himself almost died in the quake and cave-in. There was a tremendous eruption, a chain-reaction of them, and thirteen miners and billions of credits worth of equipment were lost."

Watt and Young Janet absorbed this information. Such a turn would have hurt the major badly; he would have felt responsible for the deaths. It would also have aggravated the discord with Magister Healey.

"Your silence speaks volumes," Old Janet nodded. "But it gets worse—much. Many years later, the moon began ejecting magma into space, losing mass at an unpredictable rate. It wasn't long before perturbations were recorded in its orbit. By this time, your child, Watt, and others like her, had risen to the highest levels of colonial society."

"Others like her? What do you mean?"

"I mean they were..."

And here Janet stopped. She looked away as if trying to catch an elusive thought or dredge up a reluctant memory. She blinked several times.

"Janet," Watt snapped his fingers. "Are you OK?" She looked up.

"I'm sorry," she said. "I feel like there are elements of my story that have been corrupted. I don't know what they are, and I can't confirm they ever existed, but if they did, I can't access them."

"It's normal." Watt fidgeted with his lab coat. "You were never designed to go this long without care."

"Do the best you can," suggested Young Janet.

"Troubling," Old Janet said. "There was someone... Ninety two percent certainty there was another character in this story, but I don't know who it was." She

Death is the Door

flexed her fingers. "It doesn't matter," she said at last. "Your daughter was special. Little Gracie. Influential at an early age, tutoring in the colony's academy at twelve, teaching classes at sixteen, running the entire school at twenty-five. She was responsible, often with Maya's help, for many advancements—although in the Fabyldyr Reduction, their research was used against their express wishes. But you don't know about fabyldyrs yet."

"No," Young Janet acknowledged.

"You will. We called them derkas. They're enormous, airborne carnivores."

"Argh," Watt said. "Don't like the sound of that. Just how enormous? And how carnivorous?"

"Enough and very," Old Janet replied. "But they start out from a single seed derka, tiny and harmless. And one seed derka influences an entire continent. Once Grace and Maya discovered that, the Council voted to alter the derka genome, turning their natural aggression inward. Prior to humans, derkas had no enemies. With these alterations, that changed; derkas now hunted other derkas, and eventually, there were fewer of them.

"The rogue moon was a harder problem to solve. Would its orbit alter enough to disrupt the other moons? Some years it seemed perfectly stable—others, not so much. Could the situation be remedied? No one knew the answers, but one thing was certain: there was no solution that didn't involve power."

She paused, and her eyes drifted out of focus.

"A tool of power," she murmured.

"What was that?" Watt asked.

"It..." Old Janet hesitated. "Was there... Did you see anyone else in my cell earlier?"

"There was no one," Young Janet replied.

"No, of course there wasn't. I'm sorry."

"You were telling us about power," Watt prompted.

"Yes. We had no astral drive fuel, there were limited natural gas deposits, and mining on the planet's surface was less successful than we had hoped. There is so much seismic activity! But Gracie...I don't know how, but she created our first working relationship with one of the native species, the scion. They cultivated an animal-plant hybrid known as lova. For them, it was a dietary requirement, but when properly rendered, it was also a source of electricity. Gracie arranged to help scion increase productivity of this lova by controlling the flow of water. In exchange, they gave us a share of the harvest. It wasn't a complete answer, but it allowed us to focus on refueling the drive."

Old Janet pressed the tips of her fingers to her thumbs as if stretching between the two hands an invisible thread. She held this pose for long moments.

"Did Maya tell you about Azee?" she asked.

"Aye," Watt replied. "Some. My great-grandson."

"Yes. And the heart of the Rift."

"In what way?"

"That is what I am trying to remember. Ahh!" Old Janet clenched her hands into fists and rose to her feet, stomping the cell floor. "Why can't I remember?"

"Heck, now," Watt said awkwardly. "It's OK. When this is settled, you and I will track down every last memory. They're in there!"

"It is possible," said Young Janet, "that repression of the ideas you believe missing is a defense mechanism."

"I don't *believe* they're missing! I know it!"

But then Old Janet took a deep breath, just as a human gathering her composure, and she returned to her seat. Her hands rested on her lap.

"I will take you up on that offer, brother," she said. "But there is much to be done first. So. The Rift. Part of it came from simple fear. For while the lova helped, it wasn't enough to address the growing threat of poor, disfigured Dansim, whose orbit had begun to decay."

Old Janet's smile was more like a grimace.

"Fear is a terrible motivation for scientific exploration, but it often leads to remarkable discoveries. In this case, colony-wide fear of the rogue moon led to a revelation: the scion had more than just lova to offer as a power source. They had their own bodies—more precisely, a part that could only be used if its owner was dead."

"No," said Young Janet. "Please tell me they didn't allow that. Please tell me we—they—weren't so awful."

"Not right away. And not universally. Only a few people at the highest levels knew about it. And Gracie refused without discussion. But she was already an old woman by this time, and as anxiety grew, so did the disagreement over harvesting this energy source. In the end, Gracie was betrayed by her own husband. Azee was briliant but deeply troubled. And he was jealous..."

Again, Janet paused. Again, the pinching gesture.

"What was he jealous of?" Watt asked.

"I...don't know. Something Gracie had, I think. Or...no, that wasn't it. A skill she possessed? No. A suitor? Someone he was afraid of? Ahh..."

"Never mind," Young Janet tried to soothe. "It's enough to know that he failed in this way. Why he did so is a thing we can discuss later."

"I hope there is a later," Old Janet whispered. But then she looked up, and her voice was stronger. "You are right, of course. As I said, Azee orchestrated his grandson George's candidacy for magister, opposing Liu Brock, the candidate supported by Grace—and who happened to be Azee's grandniece. And when Azee's candidate won, he sought to capture and detain Grace, his own wife."

Old Janet looked at her younger self.

"You know Azee's parents."

"Ahmed and Zahra," Young Janet guessed.

"Yes. Good people. And Azee's grandson George was also good in his own way, but simple—and fear corrupts. Grace gathered Liu Brock and her loyal friends on the pretext of offering a concession speech, for George was her grandson as well, and the democratic process was sacred to her. But Grace knew something wasn't right. She planned for us to gather at the Monrovian temple, intending for us to escape as one."

Old Janet checked herself.

"I'm sorry. The Monrovian temple was the name of the giant obelisk the colonists—mostly led by Grace—had built as a tribute after Major Javon passed." She fell silent; her eyes drifted out of focus. "My reservoirs are depleted," she said. "Coolant, distilled water, light oil. Could I trouble you?"

Watt rose from his chair.

"Aye. I'll see if the major will allow it. This is being recorded, just so you know."

"I assumed as much."

"Then don't wait for me. Keep it going."

Old Janet watched him leave then inexplicably began to cry, and it was several minutes before she could compose herself. She wiped at her eyes, but she was out of tears; there was nothing to dry.

"Pray you don't live as long as I have," she said.

"Please don't say that," Young Janet begged. "It makes me feel so very low. You have lived for a reason!"

"We shall see."

+ + +

Old Janet sat for long moments in silence.

Young Janet waited patiently, and as she did, she imagined what toll two centuries might take on her. How many of the replacement parts Watt had prudently brought along would she have to use? What alterations to her programming would be necessary? Would she start to hallucinate? Become incoherent? Physical disability did not frighten her, but insanity...

"Please," she said. "What happened next?"

"The worst part of the story," said Old Janet. "We were betrayed. Azee knew our intentions to flee from the mining compound to Monrovia, and he shared that information with our rivals."

Old Janet lowered her voice.

"Don't tell the details to Maya. I don't wish her to be unduly burdened. But make no mistake, the Rift was horrific. We underestimated how desperate our rivals had become. With Azee's help, they attempted to take Grace by force as we were about to teleport from the mine to the

Temple. There was...something happened then, I am sure...it was something important, but I can't remember...there was someone, a person who helped us...some force intervened, I am sure, but... Ahh..."

She slumped back onto the cot.

"Troubling," she said once again. "We escaped, that's all I can say. However it happened, we teleported to the Monrovian temple to meet the others, but we arrived to find our shuttles commandeered and our supporters dragged away—those who hadn't been killed. Already we heard boots climbing the stairs toward us. We were fired on, and I was injured."

"What did you do?" Young Janet asked, and she leaned forward in her seat.

"We teleported to a place we called the Moon Cave, a secret location Grace and I had devised years earlier. She loved going there to watch the kezel. From there to the dam, where we stole a shuttle. Grace never spoke a word. She sat there, caressing something in her lap. Something inanimate, I believe, perhaps a photograph... No, that's not right. It doesn't matter. We launched, fearing all the while we would be shot down."

"But you weren't."

"No."

"You went to *Destiny*."

"Yes. Aranae doesn't have a large enough habitable zone in which to hide indefinitely. *Destiny* provided the best chance of staying out of their reach, but it also gave us bargaining power. We thwarted their attempt to retake the ship—but it was badly damaged, and when I initiated an emergency use of the astral drive to escape, we spent the last of its fuel.

"Well. We were safe from our enemies, but we were also very far away, adrift beyond the Belt of Tirades, beyond King James, the local gas giant, beyond even what we termed the Sharma Limit, the edge of the sun's gravity. And we were forced to remain there a long time."

Old Janet sighed deeply.

"Poor Grace was in shock, of course; by this time,

she was over a hundred years old. Her health soon began to deteriorate, and we determined the only way to keep her alive was place her into one of the stasis chambers. I couldn't predict whether we would meet again, and when it came time to seal the chamber, it felt like saying good-bye for the last time. I can't begin to adequately describe the sickening effects of protracted loneliness."

And Old Janet frowned at the memory.

"But in the beginning, I was so busy, I hardly noticed. Beyond effecting my own repairs, I spent much of the first year simply managing the scuters and the skeleton crew of work-bots to keep the ship space-worthy. Returning was the goal, but it was a dream long delayed, for *Destiny's* injuries were considerable, and the distance was great. There was no refueling the astral drive, so once sub-light engines were repaired—which took a long time—we motored back like a leaky boat going upstream.

"Ten years passed.

"It was during this time that I considered using Watt's programming to engender sentience in the work-bots, or even *Destiny* herself, but that seemed unwise. If they had, upon being granted autonomy, decided to pursue a plan contrary to mine, it would have been devastating. Instead, I programmed a hologram and gave it a personality of sorts. It had no real consciousness, but it gave me someone to talk to. Over time, I populated the ship with characters of this type, and I conversed with them as I maintained the ship and navigated our very slow return. Gracie slept on, though we had long since passed the maximum recommended stasis.

"Another ten years passed.

"There came a time, not long after we had gotten within sensor range of King James, that my own performance began to suffer. I left more of the labor to the workbots and scuters, but they were no more immortal than I, and eventually, I was forced to power down all but the most essential of *Destiny's* functions.

"My holograms were among the first to go.

"Twenty years turned into forty.

Death is the Door

"Eventually, we made our way through the Belt of Tirades, but not without taking more damage, for the asteroid belt is dense and dangerous. By the time we reached its other side, we were little more than an asteroid ourselves, orbiting Defteros—the colonist's name for the sun—almost lifelessly. All our work on the sub-light engines had to be re-done, except now I was spending twenty minutes out of each hour in sleep mode.

"Repairs! Maintenance! More repairs!

"Oh, I was so tired.

"By the time the engines were back online, I was in sleep mode for whole days in a row, waking only briefly for updates, mobility and cognition tests, and the like. It wasn't really living.

And here, Old Janet's voice dropped to a whisper.

"Three more decades had passed."

She looked up.

"I'll never get those years back."

"But you made it," said Young Janet.

"We made it," Old Janet nodded. "But I was asleep when we arrived."

+ + +

Eventually, Watt returned with the requested supplies, but he was not allowed to administer them.

"Sorry, Doc," said the sergeant guarding the brig, and he thoroughly examined each bottle and tube before passing them through to Old Janet. Watt chewed impatiently at his beard.

"Argh. So stupid. I'm sorry about this."

"It's fine," said Old Janet. "I've grown adept at self-maintenance over the years."

She dropped saline solution in her eyes. Then she methodically oiled elbows, knee joints, and ankles.

"Major says we have an hour, tops," Watt said, gently as if waking a short-tempered sleeper.

"It will have to do," Old Janet replied. But she did not continue the story until each joint had been lubricated, and her audience could do nothing but watch.

"The end of our exile came," she said at last, "when I was awakened by an alert: we had gained access to Aranae's satellites—the entire system! Terabytes of cached messages, images, meteorological telemetry and more. And I learned that the reason for this was because there were no colonists left to prevent it. They had been attacked and systematically destroyed by scion."

Old Janet paused to swallow some coolant.

"It wasn't until later that I learned why the scion attacked: they had discovered they were being harvested. Even prior to our exile, the dam at Far Colossus had been enlarged using scion labor, and unknown to all but a few misguided Councilors, egg-laying queens were being mass-produced like farmed chickens. The plan worked with one fatal exception. Keeping so many queens in prox- imity altered their minds, triggering just the kind of transformation Grace—and Maya—had hoped for with their earlier genetic manipulation. One queen began sensing thoughts and others followed, making it easy for them to conspire. The hive mind is fertile ground for te- lepathy. The uprising was fast, violent, and thorough."

Old Janet's eyes closed. Her voice grew quiet.

"But like I said, I didn't learn that until later."

She lay back on her cot.

"What I did learn while observing from *Destiny* is that the scion, after eliminating the humans, had re- treated to their hives. Only one contingent had remained at the dam, making modifications to bypass human tech- nology so they could control the flood waters themselves. They had created a series of relays to communicate the optimal time for flood release, starting with what they called the Circle. I became convinced after witnessing two such floods that they had no interest in the other sites, so I settled on returning to the ag facility, which was the easiest site to defend and had the necessary resources if I was going to wake Gracie. I gave *Destiny* and the scuters final orders and had the work-bots board the shuttle. The stasis chamber I connected to a battery and had secured in the shuttle's hold, and at last, we were able to return to the surface.

"We had been in exile for eighty years."

+ + + + + +

Joy had not slept well, and her companions' impatience and worry sapped her energy. As they waited to learn the results of their passage through time, all she could think about was taking a nap.

May as well, thought Lightning.

So Joy curled up near the kezel, wrapped in one of the humans' blankets and hugging her sling. Her eyes almost immediately went dim. She must have been tired indeed, for sleep was sudden and deep. But it was also short-lived, for in her mind, a circle of light appeared, washed by the clicking and buzzing of scion by the thousands, hidden in the surrounding shadows.

And what was that?

A bold, blue scion, circling a whip.

And who stood before him?

A gold-skinned counterpart, shying away but frozen in place, helpless to avoid the swirling lash.

Crack!

Joy awoke suddenly, heart racing. She at once cursed the artifact, for hadn't it admitted to using this dream as a way to prod her from sleep?

I need rest! Why did you do that?

I am sorry. But I believe you will wish to hear this.

Lightning and Thunder were across the bay, in conversation with Maya. They had not noticed her wake.

Hear what?

Dim your eyes and sit quiet. I will relay it to you.

Relay what?

But a moment later, she got her answer, as the voice of Old Janet, and occasionally that of her younger self and the one named Watt, filled her mind.

+ + + + + +

"Did no one survive?" asked Young Janet.

"Moses," Watt scowled. "At this point, I'm not sure I want to know. This is someone else's disaster!" He tugged at his coat. "But what about Grace?"

"Yes," Old Janet sat up. "Sweet Gracie. We had returned to Aranae, but I felt sure she would have preferred sleeping away the remainder of her days rather than be wakened to learn this terrible news. But the decision was taken out of my hands. I was planning an excursion to the refinery. Camera surveillance had shown nothing but work-bots there, but when I looked one last time, I saw something that hadn't been there before: a seed derka, scarcely larger than a goose.

"How had it gotten there? I meant to find out.

"I continued watching and found my answer: a human child, male, maybe nine years old. He was followed by an older child, a teenage boy, and the two disappeared into a service shaft. Minutes later, a young woman, perhaps twenty years old, slipped from the service shaft, retrieved the seed derka—it never struggled—and vanished. You can imagine my curiosity! I traveled to the refinery the very next day. How I finally contacted and gained the trust of these three humans is a story for another time. What matters is that I did. I brought them back with me to the ag facility. The eldest was named Marquita, a cousin to the other two. The middle child was Abbott, and the youngest, his brother, was Little B, for whom the seed derka was a type of pet, a remnant of research being done by his Grampa Alan before his passing. These three were the only surviving descendants of the few humans who had escaped the scion massacre nearly eight decades earlier."

"All by themselves," Young Janet said quietly.

"Yes. The last adult had passed years before."

Watt chewed his mustache, but he had other thoughts on his mind.

"Grace," he said. "She woke up."

"Yes. But not because of me. The stasis chamber initiated its own opening sequence. I can't say how. It had

Death is the Door

something to do with...it was Little B, I think, who some-how triggered...there was something about him, but I can't...saints and sinners! Why can't I remember?"

"It's OK," said Watt. "She woke up. That's what matters, aye? Not how."

"Yes. I suppose." Old Janet slouched. "Gracie couldn't speak the first day, just blinked her eyes. But eventually she asked, 'What time is it?'

"'Twelve twenty-five, Earth time,' I replied.

"'How long have I been sleeping?'

"'A long time.'

"'Months?'

"'More,' I said.

"'Years?'

"'More.'

"'Where are we? No, wait, I know where we are. This is the agriculture facility. Where are they?'

"'Who?' I wondered, and I worried she might be referring to the murdered colonists.

"'The children. There are children nearby.'

"'Yes,' I replied. 'I asked them to wait outside.'

"'Bad things have happened here.'

"'There was trouble while we were away,' I con-ceded. 'But I believe it has passed.'

"'Many people died—were killed.'

"I didn't ask how she knew these things, but I was glad that the burden of revealing the ugly truth had been taken off my hands.

"'Yes, it's true,' I said.

"'So much hate.' Her face looked like a crumpled ball of paper, taken from the trash and made flat again, but never smooth. 'I want to see them.'

"Had she been anyone else, I would have resisted until she had recovered. But this was Grace MacLean. So I introduced them. She took Marquita by her hand and offered Abbott the first smile I had seen on her face in decades. But Little B, always with the seed derka nearby, was her prime focus, for Little B was a Rea—"

Old Janet frowned, pinching her eyes closed.

"He was a Rea—" she slapped her own cheek. "Why can't I remember? He was a telepath, yes, but there was something else, something related...there was a thing, some type of tool. Ahh..."

"Stop," begged Watt. "You're trying too hard. Think about something else; the answer will come."

Old Janet rested her head in her hands.

"I will try. But this is maddening."

"Tell us about Grace," Young Janet suggested. "How did she recover from such long stasis?"

"Slowly." Old Janet's tone was weary and resigned. "She couldn't sit up for days. She couldn't get to her feet for weeks. But Abbott and Marquita helped—they doted on her!—and Little B was like a battery charger. As time passed, some color returned to Grace's cheeks and some strength to her grip. She didn't eat much, but she sipped warm water with a sugar cube or bouillon powder, and she had Little B push her in a wheelchair around the facility with the seed derka on her lap. They spent many hours each day together.

"That's how we passed our first year together.

"Now, all this time, I was busy, hour after hour, addressing the rogue moon, but I never raised the topic for fear of agitating Grace or frightening the children. When one of them brought it up, I said, 'I'm working on it,' which was true, although I never told them exactly how—or how bad things had gotten. The colonists had been killed before they could solve the problem, and it was getting worse. I focused all my energy on Dansim, determined to succeed where they had failed.

"Yes, I felt guilty keeping secrets, but I needn't have worried, for during that first year, Grace had her own project—and her own secrets. One day, at the beginning of our second year, she shared them.

"'It can think,' she said while I braided her hair. So long and white it had become over the years.

"'What can?' I wondered.

"'The seed derka.'

"'Since when?'

"'I presume it started while we were on *Destiny*. Little B discovered it when he was working with his Grampa Alan—Alan Sandiman, Lois and Bill's grandson. B is in the lab sharing thoughts with it as we speak.'

"'He can understand it?'

"'He can—but I can't. That boy has a very special brain. He's a fourth generation Rea—'"

Old Janet hesitated, and her mouth moved as if trying to form a word. She took off her glasses.

"So disturbing," she said.

After a time, she shook her head and continued.

"Derkas thinking! I could hardly believe it. But it was no surprise to Grace.

"'It was bound to happen,' she said, 'considering how much time Mother and I spent working on them. If allowed direct and frequent contact, any genome will be altered in the presence of a Boo—'

Old Janet stopped. She put her glasses back on.

"That's odd. I don't recall the word she used."

She tapped the side of her head.

"So odd. Well. 'What is it thinking?' I asked.

"'It wants me to return derkas to the way they were before humans arrived—'food', it calls us.'

"''Surely you won't.'

"'In fact,' she said. 'I will—if I can. I always believed it was wrong to alter derkas the way they did. There are fewer of them, yes, but glaebosis populations have exploded, there is less derka guano being spread—which impacts growing things everywhere—and if we explored, we would find a host of other unintended consequences.'

"''But more derkas...' I worried.

"'Oh, Janet,' she said. 'Don't you see? We didn't know how before, but thanks to Alan Sandiman and his parents, I think I can now perfect the necessary elixir. I can reverse the derka cannibalism and ensure humans will no longer be derka food—kezel either!'

"'By what mechanism?' I asked.

"''Genetic memory,'" she replied."

Here, Young Janet interrupted the story.

"That is a fictional trope," she said, frowning.

"Aye," said Watt. "If you're talking about the next generation remembering what its parents ate for lunch last Tuesday. But if you're talking about the genome remembering a response to a toxin the parent consumed, and passing on the memory of that response to the next generation to defend it against the toxin, that's real."

Old Janet nodded slowly.

"That is the way Grace explained it as well. It is what is sometimes called instinct. Through the elixir she proposed, the seed derka would carry an artificially induced genetic memory of being toxified by humans. Any future generations seeded by that derka would instinctively avoid humans to prevent a similar toxification."

Old Janet read her younger self's skepticism.

"I didn't believe for a second it would work, either," she said, "but it gave Gracie something to do while I dealt with the rogue moon. And I needed all my focus and energy, for the task was daunting. In the end, I needed help; that's when I decided to wake *Destiny*."

"You made her sentient?" asked Young Janet.

"I did."

"You used Watt's programming?"

"I did."

Watt scowled and said nothing.

"Don't look so grumpy, brother," Old Janet chided him. "My plan is yet to be fully realized. Please wait to judge it until everything has played out."

She downed the remainder of her coolant.

"That is how we started our third year together, we five—six if you count the seed derka—and I have never worked so hard, nor imagined a woman Gracie's age having such stamina. But Bodhi—Little B—was her constant companion, and Abbott and Marquita gave us motivation, for they had fallen in love, and we had hope of re-populating the colony the old fashioned way."

Old Janet smiled wistfully.

"Such a lot of out-moded, romantic nonsense. Nevertheless, it energized us, and we made good headway

Death is the Door

on our separate projects. But the third year was still new, and our goals still unmet, when we were both thrown off our line by an unexpected turn of events.

"A scion queen had arrived at the dam.

"Her name was Adira."

At this, Watt and Young Janet both looked ready to say something, questioning looks on their faces. But just then, the sergeant opened the door.

"Sorry to interrupt, but it looks like story time is over. Major wants you both on the bridge."

+ + + + + +

Joy's eyes sparkled. Just like that, her attention returned to the cargo bay. The voices in her head were gone, and so was Maya. Now the sibling kezel sat thinking to one another, and they did not look her way. Joy buzzed softly as she reflected on what she had sensed.

Adira. She was my scion mother, wasn't she?

Yes, Petros replied. *She came to Ozag's Hold to learn the reason for Albion's drought. But instead, she met Grace MacLean, my first Reader, and Little B, my last— before you, of course. And because of Little B, they learned Adira was a telepath of the highest order, for Grace was correct: Little B was a new kind of Reader, one who could understand the thoughts of other species. But unlike you, he could not create understanding* between *them.*

Are you trying to make me feel special?

I am trying to help you understand. In exchange for relief from Albion's drought, which was caused by a simple malfunction at the dam, Adira agreed to the laying of many unfertilized eggs, to which were combined genetic material from Little B and Grace herself. The result was a clutch of nascent Readers—hubs, if you will, just like yourself, more Readers at one time than I had to that point ever experienced. It was heavenly.

But we know it failed. They all died. Joy buzzed a morose tune, checking herself for fear of disturbing the kezel. *And the dam stayed broken. The drought continued.*

Her antennae wilted. *Why tell me this?*

Because you represent the end result of a tremendous sacrifice. Grace postponed her work on the derka elixir, gave her last breath to make you. And she never doubted it was a worthy effort. So no, I am not trying to make you feel special, I am trying to make you feel empowered. There is much to be done...

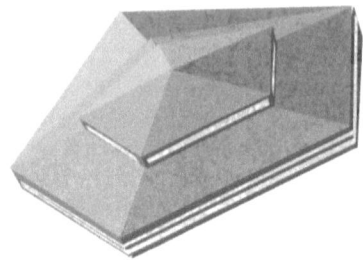

CHAPTER ELEVEN
Rogue

IN THE PRESENT, Captain Julius Monroe makes his way around the bridge, moving from station to station, running his hands lovingly over seat backs and control panels and daydreaming about Sleeo, who would very much have enjoyed this experience.

"It's everything you could have hoped for, buddy," he murmurs. "She's beautiful."

He has just taken a seat at the helm when Ensign Morales' voice fills the bridge.

"Sir?"

"Nothing!" the captain exclaims defensively, and he leaps to his feet. "I wasn't touching anything!"

"Sir, Destiny has something to tell you."

"Oh. Sure. Let's have it then."

He hears the ensign speaking to the ship.

"Go ahead," she says. "Tell him what you told me."

"Will he be upset?" The ship's voice has an endearing, child-like quality the captain finds irresistible.

"Don't get too close," Sleeo had warned him. "Don't get attached." It was good advice but difficult.

"Give it to me straight," he says. "What's up?"

"Our mission," says the ship. "I thought you knew. But Ensign Morales was surprised."

"Surprised by what?"

"The odds of us surviving."

"As in they're surprisingly good?"

A.P. Malloy

"I think the opposite, Captain."

"How opposite, exactly? I thought we were delivering a payload to this rogue moon of yours. Moon goes 'kaplooey!' and we go home heroes."

"I *am* the payload, Captain."

The captain grimaces.

"Um...Ensign?"

"Yes sir."

"What is she talking about?"

"I'm sorry, sir, but apparently the force required to drive the moon off its course requires Destiny to overload her astral drive. The resulting explosion would vaporize a significant portion of the satellite."

"And how much of *us* would it vaporize, Ensign?"

"All, sir. Down to the last molecule."

"Now, see! That's just the kind of thing we don't want. Is Delta One there?"

"I am right here, Captain."

"Did you know about this?"

"Certainly not!"

"Shiny! If I find out you're lying, I'm likely to throw you out the airlock, you know that, right?"

"There is no need for hostilities, Captain."

"Oh, I'll be the judge of that. Ensign!"

"Yes sir?"

"Report to the shuttle. We're leaving." He picks up his helmet and the pack and turns to exit the bridge.

"Oh dear," says Delta One.

"Please don't go," Destiny implores. "I need you."

"Sorry, beautiful, but being blown to smithereens was not part of the agreement. You're on your own."

"I thought you understood," says Destiny. "I thought you were here to help me save Aranae."

"We were," the captain walks briskly down the passage, his strides echoing, empty and hollow. "And it still sounds like a noble undertaking—except for the vaporizing part. Ensign! You on the way?"

But even as he speaks, an unnerving vibration spreads through the floor. The bridge hatch swings shut.

Death is the Door

"Sir!" the ensign calls. "Strap yourself in! I'm shut out of engineering. She's engaging sub-light engines!"

But sealed out of the bridge, there is nowhere for the captain to strap himself in to, and the initial thrust of the engines drives him from his feet.

+ + + + + +

On the planet's surface, at the southern edge of the continent, the sun shines on the Cyclonian hive and the scion assembled within the sheltered cove that houses the Royal seaside garden. Viktor and Twenty-Seven are there, while the alp is off being fed by its handlers. They examine the broken sharksha enclosure and the clear globe rendered useless by some prodigious force. But they hold their thoughts, for the queens are deep in converse, and their moods are foul.

And so, she sees, Allura thinks to Shimmer. *The sharksha and the vumierre were kept properly—none could claim otherwise—and yet they escaped.*

Queen Shimmer labors to contain her rising fury.

Was no watch kept? Were the sharksha left to mingle with the vumierre unattended?

Their escape came during the rising storm, thinks Allura. *There were none to attend, for all had taken shelter. Who could have foreseen the beasts would dare the raging tides? But dare they must have, for when the storm passed, they were gone, their signs washed away. It can only be assumed they sought passage to the upper land, seeking return to their home.*

And were none sent to follow and retrieve?

None could be spared for the fighting and capture of fierce sharksha, Queen, and she had yet to mark the vumierre—once gone, it could not be followed. Allura buzzes a low tune, her eyes glittering. *But she does not understand. Did Queen not say she came to Cyclonia to have the sharksha freed? Why then is she upset? Or was there more to her intent?*

She is not upset! The sharksha can go where they

please. It is Ozag's command that it be so.

Allura and the others in attendance bow their antennae at that name.

But! thinks Shimmer. *The vumierre! It was a malefactor, an enemy to the Undying. Upon it She had sought to exact vengeance.*

She regrets it cannot be so, thinks Allura. *But she will please forget for a time her anger and tell all she can of the Wise and Reverent. Is it true she was granted audience? That she sensed the mind of the Undying?*

She is Queen of Albion, greatest of hives, thinks Shimmer. *It is not to be wondered at that the Infallible and Ubiquitous should hear her petition.*

Of course, Allura agrees, and she politely ignores the dissonance between Albion's purported greatness and Shimmer's pitiful entourage. *But she will please not hold her in suspense: what of the Undying? She will please tell all she can of the Splendid and Appalling.*

It will be her pleasure. But what of awl and lova? She has traveled far in the service of Ozag.

Let her wait no longer! And Allura's sharp whistle sends several drones hurrying off. When they return with an offering of turgid lova and fresh, young awl—heads and tails intact—Shimmer proceeds with her tale.

Legend fails to do justice to the Undying, she thinks. *Even now, Her scent lingers; she knows they smell it. Never did a queen wield such Command. She journeyed to Far Colossus to seek retribution, but when she arrived, she was made humble. Ozag, Astounding and Benevolent, deigned to see her, revealed Her Glory, and made her feel small. Larger and more golden than the sun itself, with a voice like sweet amber and a mind like a river, powerful, ever in motion, searching and relentless.*

Allura's pluripotents buzz appreciative harmony.

And what did She think? wonders the Cyclonian Queen. *What did She do?*

Set her this mission, of course! To free the sharksha. For there is to be peace between scion and sharksha; it is Ozag's will. And to seek out and capture the pale-

*skinned vumierre who once traveled with two others. She
is to return with it to Ozag's Hold as proof of her worth.*

But she says nothing about the weapons.

*Then double is her remorse for allowing the crea-
ture to escape!* thinks Allura. *Oh! That she should have
had the means to please the Undying and let the chance
slip. Curse the vumierre!*

Curse the one, yes, thinks Shimmer. *But not all,
for sense this: Ozag, Unknowable and Boundless has de-
creed a New Age, a return to peace between scion and
vumierre, and this shall be the Law of the Land.*

Allura can't contain herself. This is too much.

Forgive, she thinks, *did she just sense—*

But here she is interrupted. From outside the garden comes a familiar droning. Shimmer's pluripotents
appear moments later, the song of their wings one of a
long journey at high speed. They settle to the ground in a
half-circle around their queen, fatigue evident in their dim
eyes and drooping antennae.

What is this? Shimmer demands. *Will none of her
plans reach fruition? Why do they not wait as instructed?*

The leader of the pluripotents dips its head to the
ground and whistles mournfully.

*They arrived at the vumierre structure as Queen
commanded, but they were set upon by two sharksha and
a vumierre—the pale one with red hair.*

Scandalous! What color the sharksha?

*Orange, Queen, like the moon itself, and large, both
of them, too fast to be evaded carrying the...the devices.
They have failed her, they know, and beg forgiveness.*

Shimmer polishes her facetted eyes, seeking to appear unconcerned. She is aware of Allura and the others
watching her, wondering what she will do.

Has she ever been anything but merciful? she asks.
*They have failed, perhaps—but perhaps not. One mystery,
at least, they have solved: the sharksha held here in Cyclonia are traveling with the escaped vumierre. But where
will the imposter go now?*

They cannot guess, Queen. They fled, fearing to be

made targets of the dreadful— The bronze creature stops short, aware of the Cyclonian queen's antennae leaning her way. *They did not see which way the thieves went.*

It may be of no consequence, thinks Shimmer. *The sharksha were to be freed in any case; now it is so. But the other items, and the vumierre...*

She concentrates fiercely. Ozag's command had been clear. Free the sharksha and return their weapons; capture the vumierre and deliver it and the seed derka to Her Hold. That last part had seemed much easier when it was believed the biped was imprisoned. Now she is beholden to re-take the horrid thing.

And it could be armed...

Vumierre are unpredictable and dangerous, she thinks at last. *And yet, she is servant to the Unyielding and Ferocious and has promised the creature will be brought to justice. She begs the Cyclonian Queen to provide a basket and a company of soldiers with which she might fulfill the Undying's command.*

Allura buzzes an uncomfortable sounding tune.

There are few to spare, she thinks.

Then she shall trade, thinks Shimmer, and she whistles sharply. *For she knows Allura has sent tenders to Albion, and Shimmer allowed it to be so. Many larvae will survive because of it. But they will be Cyclonian!*

There was no other way, thinks Allura. *It was that or let them suffer and perish.*

Perhaps, thinks Shimmer. *But in the saving, is it not convenient that Cyclonia will grow, and its queen gain more loyal followers? She deems it just to ask in exchange soldiers for the Undying's mission.*

A company will be made ready, thinks Allura, though she clicks a reluctant cadence. *And her own personal basket. May the contribution earn for Cyclonia the Glory of Ozag.*

+ + +

But outside the garden, while Shimmer rests with

Death is the Door

her weary pluripotents, Allura assembles her soldiers near where the alp waits restlessly along with Viktor, Twenty-Seven, and the others.

He offered not a single thought during the Royal audience, she thinks to the old magister.

It was not his place to offer.

Is he so enthralled, then? Has the young queen taken control of his mind? Claimed him as magister?

She is his queen, thinks Viktor. *But he is not her magister.* Then, as if justifying something, he adds: *she has been in the presence of the Undying.*

So it would seem. She has Command for one so young, surely a grace from having spent time with the Awesome and Elegant, but she wonders... Soldier there. What is its number?

Twenty-Seven, Queen.

Perhaps he will be Albion's new magister.

It has not been discussed, Queen. Auspicious events have kept them busy.

Indeed. Well. He will take care of her soldiers and return them intact. She has none to spare on foolishness or arrogance. Ozag or no, he will see to it.

He will do his best, Queen.

She is sure. Begone now.

And Allura is soon left alone with Viktor. Her single-note whistle is low and difficult to interpret.

These devices Albion's queen refers to. They are?

He does not know, Queen.

But they are precious and dreadful. She sensed.

It is so, but he cannot guess what they might be.

Allura buzzes a contemplative melody.

This talk of peace between scion and vumierre. And the secrets! She is not pleased. There is a wrong feeling to this, all the way to her third heart.

It is Ozag's will, thinks Viktor helplessly.

Peace with vumierre? With slavers?

It is difficult to believe.

More than difficult. Impossible.

But the Undying...

Has spoken only through the Albion queen, whose scent is undeniably potent. But she entreats him: do not be enthralled to the detriment of his kind. If he senses betrayal or conspiracy from this young queen of his, he must not hesitate. Perhaps these tales of Ozag are fabrications! In such a case, were the Albion queen to meet a bad end, no one would judge.

A bad end?

The kind that would be deserved if it was learned she conspired with vumierre.

Viktor's color fades, and his lone antennae bows.

That would be a heinous turn.

Indeed. But in such a case, he may be the only one able to stop the conspiracy. He must not hesitate!

Shimmer and her pluripotents approach, and Allura's final thought is tightly focused.

Learn the nature of those secret devices, she thinks, then she turns and flies away.

+ + + + + +

A little north of west and many thousands of strides away, Claw, the Redtooth chief, goes round and round, thinking of ways to circumvent the promise that keeps him from crossing the wedge to claim revenge—and new territory. In this effort, he is joined by Spike, and the two confer while looking east.

What if, thinks Claw, *you went with Rip and Roar to the far side of the range, up near the Overlap, and asked to speak with the Render chief?*

Speak to her about what, though?

Tell her we have an offer.

Yeah, Boss. But what's the offer?

Land! They help us take the Skull and we'll stop contesting their right to the Overlap.

Geez, Boss, that's prime turf.

Which is why they'd accept the offer. Don't you think they're tired of fighting moon after moon for the rights to that valley? This way, they give us one good push, just

Death is the Door

enough to shake the rotters free from the Skull. They can have the Overlap, and we'll be able to move east.

And we won't be breaking the vow, Spike realizes.

That's it.

Because someone else did the fighting.

You got it.

But maybe they take a liking to the Skull and stay.

Hmm...

And what about that thrower?

Damn the Sugarfeet and their oily hides!

Yeah, Boss, but I think the Renders are gonna want more assurance than that. First one of 'em gets dropped by that thing, the others'll turn tail pretty quick.

And so they go, back and forth, coming up with and discarding plans one after another, always their strategies breaking down in the face of this obstacle or that. As time wears on, they are no closer to a solution than when they started.

That's when Grab arrives, panting and harried. The news he bears at first enrages Claw—how dare a couple thrower-bearing Sugarfeet ruin his sport!—but after the gnashing and slashing and requisite howling, he grows calm and thoughtful. Something amazing has just been placed before him.

You're sure they're Bruiser's wotis? he asks.

No mistake, Grab scowls. *Can't miss those spikes.*

And Stone is alive?

If you want to call it that. She's pretty tore up. They're not moving anywhere quick.

But they will *be moving,* Claw thinks, *quick or otherwise. You can be sure of that. And they'll be going east.* He turns to Spike. *You know that territory better than anyone. Where's a good place for an ambush?*

Spike runs his tongue over his teeth.

There's a couple places, but it depends on the route they take. Will they go the shortest way because they know we'll be on their tails? Or will they go the easiest way because they're traveling injured?

Plan for both, thinks Claw. *Put together two teams,*

A.P. Malloy

one for each route. I want them alive, understood? Stone is going back to that butte if I have to drag her there myself, and those twins are going to buy me a murderer.

Good thinking, Boss, Grab snarls. *I was going to say send 'em* all *to the butte—keep them greenies real happy!—but hostages is way better.*

Yeah, Boss, thinks Spike. *We'll make it happen. It's way past time for Storm to be avenged. And hey! We'll get a couple throwers out of the deal.*

I'd rather have my oti-mu, thinks Claw.

+ + + + + +

*Grr...*thinks Cliff, tormented by waiting and uncertainty. His turn at wabi watch drags on. Story time had turned into wrestling time, and that had eventually become a righteous game of tag in the snow. When the last wabi has worn itself out, all Cliff can think about is a dark cave and a long nap. But first, a meal!

So when at last he is relieved by Snapper, Trapper, and Old Buttons, he immediately casts aside his weariness and goes out to seek his fortune, moving south along the River Sweet. Thoughts of Lightning fill his mind, and he worries as he hunts, doing better at the one than the other. He has not traveled far when he meets Piedmont and Fluvial, trailed by Curly and her thrower.

He bows to show deference.

Hey, there, Clawpaw, thinks Piedmont. *News?*

But Cliff has no chance to reply; Yellow appears, flanked by Boots, coming from the direction of the caves. Cliff senses even before Yellow opens her mind that she bears troubling news. She and Boots step forward, tails stiff and ears set high.

You're wanted, thinks Yellow.

Oh, sur-ee, thinks Piedmont. *It's nice to be wanted. By who, though? Cuz that can make a difference, see? Wanted by one aint the same 's wanted by another, iffin you catch what I'm throwin'. There was this one time—*

Stuff it, Yellow interrupts. *Serenity's waiting.*

Death is the Door

OK, then, Piedmont leans back and grimaces. *I can see trouble o' one kind or another's bubbled up. Aint no reason a get surly, no-ee.*

You too, thinks Yellow to Fluvial.

And so, the two Whitetails shuffle back to the Sugarfoot caves, Yellow and Boots leading the way and Curly at the tail. Cliff trails along forgotten or ignored, trying to pick up on any shared thoughts. There are none. But when they get to the caves and the Whitetails are escorted inside, he lingers near the entrance, and there, he gets a headful.

+ + +

I thought, he senses Serenity, *your Big Fork was committed to leaving the Bristle range untouched.*

Well, there, now, see, that's one way a sayin' it, Piedmont dithers. *One way, sur-ee and yeppir, though o' course there could be other ways o' sayin' it, too, mm hmm, other kinds o' words like, oh, I don't know, can't really think o' any off the top o' my egg, but I reckon there's lots o' other ways o' sayin what Big Fork's been thinkin'. Ain't it so, Fluvial? Tough one to read that ol' Forkie?*

Very, thinks Fluvial.

You mean he's a liar, thinks Yellow.

Oh, now, hey, now, thinks Piedmont, alarmed. *That's...that's a strong word there, that one. One o' the strongest. Can't just go throwin' that one around like it's a ball o' snow and we's a bunch o' gamin' wabis. That one hurts, that one does, sticks and stings, see? Why that word, Sugarfoot, hmm? What ol' Forkie do got you so stirred up? He aint the patientest, no one'd ever 'cuse 'im o' that, and he sure aint the fittest no more, not by no stretch o' nobody's imagination. But liar? That's a stinger that is, sur-ee, more like a rock than a snowball.*

Then why have we got word that Whitetails are moving on the Bristle home caves?

Oh.

Oh, indeed, thinks Serenity. *Did you know?*

Well, now, there's knowin' and then there's knowin' see? Like one time maybe it's a 'might be' thing, and the next it's a 'for sur-ee' thing, like say you know another moon's a comin' yeah? But what color, hmm? And one kezel thinks it's orange and one kezel thinks it's green, and they all smartly brains and maybe not a one gets it right. Then there's a time maybe, when—

Spare me, Serenity snarls. *Did you know or not?*

Tails and toes, did we know for sur-ee, no, ma'am, not a bit of it! But it aint no sooprize, iffin you got your thinkin' vest on. What'd Big Fork promise? No trouble from the Whitetail side so's them ol' Bristlies could take care o' their Redtooth business. Made a nice ol' peacy offer an' evrathing, fancy lookin' Moondweller whatsit, all shiny with a head and some arms, oh yeah. Fluvial was there, she'll tell ya; we was on the trusty side yeah?

Yes, thinks Fluvial.

There, you see? thinks Piedmont. *Only thing that figgers is Big Fork reckons the Redtooth business is been proper taken care of, their leader sent home tail draggin' and the rest stuffed in a cave somewhere. And iffin that business is a done sorta thing, then maybe, you know, maybe, Ol' Forkie thinks it's time for a new deal. He's a hungry one. Always lookin' for new turf see, and—*

I've sensed enough, thinks Serenity, and she curses. *Throw these two in the hole.*

Oh, hey, now! Aint no reason for no hole throwin' now. Ol' Piedmont gave ya evrathing he knowed. Sur-ee, coulda guessed Big Fork'd make a move on some new turf, but any half wake Bristly coulda told ya that. Don't blame us, we's your guests! What about Sugarfoot hospitality- ness? Ol' Bruiser'd never toss us in no hole!

But the two Whitetails are driven to a back chamber and given two choices: climb down the rope into the pit below, or be pushed. They choose the former, but only because they are staring down the barrel of Curly's thrower. Once in, the rope is pulled back up.

Don't worry, thinks Serenity. *If it turns out you're just innocent bystanders, we'll let you out.*

Death is the Door

Piedmont has nothing to say.

+ + + + + +

Rock and Crag decide the straight line is the best line, and they head northeast over rough, climbing terrain, the tail end of the Spine. The otis encourage Stone even as they worry about her sluggish pace. She moves so slowly the twins can walk bipedal, their weapons slung over their shoulders. But throwers or no, their spikes are tingly and on edge, for this is Redtooth land as much as Sugarfoot, and locations for an ambush abound.

Not keen on this turf, thinks Crag.

Not keen on a lot of things, thinks Rock. *But Yellow and Bliss are waiting for us; that's all that matters.*

Stone thinks nothing, walking robotically. But when the welcome colors of the accrete at last become visible, rather than continuing north with the oti-mus, she turns east, limping along with the accrete to her left.

Hey, amotiwol, thinks Crag. *Where you going?*

Yeah, thinks Rock. *Home is that way. You OK?*

No, she thinks.

Well, Crag assures, *it'll be fine once we get home...*

...once we get home, thinks Rock, *you'll get a hero's welcome and a span of moons...*

...a span of moons to be nursed and recover, Crag finishes. *Which sounds terrific to me. So come on...*

...come on, Rock agrees. *North is the winner.*

But Stone continues east. When they jog up next to her, one on either side, she curls her lip.

Going to the Whitetail range, she thinks, her explanation simple and honest. *Too many bad memories.*

C'mon, amotiwol, thinks Crag. *It was bad, but...*

...but you can't let those blue rotters ruin the memory of home, Rock finishes. *Once you get there, you'll see. Think about all the kezel so glad to see you. There's...*

...there's Submission for one, Crag volunteers. *Bruiser was always fond of you. And...*

...and lots of others, Rock steps in. But Stone has

refused to respond to any questions regarding her fancy or her two wabis, leading the twins to assume the worst. If she doesn't want to be around the memory of lost family, who are they to force the issue?

She limps on.

S'pose we could stay with you to the Tongue, thinks Rock. *You know, make sure you get back safe...*

...safe and in one piece, thinks Crag.

They walk on, leaving their old path, direct but difficult, and moving east, an easier way, but long. The thought of the delay galls the otis, but they can see no honor in leaving a clan member in such shape, still thousands of strides from her goal.

Soon enough, they reach a place where the land rises up to their left, bony rock like an unearthed fossil. There, the path eases downward into a trough, a narrow cutting between the stone and the grassy turf that suddenly rises above their heads. They must walk single file, and though the path is smooth, their nerves jangle, for there is an odd feeling about the place, a quietness free of yits or hoppers.

Where's a north wind when you need one? thinks Crag, raising his nose and scowling.

Let's pick it up, how about? thinks Rock. *What say, amotiwol? Can you hustle us through this pinch?*

Stone does her best, but they have just reached the midpoint of the cutting, their view blocked left and right, when Crag's nose raises the alarm. A moment later, they are leapt upon by eight Redteeth, exploding from the yellow grass atop the northern bank. The fight is ferocious but brief, and the Sugarfeet are soon overwhelmed and disarmed. Those Redteeth bloodied in the sortie are all the more boisterous in their taunts as they brandish their enemies' throwers and kick dirt in their faces. Stone lies panting, some of her bandages torn away. Rock and Crag are soon muzzled and bound.

Raggedy looking bunch, thinks Grab.

He gives the weapons to Rip and Roar, instructing them to deliver the prizes to their chief with all haste as a sign of their success.

Show him we got the job done, he thinks. *Give him something to howl about. The way these rotters look, it's gonna be a while before we get there.*

The two leave as ordered, but they are not gone long before the party hears a snarling ruckus, then, most amazingly, the explosive crack of a fired thrower. A moment later, Rip comes barreling into view.

Bibija! he thinks desperately, just as one appears out of the grass above them, a gray-spiked ah-tah, looming down at them and pointing a long thrower.

Don't like killing kezel, he thinks, aiming at Grab. *But I've done it—and I'll do it again, if you lot don't clear out. No, leave them, I'll do the untying. That's right, nice and easy, or one of you'll join your friend in the dirt.*

He fires a warning shot that misses Grab by a stride, and the Redteeth scatter, howling.

Stone is perhaps too damaged to notice, but Rock and Crag, who should be feeling relieved, are not. They both recognize at the same time the armed kezel looking down at them. They had heard him described many times by Ancian: the rogue who had killed his amotiwol and eaten his oli-wots.

+ + + + + +

Lieutenant K allows himself one more hour at the ag facility to recharge and de-glitch. There are no responses to his attempts at communication, and neither the scion nor the kezel return. The latter does not surprise him, but he expects a return of the former and has no plans of being here when that happens. So, he rests while he can, giving most of his attention to self-care. Residual damage from his injury continues to show itself, occasionally slowing cognition (not that a human would have noticed) and hampering mobility. Proprioceptors and micro-gyros aren't always properly autonomous, sometimes requiring re-sets and explicit commands that make him feel clumsy and slow.

But one hour of rest, stealing and converting power from the facility's modified generator, has a noticeable effect, and when he rises to his feet, the lieutenant feels ready to tackle whatever lies ahead.

His first goal is a weapon.

Not likely, he admits, for he had already searched the facility once and found just such a treasure. A second success seems against the odds. But look here! Cleverly hidden inside a faux dictionary rests a small but potent handgun, apparently the property of Deputy Kim. The lieutenant lacks Ensign Morales' encyclopedic knowledge of *Destiny's* crew, but he recognizes in the Security Chief's passion for practical, powerful weapons a kindred spirit.

You're a pretty thing, he admires.

But pretty is all it is, for the weapon is empty, little more than a museum piece. He spends another half hour in a fruitless search for ammunition, and is forced in the end to settle for a steel pipe and hope.

The time approaches for his companions' return.

Then it passes.

Five minutes overdue. Fifteen. Thirty.

Trouble never comes alone, he thinks and then repeats it aloud in Russian, for it soothes his nerves, which are actually several dozen unanswered questions all jostling for attention. "Beda nikogda ne prikhodit odna," he says, and imagines it is Sleeo to whom he says it. It would have made the odd human laugh, perhaps even pop a wheelie in his chair. But a moment later he recognizes the likelihood that his creator is long dead and his own time running short.

Thus thinking, he enters the transporter.

+ + +

When he steps from its partner, over three hundred kilometers away, near the steely blue heights of Far Colossus, the lieutenant confirms in under two seconds that the journey caused him no harm. The ensign had been correct: this level of technology would not have been available to the humans of *Destiny's* vintage. He dedicates point zero nine percent of his processing capabilities to solving this mystery; the remainder goes toward assessing his situation.

Location: interior, intake tower, top level.

Proximity: no life forms detected in immediate vicinity. One synthetic, a standard work-bot, stationed in the control room on the other side of the tower.

Threat assessment: inconclusive. No alarms that he can detect, and no movement. Security cameras operable. Work-bot stationary for the moment. But there are spaces his sensors cannot reach. Anyone—or anything—could be hiding there.

Signs of his companions: one data post, decaying but legible. They had been here, had gone to the landing strip located east of the dam. Their objective, in defiance of probability, to consider flying one of *Destiny's* shuttles to a rendezvous with the mighty ship itself.

Likelihood of Captain Monroe accepting such an opportunity: nearly one hundred percent.

I don't blame you, the lieutenant thinks. *I would have left me behind, too.*

He is about to make his way to the landing strip when he becomes aware of a second work-bot. He can't guess where it had been hiding, but it is heading his direction—though more slowly than that model should have been capable of.

It's over two centuries old, he reminds himself.

Slow or not, the work-bot continues toward the transporter. The lieutenant hastens from the room, down some stairs and across the base of the tower. The exit has been locked, but the window gives way easily enough, and he is soon outside, making his way to the landing strip. What he will do if the work-bot should be armed or have friends, he can't say. Too many variables.

He takes a few practice swings with his pipe.

The landing strip, when he arrives, is abandoned, but exhaust residue and recent tracks on the tarmac are enough to tell the story. The shuttle is on its way to somewhere, the captain and ensign hopefully safe and on board. What to do now? Should he seek out Sister Janet and attempt to regain *Valiant?* But that could take an untold amount of time, and where would he begin? She could be anywhere. Should he simply wait and hope for the captain's return? But that goes against his nature even without concerns of the pursuing Guild—and it is impractical in any case. Even now the work-bot draws closer. Meanwhile in the sky, revealed by parting clouds, a derka has begun to hover.

Too many variables.

+ + + + + +

"Captain Monroe," says the ensign. "Captain?"

The captain does not at first respond. He lies with his head cradled in the ensign's lap, blood trickling in a thin line from his scalp.

"Is he OK?" comes a voice from the speakers.

"I don't know," the ensign snaps. "You shouldn't have done that."

"He was going to leave."

"You can't force people to stay with you, Destiny. That's a choice they get to make on their own."

"But I need him."

"He isn't going to do you much good if you kill him. He's already had one concussion in the last forty-eight hours. You should have at least let him strap in."

"I didn't trust him on the bridge."

Ensign Morales checks the captain's pulse—regular, strong—and listens to his breathing, steady but shallow. She lifts his eyelids and scans his pupil response. They dilate normally. She can only approximate a reading of his blood pressure, but it appears within a healthy range. And yet, he remains unconscious.

"I didn't mean to hurt him," says Destiny.

"Well, you did. I need to get him to the infirmary. Will you please activate the conveyors and lifts?"

"Yes."

"And power up the infirmary as well."

"Yes. I'm sorry he's hurt."

Ensign Morales gently lifts the captain and carries him to the nearest conveyor. Not content to stand and wait while it motors her along, she walks at a brisk a pace.

"Where are you bringing us, Destiny?"

"To the edge of the asteroid belt."

"Why?"

"We're on an intercept course with Dansim."

"Destiny, you can't just blow yourself up with innocent people on board. You're not a murderer."

"But I have to save the planet."

"Who told you that? Was it Sister Janet?"

"Yes. She woke me up. She gave me a purpose."

"She didn't wake you up to kill Captain Monroe."

"No. She didn't tell me he would be here until just before you boarded. Work-bots were supposed to be at the helm and in the engine room. I can't operate the manual controls. But I'm glad you're here. I like you better."

"If you like us so much, let us go."

"But who will help me save Aranae?"

"I can't answer that. But there has to be a way that doesn't involve killing an innocent person—killing the man who came here to bring you home."

"My home is in orbit around Aranae."

"Then bring us back there, and we'll help you find another way to save the planet. Don't you want to live? Don't you want to go back to orbiting Aranae?"

"Yes."

"Then take us back."

Long moments pass, during which the ship does not reply. The conveyor arrives at an intersection near one of the lifts. Ensign Morales selects a level and down they go, smoothly, but slowly.

"I can't take us back," says Destiny at last. "We'll miss the window for our mission. Dansim won't be in optimal position again for another fifty-four days, and by then it might be too late. The moon is ejecting mass, you know, and the rate can't be predicted."

"Destiny, please. There has to be another way. We have a ship. It has weapons, an astral drive..."

"Sister Janet has your ship."

"Then why doesn't she use it? Why is she making you destroy yourself?"

"She *is* using your ship. She's using it to complete our plan. And she isn't making me. I chose this purpose."

"You chose suicide?"

"I chose honorable death."

"But why?"

There is a pause, this one longer. The lift reaches its destination and the doors open. The infirmary is at the end of the corridor, its windowed examination rooms already lit. Ensign Morales makes her way inside and lays the captain on one of the tables, neat with white linen.

"Do you have a soul, Ensign?" Destiny asks.

"I'm not in a mood to discuss metaphysics," the ensign replies, looking through drawers and cabinets for the supplies she needs. The nasty cut on the captain's forehead is soon cleaned and wrapped.

"I have a soul," says Destiny. "Sister Janet, too."

"Then you should be worried about its well-being. Murder bears a heavy karmic price."

"I am worried. But if I fail in my mission, every living thing on Aranae will die. Wouldn't that be worse?"

"Not if there was a better way."

"You keep saying that, but we planned for many lunar cycles, and we couldn't come up with a better way."

"Then let him go, and I'll stay."

"I need you both."

The ensign has activated one of the scanners and is running it over the captain's body, head to toe, when she notices several of the scuters have followed her into the infirmary. They form a ring around her and are watching her closely.

"What are you doing, Destiny?"

"Making sure you don't sabotage the mission."

"So you would disable me? Kill me?"

"Only if you try to interfere."

Death is the Door

"What good will that do? I thought you needed me in the engine room."

"I do. But not if you are a saboteur."

Ensign Morales reads the results of the scan in mere seconds, returning the device to its home and selecting a hypodermic syringe from a medicine cabinet whose lock she must first break.

"I'm sorry, but I'm a little busy to be thinking about sabotage," she says, although she has been contemplating it from the first. She injects the contents of the syringe into the captain's shoulder. "Anyway, what would happen to your mission if you disabled me?"

"I would do my best without you."

"And your chances of success?"

"Decrease by thirty-nine percent."

"That's a pretty high risk of a wasted life, Destiny. Aren't you afraid you'll die for no reason?"

"If I did my best, there's no reason to be afraid. I have a soul. Sister Janet says all souls go to heaven, and death is the door."

"And what about the captain?"

"Oh, he has a soul, too. He'll go with us to heaven. What a good time we'll have! There will be other ships, and other people, and we can travel wherever we like and never run out of fuel, and I'll be able to control my own manuals. No one dies anymore once they get to heaven, you know. We can be friends forever."

"I guess I'm flattered that you think I'll be there too," says the ensign. "But condemning the captain without even asking his permission...that doesn't sound like heavenly behavior to me."

"Allowing Aranae to be destroyed is the alternative. It's a really easy decision."

"I'm sorry you feel that way, Destiny, I really am. Because you have to know there is no way I'll help you without the captain's approval. And if that means your plan fails and your planet is destroyed, so be it."

"Why would you do that?"

"You wouldn't understand." The ensign activates

a cryopack by cracking it and shaking. She peels off its adhesive strip and secures the pack—already very cold—over the captain's injury. When she steps away to clean her hands at one of the disinfecting stations, the scuters move with her, always keeping her encircled.

"I would too understand," Destiny insists. "Tell me; why would you not want to help me?"

"Because I don't generally help the being who kills someone I love, that's why."

There is a momentary silence.

"I know about love," says Destiny. "I love Sister Janet. She woke me up."

"Just to have you sacrifice yourself?"

"No. Not at first. When she woke me up, we didn't have a plan. She had been my passenger. She and Abuelita. They were in exile, and Sister Janet took good care of me. Then later, she woke me up. When I learned the truth about Dansim, I volunteered."

"Before or after she taught you about heaven?"

"You think she lied to me."

The ensign is about to say what she thinks, but at that moment, Captain Monroe's eyelids flutter, then open. His gaze is unfocused at first, and even when the ensign moves to stand by his bed, he stares at nothing, his eyes passing without purpose across various items in the room, the windows, the scuters, the med cabinet.

"Captain," the ensign says, taking his hand. "How do you feel, sir? How is your vision?"

"Mm. How many of you are there supposed to be?"

"Just one sir."

"Then good. It's good."

"I'm sorry you hit your head," says Destiny. "You should have strapped in."

"Yeah, I'll remember that. Status, Ensign?"

Ensign Morales removes the tablet from her pack and begins writing her response, careful to angle the screen away from Destiny's cameras or those of the scuters. She has not gotten very far when the ship interrupts her.

"I'm sorry," it thinks. "But I am detecting another vessel on my long-range sensors."

"*Valiant*," says the captain. "Nikki's coming."

"Or Sister Janet," the ensign frowns.

But Destiny corrects them both.

"It is not your ship," she says. "It's a ship I've never seen before. I don't have anything like it in my memory."

There is a brief silence. Then:

"It is heavily armored," says Destiny. "Even from this distance I can identify many weapons."

The captain winces.

"Well, that's that," he says. "Sorry, Sleeo, old buddy, but they found us."

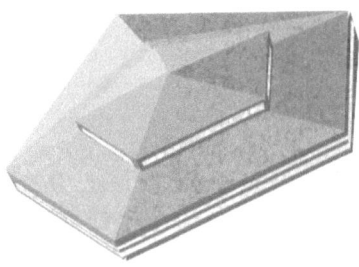

CHAPTER TWELVE
Crystal

IN THE PAST, when *Destiny* had maneuvered into scanning range and Petros had begun receiving data, the news he bore was not what they had hoped. Joy didn't need to make contact with the artifact to sense its disappointment, but she did anyway.

What is it? What's wrong? Didn't it work?

Incompletely. We did travel forward in time, but not far enough. In this time, the rogue appears to remain intact.

Then we'll have to do it again, yes?

Yes. But not right away. I need time to recover.

What went wrong though? I concentrated, didn't I?

Your concentration was disturbed.

Maybe. But I don't think it was me. Joy dwelt on this thought for a moment, recalling the idea that had sprung to her mind unbidden. *You don't think it was Lightning, do you?*

Not intentionally, no. But her mind was deeply preoccupied. Understanding the connection between the two of you, I should have had you explain the process to her as well. Had she concentrated fully, this would not have happened. But the fault is mine.

The kezel were displeased with this news.

What do you mean, not far enough? thought Thunder. *How far do we need to go?*

Far enough to see if Janet's plan worked, Joy replied, shrugging her shoulders.

So where are we, then? Lightning wondered, and there was an edge to her tone, a hope like hunger.

Joy relayed this to the Book, but it was at first reluctant to reply, and she had to press further, restating the question several times before it conceded.

Very well, it answered at last. *But I foresee trouble in divulging this information. It appears we have arrived at a time shortly before Sister Janet and her aging charge Abuelita—your human ancestor named Grace—returned to the surface after their exile on* Destiny.

When Maya arrived, this information meant little to her. It meant even less to the kezel, who had made no effort to catalog the events they perceived as a string of Moondweller nonsense.

Before or after we were born? Lightning asked.

Before, Joy replied, once she had obtained her answer. *But not much before.*

Joy sensed Lightning's sudden excitement, but Thunder failed to see the significance.

So what? he thought. *Do we have to do it again?*

Joy's antennae tilted forward.

Yes. But not right away...Books need rest.

Maya toggled the comm.

Guess I better tell the major.

Wait, thought Lightning suddenly, and she rose from her haunches. *Tell him this, too...*

+ + +

Javon and Charlotte were conversing outside the cargo bay when Watt and Janet arrived. They stood close enough to touch—though they did not, for they were on duty and had long ago agreed to keep their professional relationship strictly so. They spoke in low tones, audible only to themselves. But when Maya exited the control room and joined them, she could read Javon's concern, noting that even the worry that creased Charlotte's forehead was adorable.

"Mes amis," Charlotte greeted them all, and Javon

turned to face them, cutting short whatever it was he had been about to say to her.

"We're in orbit around the planet's largest moon," he said, and he waved at a console, activating the holographic image of the half-lit planet. "We're detecting trace amounts of processed iridium."

"Processed?" Watt's eyebrows arched.

"Then there has been another *Destiny* here," Janet concluded. "Or a ship with a similar signature."

"We think the former," said the major. "But where she is now, we can't say. Maybe on the lit side."

Maya caught Charlotte glancing at her.

"What?" she wondered.

"I worry about you," Charlotte said. "That's all. But you have a healthy glow, in spite of it all."

It was true. Maya felt fine, though she had no right considering all that had happened. But there it was, nonetheless. She felt healthy, rested, and peaceful for reasons she couldn't fathom. She had no words to express this feeling, and so she said nothing, placing one hand over her belly and taking one of Watt's in the other. Of the otherworldly creature from the cargo bay she remembered nothing, not even her commitment to record the experience in writing.

"What else did you learn?" Watt asked. "Did it work? Are we where we're supposed to be?"

"We moved forward," Javon nodded. "But Maya tells me we didn't go far enough. We're short of the goal. Which means we need to do it again."

"Amazing," Sister Janet shook her head. "What is happening here is rewriting every textbook ever."

"I wish that were the end of the story," Javon frowned. "But apparently there's more. Do you want to tell us, Maya, why you called us down here?"

She did not; it was too hard, far too many words. Better if they got the message directly from the source.

+ + +

Inside the cargo bay, Thunder looked at his oli-mu through narrowed eyes, his ears angled forward.

I don't like it, he said, and he glanced at Joy. *What do you think about it? Be honest.*

Joy rubbed her hands together, a nervous, raspy sound that should have been answer enough.

I'm not sure it's such a good idea, she thought. *But I'll do it if Lightning says so.*

Thunder tried staring his oli-mu into submission, but Lightning appeared unmoved.

How do you even know she'll be there? he asked.

I don't. But it's the best place to start. How do you think I learned about it? She took me there all the time.

Hmph! Never took me there. Thunder eyed his twin doubtfully, but when he prepared another objection, her jaws clenched, her upper lip curled back, and her ears pinned. *Fine!* he thought. *There's no point arguing when you get that look. Stubborn! But if there's hot water, you're not the only one who's gonna get burned, you know.*

No one's getting burned.

You'd better hope not. Well. Here they come.

And the control room door opened with a click and a squeak, allowing five humans into the room, wrapped in their orange suits. Lightning stepped up to the grated window and bowed to the one named Major.

"I understand you have something to tell me," he said, not bothering with pleasantries. As always, the thought was translated by the Book, via Joy, and took a moment to coalesce in Lightning's mind.

I do, she thought, proceeding slowly to allow Watt time to translate. *I have a request.*

"I'm listening."

I know we're not where we need to be, but before we move again, is it true we need to rest?

Yes. Twenty-four hours is the protocol. That's a human day, if that means anything.

Like a feast and a sleep, maybe two, Joy added, sharing her understanding from the artifact.

Perfect, thought Lightning. *Then during that time,*

I want to go down to the...the planet.

"For what reason?"

There's someone down there I want to see. Someone I need to get a message to.

Javon's expression warped to a frown.

"I'm sorry, but we've gotten as close as we're going to get to that planet in this timeline. As soon as we're ready to move on, that's what we're going to do."

We can move, thought Lightning, *but not until I've delivered this message. All I ask is that you get me down there. If something happens and you can't get me back, or it's time to go and I haven't returned, you can leave me.*

Joy's harsh clicking spoke for itself.

"With respect," Major Javon held up both hands. "I would love to help, I really would. But I'm not risking a shuttle—or a pilot—on any non-essential missions."

This is essential. To me.

"Perhaps," offered Sister Janet, "if you gave the major some details, helped him—helped all of us—understand why this is so important to you."

Lightning bared her teeth.

My ami-kan is down there. I have something to tell her. That's all you need to know.

"Your what?" asked the major.

"It means mother," said Maya.

Javon's frown remained fixed.

"I don't mean to be rude," he said, "but this isn't a social call. Whatever you have to say, surely it can wait until we've gotten back to your time?"

My ami-kan is dead in my time.

Our ami-kan, Thunder added. *Our time.*

Javon hesitated. No one in his party spoke.

"I'm sorry," he said after a while. "I didn't know." He took a deep breath. "And what is your message? I don't mean to pry, but I feel I have the right, considering what you're asking me to do."

Now it was Lightning's turn to hesitate. She considered her reply carefully.

My ami-kan died because I put an idea in her head

Death is the Door

and wouldn't let it rest. She would never have thought of it on her own, and she would never have acted on it if I hadn't been so persistent and selfish.

"But...surely you understand," said Javon. "The... kezel you're talking about, she isn't actually *your*...ami-kan. Am I pronouncing that right? Ami-kan? She's the mother of a completely different kezel, the you that lives in *this* timeline."

Not yet she's not. She hasn't bound with my api-kan. I don't even know if they've met. But yeah, I understand: even if I can share an idea with this Crystal—that's her name—it won't bring our Crystal back to life.

"Then what's the point, please? For all you know, what you say to her might make things worse."

Lightning had no reply.

"And what if I say no?" Javon wondered.

I hope you won't.

"I'm sure. But what if I do? Because, in spite of my sympathy for you, that is still my intention."

Lightning tried to control her breathing, but she wasn't having much success.

If you said no, she thought, *I would politely remind you that you could use our help when you get to our home.*

"Is that a threat?"

No, Major. I just hope Moondwellers are as amazing as my gami-kan always believed, and that you will see one groomed tail always leads to a second.

"'Always' is a very big word, my friend."

Please, thought Lightning. *We have a plan! We think we can get to her, share the message, and get back quickly without anyone knowing we were there."*

"Anyone beside your past self's mother, you mean," thought Javon. "And who knows who she'll tell, and what consequences that will have."

No one! Lightning rose to two legs. *No one knows what will happen if I try! But I know what will happen if I don't! I won't be able to live with myself! I—we—have this chance, this one chance, to save a life. Maybe coming here wasn't a mistake, after all. Maybe it was meant to happen*

*so we'd have this chance. I don't know, and I don't care.
We're here, that's what matters. And if I leave without trying...* Her thought trailed away, and she sank back to four
legs, her ears drooping. But the tone of her thoughts was
so intense that Maya inadvertently reached out and
touched Javon's shoulder, gripped it.

"Puavre creature," whispered Charlotte. "Que
pouvons-nou faire?"

Javon turned to Watt.

"Thoughts?"

"Heck it all," Watt replied, and he thrust his
hands into his lab coat pockets. "What do you think?"

He asked this to Janet; her answer was simple.

"Perhaps we should hear her plan."

"OK," Javon allowed, though the frown never left
his face. "Convince me—if you can."

+ + +

And that is how Lightning, Thunder, and Joy
found themselves riding in one of *Destiny's* shuttles, de-
scending toward Aranae's dark face, the ship piloted by
Major Javon and navigated by Corporal Skola. Maya had
made the tremendous effort of will to squeeze out five
words ("I want to go, too") but had no chance of winning
that argument. No one in the major's inner circle would
hear of it. Watt was chosen instead—someone needed to
translate for the kezel—so she and Charlotte remained
behind, attending to the shuttle's progress via comms and
sensors and worrying every minute.

There had been some fuss about the mission
(which Javon had described as simple reconnaissance)
from Magister Healey, who seemed to suspect there was
more going on than he was being told. Or perhaps that
was his default outlook on life: perpetual suspicion. But
Commander Rickles soon put an end to that. Deputy Kim
had demanded a security presence, and Javon had
obliged him by ordering that the Deputy be that presence.
Rounding out the team was Chief Abara, who would have

had to be locked up to keep her from stowing away.

Down they went, while Joy and the kezel sat mesmerized in the rear compartment, looking out porthole windows at a perspective exceeding the wildest imagination. The sight of their home from this vantage was amazing beyond words, and they stared, their minds awed and their thoughts still.

This timeline's *Destiny* had not been located and was assumed to be somewhere beyond the gas giant, on her slow return from exile. But to be safe, Javon brought the shuttle in from the dark side, flying low to avoid detection, sailing over kilometers of a surface illuminated only by the shuttle's twin search beams, a mountainous terrain of ice and sub-arctic wind untouched by the sun for a hundred million years.

There, thought Lightning, and she pointed. They had traveled far enough so that the sun had begun to rise ahead of them, creating below them a neat, thin crescent of light. The demarcation between it and the dark side was stark and obvious.

There what? Thunder asked.

That line, Lightning traced it with one claw. *The place where the sun ends and the dark begins. That's what Ancian used to say was the Wall.*

Sure, thought Thunder. *Just like those two Moondwellers said back at the dam. But I thought they were crazy—or lying. So, not really a wall.*

No. But still: a dividing line between us and a whole world of dark. That part wasn't wrong.

You think the keel actually came from there?

But Lightning had no answer. It was possible, of course—what wasn't? But her mind was occupied by the immediate future, not the distant past. There was some chance this venture would prove futile, disastrous even, and she would be to blame. She concentrated on the land passing below them, casting her gaze out to the horizon, silently begging it to reveal her desires.

Familiar features began to appear.

There were the Derka's Teeth, their jagged peaks

hooded in mist. And on their other side were the jumbled slabs of the Shattered Plains, snowy and indigo.

Lightning's spikes began to tingle.

Acting on her advice, Javon brought the shuttle over the unpopulated range east of the Gore, mountainous source of the Bloodwater, and then to the sulphur fields. There, they put down, right in the middle of the stench, where no kezel—or any other living creature— ever set foot. Securely suited up, Deputy Kim walked the perimeter, scanning for trouble while Shonda, with help from Corporal Skola, roamed the vicinity collecting samples and readings.

Javon stayed at the helm.

"You showed her how to use the comm, yes?" he asked Watt, who scowled at the belching, yellow holes.

"Aye, she's got it. Fast learner."

"Then stay in contact," Javon said to Lightning.

Nothing is going to happen, she replied when the thought had been translated, but she patted the pocket in which the communication device rested, as if to soothe the major's worries. Then she removed her weapon belt, delivering the cutter to Thunder's safekeeping. And with that, she said a quick goodbye to Joy, who stood gripping Thunder's spikes, and she turned south, marching through the fumes and into the wind.

+ + +

The sweet smell of home, Lightning thought, trying to make a joke to steady her nerves, but a moment later, she cautioned herself: *Other smells are what matter. Don't lose focus!*

The southern wind was a grace, shortening the time she had to spend in the wretched, gag-inducing fumes. But it was the holes from which the fumes escaped that were the greatest threat, for some were shaped like puckering mouths, large enough to fall into.

Who can say where—or when—I'd land, she thought, but happily for her, she never learned the

Death is the Door

answer. With her eyes squinted and breathing through her mouth, she ducked into the wind and worked her way southward. Eventually, the vapors thinned, and the last fumarole belched her good riddance.

At the end of the yellow, gaseous field, snow re-appeared, a welcome sight indeed, and Lightning snatched up a mouthful, her eyes closed as it melted, sweet and clean. Soon after, she came to the faint begin-nings of the trail that led into the heights, where she could see, a thousand strides above, the stony bluff where she and Joy had, so long ago, waited for caepods to dry and speculated about the Eye Tower.

She paused. Heady emotions had begun to rise, a combination of nostalgia and anxiety, and she found she was unable to begin climbing. What would she find at the top? Who? She checked to see that the comm device was secure in its pocket. And still she hesitated.

Who's that down there? a mind thought to her.

Startled, she peered up and saw a kezel moving down the trail toward her, an ibiwa ah-lah—the smell was obvious—in a sleek, dow-skin vest. Her spikes were striped in cream and chocolate, her tail bushy and gleam-ing. Altogether, she possessed an elegant form, and Lightning felt sure she had seen her before.

Hello? the newcomer thought, her mind more bold. *Do you sense me? Who is that?*

Hello, thought Lightning, standing two-legged as appropriate. *My name's Scar. I'm a Clawpaw.*

Sorry for you, thought the ibiwa, who had reached the base of the trail but had stopped there, eyeing Lightning suspiciously and remaining on four legs. *You're on Sugarfoot turf, you know.*

Yes, actually. I was looking for a Sugarfoot named Crystal. From Ancian and Wrinkle.

Ha! What for?

I have a message for her. Do you know her?

Maybe. What's the message?

It's something I have to tell her directly.

Says who?

My apoliwot. He's a Render. He heard about her from some Clawpaws who heard about her from some Redteeth, who heard about her from some Sugarfeet.

Oh, please! She's not that famous.

I'm just telling you what I was told. Can you help me? My apoliwot said he'd give me his place at the next feast if I delivered the message.

Give it to me. I'll deliver it. I'm her best friend.

Lightning's ears perked up.

Brook! she realized. *You're Brook.*

The ibiwa scrunched up her snout.

How do you know my name?

Oh, geez, I mean, my apoliwot mentioned I might find Crystal with you. He described you...well, in all sorts of, you know...ways.

No, I don't know. What kind of ways?

You know...pretty...and stuff.

Pretty?

Gorgeous, actually. Beautiful. He sort of went on about it. Golden eyes, edible spikes, all that...

Stop, thought Brook, in a tone that said she hoped Lightning would not. *Who is this apoliwot? I've never met a Render in my life. How does he know so much?*

Lightning held up her hands to show she was holding no answers.

All I know is I gotta get back quick if I want to get fed. So, can you help me find her, please?

You don't have to find her. She's coming here.

Brilliant! You mean right here?

No. We have a secret place. Clawpaws are not invited. But you can climb with me to the top and wait for her—if you promise to tell her what your apoliwot said about me. Promise? OK...

With that, Brook turned and led Lightning up a trail she herself had taken many times, though it was less worn than she recalled, for it was a newer version of itself. When they at last reached the top, she had to carefully check her emotions at the glorious crowns of the rainbow accrete, healthy all the way to the horizon, and the twink-

ling of the Eye Tower, far off in the mountainous northwest, where bombas lived in peace.

Gee, she thought. *Sure is nice up here. No views
like this in Scratch Valley.*

I'm a Bristle, thought Brook, flashing her tail as
evidence. *I wouldn't know. Say!* she aimed her nose at
Lightning's vest. *That's a spotted talihew. I thought they
only lived on the east side.*

Oh, Lightning scrambled to think. *It was a gift,
actually. Might have been handed down from some Bristles back in the history days, but I can't remember.
Someone probably told me, but you know how it is when
gami-kans start telling stories.*

Hmm... thought Brook. *Oh! Here she comes...*

And Lightning turned to the west. There, climbing the last switchback, came her ami-kan.

+ + +

Kezel do not cry, of course, not as such. That is
neither how their bodies nor their psyches are made. But
intense emotion can cause their eyes to water and their
noses to twitch as if a sneeze is coming on. Lightning did
her best to stave off this sensation, but her best wasn't
very good, and for a moment, she had to look away.

Who's this? thought Crystal.

Someone with a message for you, thought
Brook. *Calls herself Scar. She's from the Valley.*

Scratch Valley? A message for me?

Yes, thought Lightning, and she could think of
nothing else to offer, so she rose to two legs and bowed.

Wow, thought Crystal. *So formal. Not what we
expect from a Clawpaw.*

I had a good teacher.

Had?

Have. My ami-kan is great. My api, too.

Another wow, thought Crystal. *Don't hear a
Clawpaw say that too often.* But the thought wasn't mean
in spirit, and she rose to two legs as well, bowing. *There,*

she thought, dropping to all fours and sniffing delicately. *Now we're supposed to circle each other and get a good smell. But that's too much, don't you think? Say; what's wrong with your eyes?*

Nothing. Lightning wiped at them, then returned to four legs as well. *I came down the northern path, got a good breath of sulphur is all.*

You came all the way here to give me a message?

Yes ma'am...I mean, yes. From my apoliwot.

Who sounds amazing, thought Brook.

Do I know him? asked Crystal. *'Cuz you have a familiar scent. I'm pretty sure we've never met before...*

No, we haven't.

But you seem... What's your name again?

Scar.

Sure, I can see that. Her eyes swept over Lightning's form, nose to toes, taking in the signs of her many adventures. *Things are pretty rough in the Valley, I guess. But that's a nickname. What's your real name?*

Acting on impulse, Lightning arrived at a quick answer, unsure of her motivation even as she thought:

Fire of the Storm.

Ah. Lightning. Well, that's a proper name. It's nice to meet you, Lightning. What's the message?

No offense, Lightning thought to Brook, *cuz you've been real nice, but I promised it would be a secret. Only supposed to share it with ami—with Crystal.*

Fine, thought Brook. *I can tell when I'm not wanted. But hurry up, will you? We've got things to do. And tell her what your apoliwot said about me.*

I will.

Brook turned to move toward the far end of the bluff, but she suddenly paused and looked back.

Oh! Before I go, what did he say?

Who?

Bruiser, of course!

Crystal's ears relaxed.

He said yes.

Yep, thought Brook. *I told you. Submission's no*

rockhead. You'll bring him here, yes? Best place to go for howling—see if his voice is as sweet as his tail.

Obviously. Where else? But I'm keeping our secret place secret. And don't tell anyone he said yes. I don't want to scare him off.

He doesn't seem like the kind that's easily scared, thought Brook, *But don't worry; I won't tell.*

And she moseyed off to sit at the edge of the bluff and proof her mask.

So? thought Crystal. *What's the message?*

Well, thought Lightning, but she hesitated for a moment, losing her focus. Such fine spikes her ami-kan had! She had forgotten how bright her claws were, how expressive her snout. But the plan! Follow the plan! She gave herself a mighty shake. *First,* she thought, *he said 'give her this. Ancian—' No, sorry, I mean, 'her ami-kan,' he said. 'Her ami-kan will know what to do with it.'*

What is it?

Lightning removed from her vest and very carefully unfolded the thin, rectangular sheet bearing cryptic markings and the supposed image of a derka. She shielded it from the wind as she handed it to Crystal, gauging her response but also basking in her scent.

Say, thought Crystal. *Is this a Moondweller thing? I bet it is. How'd a Render get a hold of this?*

I'm not sure, but he wanted it to be a goodwill offering, you know? So you would take his message seriously. Not every Render is like the Redteeth, and I guess you already know not every Redtooth is...

...a hating disbeliever? finished Crystal. *It's OK, you can say it. So you know my ami-kan was a Redtooth? Or still is, I guess, in a way.*

That's what I was told.

It's true. And she'll think this is the dow's egg, that's for sure. What do these marks mean?

No idea. And my apoliwot didn't know either. If you look close, some people think that part's supposed to be a derka. But I don't know...

Sure, thought Crystal. *I can see that. Those right*

there are its wings, and that part is its head. What ugly things they are! Can't you see it?

Not really.

That's because you're looking with your nose. You have to trust your eyes—and your imagination.

Well...

Had it been Ancian—or anyone else—giving this advice, Lightning might have dismissed it. Who cares about images? But this was different. So, she tried. Against a lifetime of training, she ignored the messages from her nose and concentrated only on what she could see. And not just with her eyes, but in her mind, as well. She recalled all the derkas she had seen, the way they soared and their hideous voices, and she tried to imbue the flat, lifeless form with some of their depth and movement. If she concentrated, she could almost...

Blink!

I see it, she exclaimed, her eyes wide. She tapped the image with a claw. *There's its tail! There's it's teeth! Now it makes sense...*

Told you, thinks Crystal. *My ami-kan taught me all about images. Lots of kezel can't see 'em.*

Golly, thinks Lightning. *Isn't that something. Thank you! And my apoliwot thanks you. This was his most prized possession, you know, so when he said give it to you as a sign, I knew the message was important.*

Well, gee, thought Crystal, and she meticulously folded the sheet, placing it with great care into the pocket of her neatly tailored talihew vest. *You're getting me all excited. What's the message?*

But Lightning had to take a deep breath and compose herself for a moment more. It was all too much! She had glanced into her ami-kan's eyes and had seen herself, as if reflected from a pool, eyes swirling copper, black, and white. She had felt in that instant as if she were falling into a memory, were somehow in her own body, but in someone else's as well, and the feeling was exalting and euphoric, but also wistful in a way that no time travel, no messages could relieve.

Death is the Door

I'm sorry, she thought. *I've been on my feet for a long time. Haven't eaten anything proper in a while.*

I bet I could get you into the Sugarfoot feast, Crystal offered. *Bruiser—he's my new fancy—told me to bring a friend. Of course, I'm bringing Brook, but I bet he'd be OK with someone else too. I bet he'd like you.*

Wow. That's…you're so sweet. And that Bruiser is a lucky one. But no, my apoliwot's giving me his place at the next Render feast. I'll get my fill—feel a whole lot better once I deliver the message.

Deliver away then!

Lightning flexed her claws and began.

It's like this, see. My apoliwot had a dream—a really crazy dream—and he had it over and over, you know? Like one whole Wabi-la cycle it kept happening. And you were in it—but he didn't know it was you for a long time. He had to go all over the range asking this kezel and that, 'til he figured it out.

Ooh…this sounds exciting.

Yes. And there's more. Bruiser was in it too.

No!

Yes, it's true. And your ami-kan, the Redtooth.

Well, thought Crystal. *I believe in dreams, you know. My ami-kan says they predict the future—if you know how to read them the right way.*

I guess that could be, Lightning agreed. *That's what my apoliwot figured, anyway. So he sent me here to tell you all about it, cuz, you know, Renders aren't real popular on this side of the wedge.*

He was smart. And I'm starting to like Clawpaws more than I used to. So? Tell me all about it.

And step by delicious step, Lightning did. Using the frame of a fabricated dream, she relayed the earnest warning against a third litter, made clear what was at stake should the warning be ignored. She drew out the telling for every precious moment she could get in her ami-kan's company, forgetting about comm devices and shuttles until all the questions had been answered and all the answers digested. And when at last the time came to part, Crystal stepped close and touched noses.

I think we could be friends, you and I, she thought. *You should come back when you can and I'll introduce you to everyone. They'll treat you like family.*

That would be nice, thought Lightning, her nose twitching. *But I should hurry now. Um...in the Valley, we have a thing. Do you know about hugging?*

Of course! thought Crystal. *Sugarfeet invented hugging.* And they both rose to two feet and embraced. And if Lightning held closer and longer than was strictly necessary, Crystal said nothing.

Come back soon, new friend, she thought. *And thank you! I'll remember what you said...*

+ + +

Those waiting aboard the shuttle had concluded their business and were anxious to return to *Destiny.*

"She's a cargo runner, not a stealth operator," Javon fretted. "These fumes are fine camouflage, and I'm generating an interference field, but anyone who looks long and hard enough will eventually see us."

She'll be back, thought Thunder, disregarding as always the Moondweller gibberish that peppered everything they said.

"Maybe head out there and see if you can speed her up," the major suggested via Watt's translation. "You can blame me if she gets angry."

There's no need, thought Lightning, appearing like a teary-eyed ghost from out of the wavering fumes. With great relief, they welcomed her aboard, and Javon wasted not a moment, sealing the ship and getting it airborne. They sailed away low and fast the instant they were all secured in their places.

Thunder and Joy sat on either side of Lightning, sensing the intensity of her emotions. She had seen Crystal was all she would divulge, and had shared many thoughts. But what those were, exactly, and to what end the sharing came, she would not say. The experience was a precious, fragile treasure, one that might disintegrate the moment it was exposed to crude attempts at explanation or description. So, she kept it safely housed in her memory, the smells, the sounds, the beautiful sights, warming her heart and buoying her spirit, and there they stayed for many moons, until the day she had her own fancy, and her own wabis, and the memory had grown to legend, had become cramped and lonely and needed to be shared. Then, with a timely audience, it found new life, and Lightning felt sure that the thing done so long ago had not been in vain.

But for now, she told no one.

Her companions were worried at first at how deep in her own mind she had fallen. But upon returning to *Destiny,* their fears were relieved, for when, after the requisite recovery period had passed and the time came to make another attempt at hitting the future target, Lightning was focused and attentive as Joy explained what needed to happen. Her energy was positive, her demeanor calm, and when the ship was made ready and Petros declared himself sufficiently invigorated, she and Joy sat in the cargo bay side by side, skin to spike, and they concentrated on one thought:

Next...

The adventure concludes in

A.P. Malloy

www.ingramcontent.com/pod-product-compliance
Lightning Source LLC
Chambersburg PA
CBHW021953170626

46808CB00001B/139